Have Your Cake and Kill Him Too

**Center Point
Large Print**

**This Large Print Book carries the
Seal of Approval of N.A.V.H.**

Have Your Cake and Kill Him Too

A Blackbird Sisters Mystery

Nancy Martin

CENTER POINT PUBLISHING
THORNDIKE, MAINE

This Center Point Large Print edition
is published in the year 2006 by arrangement with
New American Library, a division of Penguin Group (USA) Inc.

The text of this Large Print edition is unabridged. In other
aspects, this book may vary from the original edition. Printed in
Thailand. Set in 16-point Times New Roman type.

ISBN 1-58547-773-7

Library of Congress Cataloging-in-Publication Data

Martin, Nancy, 1953-
    Have your cake and kill him too / Nancy Martin.--Center Point large print ed.
        p. cm.
    ISBN 1-58547-773-7 (lib. bdg. : alk. paper)
    1. Blackbird Sisters (Fictitious characters)--Fiction. 2. Bars (Drinking establishments)--
Fiction. 3. Businessmen--Crimes against--Fiction. 4. Philadelphia (Pa.)--Fiction. 5. Women
journalists--Fiction. 6. Pregnant women--Fiction. 7. Socialites--Fiction. 8. Sisters--Fiction.
9. Large type books. I. Title.

PS3563.A7267H38 2006b
813'.54--dc22
                                                                                    2005035837

*The Book Tarts have become my daily companions
despite our living all over the country.
Harley Jane Kozak, Susan McBride, and Sarah
Strohmeyer are my sisters at heart.
See you on the blog, ladies!
Check us out at
www.TheLipstickChronicles.typepad.com.*

Acknowledgments

I can't imagine writing a book without help. This time around, Veronica Henrick and Mary Anne Donnelly became my Philadelphia transportation experts. Hilde Terpeluk Kern is the wonderful reader who came up with the perfect name for Libby's baby. Various Sisters in Crime helped with the diet ideas. (Special shout-out to Gina Sestak, who knew all about the cabbage soup and chocolate-cake diets!) As always, Ramona Long, Sarah Martin, and Barbara Aikman provided fresh eyes along the way. And many readers have dropped me notes of encouragement. I so appreciate your kind words! Thanks, everyone!

Chapter One

*M*y sister Emma blew into the country-club dining room and conned the waiter into bringing her a bloody New York strip. Then she planted her elbows on the pink tablecloth and laid down the conversational ground rules. She said, "I'll choke the first person who brings up carbohydrates as a topic of serious discussion."

Which caused the fur-and-face-lift ladies to take their coffee cups and flee our table at the Daffodil Luncheon, leaving the three of us alone for a sisterly squabble.

"Oh, Em," said Libby, who had called us together to mend fences. "You couldn't have worn a decent pair of shoes?"

Emma had obviously come from the barn, because her riding boots were caked with a spring-scented substance that she was gracious enough to disguise by lighting a cigarette—against club rules, of course. "At least I wore a brassiere. You, on the other hand, look like a Playboy bunny who spent the winter binging on Krispy Kremes."

Libby sported a snug mohair sweater with a neckline that plunged down the ski slope of her bosom. The décolletage was edged in a perky white fur obviously intended to distract the eye from the few pounds

9

of loveliness that had crept onto her figure in the last year.

"At least I didn't come with a Band-Aid on my nose," said Libby.

"Let's not make a scene," I said, having already decided not to mention Emma's dubious fashion statement, no doubt the result of some barnyard accident.

At the front of the room, local blond network affiliate newsreader Bebe McCarthy took the microphone and sent an electronic shriek bouncing around the room. As Bebe began her thanks-to-the-committee speech, Libby said, "You're right, Nora. Some of us must reserve our positive mental energy for more important issues."

"Yes," I said.

"It's not a diet, of course," Libby explained for the third time. "It's a healthy lifestyle change. And you'll benefit, too. It's time to take off those few pounds you put on lately."

Emma made a noise like a cat with a hair ball, and I sighed.

Libby ate the last crumb of slivered almond from her spinach salad with dainty precision. "I understand completely. Like you, I refuse to be made to feel inadequate as a woman, enslaved by current fads in body image or temporary ideals established by a punitive fashion industry that actively destroys a woman's confidence simply to sell their products. I'm perfectly happy with myself. Delighted, in fact. But a few changes once in a while make life interesting."

10

Emma pushed back her plate, picked up her cigarette from where she'd left it balancing on the rim of her saucer and asked, "What's for dessert?"

Libby dabbed her napkin to her lips. "Why don't we split the mixed berries? A few raspberries would satisfy me."

Emma blew a seductive smoke ring up at the waiter as he bent to refill her coffee cup. "How about finding me a chunk of chocolate cheesecake, big boy? Extra whipped cream."

"Em," I said. "Let's be supportive."

She noted my untouched plate as the waiter whisked it away, and she frowned. "What's the matter with you?"

"I'm fine."

Libby patted my hand. "I appreciate your support, Nora. I'm glad you're taking control of your food issues."

"But—"

"Let's hear why we're really here." Emma flicked ashes into the centerpiece. "What's the story, Lib? You didn't invite me to the Daffodil Luncheon just to cheerlead your diet. What do you want?"

"Can't I simply enjoy the company of my sisters as we prepare to welcome spring?" Libby looked prettily affronted. "After our little argument, Emma, I thought we'd join Nora at her social engagement in the spirit of sibling—"

"You and Em argued? About what?"

Emma checked her watch, clearly not allowing the

11

subject to be reopened for discussion. "I've got things to do this afternoon."

"Anybody we know?" Libby asked tartly. She checked her lipstick in the mirror of her compact. "Someone you met at work, perhaps?"

"Jealous?"

Since the festive night our parents threw their last cocktail party and pulled a disappearing act with the last of the Blackbird family fortune, our situation had pulled my sisters and me together rather like desperate souls clutching the gunwales of a fast-sinking lifeboat. While Mama and Daddy enjoyed their tax evaders world tour, the three of us took turns wrestling with the impulse to throw a sister overboard.

Emma and I both suppressed the urge to give Libby the heave-ho unless she revealed her agenda pronto. The postluncheon fashion show music began, but the two of us glared meaningfully at Libby.

She snapped shut her compact. "Oh, all right! You know I'm a founding member of the Erotic Yoga Society."

"That bunch of nutcases," Emma muttered. "I'd never seen so many loons in one room until you invited us to your Christmas party."

Libby bristled. "Our group is firmly committed to the sensual melding of mind and body for the—"

"We've heard that crackpot mission statement before and it still doesn't make any sense," Emma said. "What happened? Somebody sprain his privates while saluting the sunrise or something?"

Sensing the imminent arrival of a headache, I intervened. "What's going on with the Erotic Yoga Society, Lib?"

"We lost our lease." Libby ignored Emma and focused on me. "For years we've been meeting in the basement of Larry's Laundromat, but Larry's pipes burst over the winter, and there's been terrible water damage. All our mats are mildewed, and—well, it was a total catastrophe. The feng shui has been permanently compromised."

I asked, "What are you going to do?"

"We need to raise some rent money for a new location. Larry always let us use his basement for free, so—"

"Hold it," Emma said. "You mean Larry Wolmeister? The owner of the Dungeon of Darkness?"

Libby's face went slack. "Larry owns the Dungeon of Darkness?"

"Of course he does!"

"Well, you would know, I suppose. Has he given you a raise lately?"

"Yes, as a matter of fact. I'm Employee of the Month."

"What's the Dungeon of Darkness?" I asked. "One of those stores that sells hobbit games for teenagers? Is that your new employer, Em?"

Libby glared at Emma. "Just because Larry happens to own that den of—of—who knows what doesn't mean he can't operate a legitimate business, too."

"The Dungeon is a legitimate business," Emma said. "Do you know how much people pay to get inside?"

"How much?" I asked.

Libby sniffed. "Do you run the cash register now, too?"

"I do lots of stuff for your pal Larry. All of it legal. Maybe you should stop in to check out the scene?"

"Is anybody going to tell me what's going on?" I asked.

"No," they said together.

"Is this what you've been arguing about? Em's job?"

"Yes," in unison.

"And I'm still not allowed to know about it?"

"It's no big deal," Emma said, but she and Libby were seething at each other like boxers before a title match.

"All right, then, let's get back to the Erotic Yoga Society." I was determined not to let either one of them make me crazy. "How are you going to raise the rent money, Lib?"

Libby delicately laced her fingers together and created a hammock for her chin as she turned to me again. "Larry is a very generous soul who appreciates the nature of our spiritual quest. He suggested creating a calendar to raise the rent money. The volunteer firemen did one and made a fortune last year. They bought a new truck with their profits."

"Photographs," I said. "Of what?"

"Who," Libby corrected. "Of our group members. We're all posing."

14

"Aha," said Emma. "I knew there was a reason for the diet."

Libby's eyes blazed. "It's not a diet! It's a healthy lifestyle—"

"Exactly what kind of photographs are we talking about?" I asked.

Libby stopped glaring at Emma and took a cleansing breath. "We are the Erotic Yoga Society, after all. So naturally, the photos are supposed to be . . . well, natural."

"You mean naked."

Emma laughed. "I saw the fireman calendar. Those guys squirted their muscles with so much PAM they could barely hold on to their hoses."

"Our calendar will be *tasteful*. And I'm the month of June. Maxine Peeples already grabbed July, which is right on the staple, damn her. It's the month everybody will look at right away. The centerfold! Thing is, she's got a twin. And they're posing together." A peeved frown appeared between Libby's brows. "You'd think Maxine had invented twins—she's getting so much attention. And she's not nearly as attractive as she thinks she is. Her bottom looks like cottage cheese, which I presume is genetic, so together they're going to look like—"

I had already completed the mental equation and began to shake my head. "I'm afraid not, Libby."

"I haven't even suggested anything yet!"

"We're not posing for naked pictures with you," Emma said. "No way, no how."

15

"*You* object?" Libby demanded. "You, of all people, who rents your body out for sushi parties, not to mention your latest—"

"I only did the sushi thing once," Emma snapped. "The caterer paid me three hundred dollars to lie on a table with raw fish all over me. What's your beef?"

"You were stark naked then, too!"

"There was seaweed!"

"Libby," I said. Their raised voices had begun to attract shushes from nearby tables. "The point is, Emma and I aren't even members of the Erotic Yoga Society. And we're not as—as photogenic as you are."

"Of course you are! You just need to firm up a bit, and Emma needs a couple more pounds to round off her edges. Most men like to be able to hold on to a woman, not dodge lashes from her whip."

"What does—"

Emma said, "We're not posing for pictures."

"Nora will, won't you? I've already scheduled a preliminary session with the photographer Larry suggested."

"Larry suggested a photographer?" Emma cried. "Are you nuts?"

"I'm told he's very accomplished and artistic!"

"I work for Larry," Emma snapped. "And his idea of artistic is changing the letters on the marquee."

"Lib," I said as calmly as I could manage, "I'm sorry. No matter who the photographer is, I just don't see myself becoming Miss July."

"June. Look, I know you're reluctant to show your body. I can help! I'll be your diet coach! It will be fun!"

"No," I said.

"Dieting doesn't have to be painful. Here, I've brought you a little present! See? It's a notebook to write down everything you eat. Isn't it pretty? Hand-made by Navajo tribeswomen."

She handed over a small notebook decorated with plastic beads. I looked at it suspiciously. "Is this something you picked up on your trip to the Grand Canyon a few years ago?"

"The point is, you keep track of your food for a few days and voilà! The pounds just slip away."

"I don't think that's quite how it works, Lib."

"I recommend the Cabbage Soup Diet," she continued. "You eat nothing but cabbage soup. I'm told it's miraculous. I'm not crazy about cabbage, so tomorrow I'm going to make a big pot of potato soup instead. Shall I make extra for you?"

I lost control. "Libby, I'm not posing naked!"

Heads turned. Disapproving looks were cast my way.

Libby pouted. "I thought spending time with the Mafia Prince might have loosened you up a bit. I thought he was revitalizing your sensual side."

"Yeah," said Emma. "Doesn't the Love Machine make you take off your clothes while he opens the beer with his teeth?"

"I'm not seeing Michael anymore," I said.

Both my sisters forgot about their differences and blinked at me. "What?"

"That relationship is over."

My on-again, off-again romance with Michael Abruzzo had escalated to the live-in stage over the holidays, but imploded. I was a single woman again.

"Oh, Nora, I wondered why you look so awful! What did he do? Was it disgusting?" Libby seized my hand. "Tell us everything!"

"It wasn't—look, I don't want to discuss this. It's over, and that's the way it is."

"It's about time, of course." Libby patted me gently. "Despite a certain animal magnetism, Mr. Abruzzo was not right for you, Nora. I spent three terrifying days with him after that misunderstanding I had with the police, and I'll never forget my brush with death while under his protection."

"Brush with death?" Emma said. "You got a back-stage pass to the ultimate testosterone festival, and you didn't like it?"

Libby sniffed. "I believe Nora needs someone with more polish than That Man. Someone who can be taken out into polite society now and then."

"A court-sealed criminal record would be a plus, too." Emma stamped out her cigarette. "You serious this time, Nora? You gave Mick the boot?"

For some reason, my throat had begun to swell shut, so I reached for my glass of ice water, conscious that my sisters were watching me for signs of hysteria.

I was saved from further cross-examination when

Libby's cell phone chirped from the depths of her handbag. She rummaged through a jumble of nutrition bars before snatching out the phone.

"Hello?" she asked with a musical lilt. Then her expression hardened into the face of a woman with five children. "No, Lucy, you may not paint the living room carpet."

While Libby conducted détente with her six-year-old daughter, the waiter came with Emma's cheesecake, looking relieved to see she had extinguished her cigarette. Emma tapped her fork on the table, staring meaningfully at me until the waiter went away.

"Well?" she said, keeping her voice down so Libby couldn't overhear.

"Well, what?"

"You hardly touched your lunch. You turned green at the slightest whiff of salad dressing. It's official, isn't it?"

"Emma—"

"Just because Mick's out of the picture now doesn't mean you weren't doing it like bunnies all winter. You're pregnant."

The word simply spoken aloud made my heart seize. Around us, the fashion show froze. The luncheon lurched. It had taken three pink strips to convince me of the irrevocable truth, and even weeks later, I hadn't been able to bring myself to speak the name of my condition. And now that Emma had said the word, I had no choice but to kill her.

I throttled back the tidal wave of terror. "Em, if you

breathe a word to Libby, I swear I'll—"

"What's the matter?" Emma grinned, but obliged me by lowering her voice another notch. "Afraid she'll give you daily pointers on how to have satisfying pregnant sex? Or is it her lecture on the orgasmic vaginal delivery that has you so worried?"

My current state of catastrophe was almost complete, but the thought of unleashing Libby's full store of appalling gynecological information—each factoid less appetizing than the one before—nearly gave me a panic attack.

"I just can't face telling her." I abandoned my last iota of pride and begged, "Not yet, please. At this point, I can barely cope with the morning sickness."

"Be glad it's just nausea. When Libby gets pregnant, she turns into a nymphomaniac. Remember how exhausted Ralph looked the last time she was fully fertilized? Like he just staggered off a chain gang. That's not one of your symptoms, is it? Perpetual hots? 'Cause that would be pretty funny, considering."

"Your sympathy is heartwarming. Just let me tell Libby in my own time, will you? She's going to go berserk. You see how excited she can get about making me diet?"

"Yeah, that's nothing compared to how nuts she'll go if there's a vagina involved." Emma grinned. "But at least she'll be off my case."

"You're no help!"

"Maybe we can strike a deal. Been to the doctor yet?"

"Twice."

"What does Mick say about the baby?"

I did not respond.

Emma put down her fork and sat back to assess me with a more serious look in her eye. Usually a party girl in search of rowdy redneck love in the back of a pickup truck—she could walk past a Jiffy Lube and leave a dozen men drooling on the pavement—Emma didn't often take charge. But when she did, it was with the air of a strike force commander. Hard-voiced, she said, "You're keeping this a secret from Mick?"

"For the moment, yes. I have a few things to figure out before I—before he can know."

Emma shook her head. "If I had to guess which one of the Blackbird sisters was going to totally screw up her life, you would have been my last choice."

When our parents saw fit to leave the Bucks County family estate in my hands—probably because I had heretofore been seen as the sensible sister—the farm had come into my possession along with an unpaid tax bill for a heart-stopping two million dollars. Since Blackbird Farm was the last vestige of our once proud family legacy, I was determined to hang on to the place. But my job wasn't going too well, and my affair with the son of a New Jersey crime boss had turned my social circle on its collective ear. And now this. To my own surprise, I wasn't the sensible sister after all.

Considering the competition, that news bulletin was pretty upsetting.

Emma took a slug of coffee. "Seen today's newspaper yet?"

"You mean there's another disaster on my horizon?"

"Mick's picture's on the front page again—with his dad, Big Frankie. The story says the Abruzzo crime family are the last remaining gangsters in Jersey. Except for some rinky-dink crew that runs a garbage syndicate up near Paterson."

"Why are you telling me this?"

"Mick's back in the mob."

I had understood that fact the first twelve times people told me that my sometimes lover had rejoined his family business. After several years of going straight, he had answered the call of the wild or succumbed to his instincts and gone back to a life I did not understand. And could not accept. Illegal gambling, some loan-sharking and a few other felonious activities involving stolen cars and chop shops had appealed to him more than making a life with me.

I cleared the lump in my throat. "In case I didn't make it clear before, Michael and I are not together anymore, Emma. I finally figured out that associating with a criminal isn't the yellow brick road to happiness. And he seems to feel I don't fit into his plans anymore, either, so it ended on a civil note, quite calmly."

Emma looked at me as if I'd tried to take a trip to Pluto on a pogo stick. "So you're not telling him about the kid?"

I folded my napkin.

"It's either that or . . ." Emma sounded mystified, and then the other possibility finally hit her. "Holy shit! The kid isn't Richard's, is it? Nora, have you been doing the hokeypokey with the reporter, too?"

Libby was coming to the end of her phone call, and rather than explain the mess that was my life to both my sisters, I decided to escape while I could. I dropped my napkin on the table and stood up. Libby signaled that our conversation wasn't over yet, but I decided to run while I could. I departed, winding my way through tables of Daffodil luncheoners.

The fashion show models milled around in the lobby of the country club, too busy checking each other for lipstick on their teeth to take notice of me. I over-tipped the teenager at the coat check, grabbed my coat and headed across the tartan carpet. The club was very faux Scotland, with a mural of the Highlands painted along the hallway and dozens of tarnished golf trophies in a glass case. I rushed past as if pursued by a regiment of demonic bagpipers.

I paused in front of a mirror by the double doors to slip on my grandmother's vintage swing coat, the perfect garment to hide my coming figure flaws. Before I buttoned up, however, I looked at my reflection and found myself involuntarily exploring the new topography of my body. I put my hand on my thickening waist. In the mirror I looked very different already. In just two and a half months, I'd lost weight in my face and gained incredibly round and tender vulnerabilities elsewhere. All my bras were tight, and I felt constantly hot and swollen with hormones. My stomach had a distinctly new silhouette that the clothes from my grandmother's closet didn't quite conceal anymore. And although I prided myself on remaining steady in a crisis, lately I'd become more temperamental than an alien monster worthy of Sigourney Weaver's rage.

And within my now frequently uncontrollable body blipped the heart of a human being who planned to spend the next twenty years relying on me—a woman with equal quantities of financial stability and common sense. Zilch in both categories.

The baby's father? I hadn't come to terms with that yet. I wasn't ready to admit—even to myself—who had helped me mix the magic that resulted in the child I carried.

It was all a terrible mess.

So how come my mirrored reflection was smiling?

"If you're hallucinating," Emma said behind me, "do I get to slap you?"

She had come up quietly and was watching my face in the mirror. I quickly fastened my coat. "Don't start anything you can't finish."

She followed me out the door into a cold blast of March wind. "Where are you going?"

"To work."

"Let me drive you."

"I don't need a babysitter."

"Yet," said Emma.

"Take a hike!" I snapped.

Emma laughed. "By God, I thought you never lost

24

your cool. Come on. You need a ride, don't you? I'll drive."

We were on the sidewalk by then, and the March wind whipped my hair across my face. I pushed it aside with irritation. "Don't you have to punch the time clock somewhere?"

"Not for hours. Are you okay?" She squinted at me. "Healthwise, I mean."

"Emma—"

"Because the last time, remember," she said, "you had a miscarriage."

Years ago, when my marriage to Todd had been at its worst, I'd gotten pregnant, but lost the baby within a matter of weeks. Except for my sisters, I hadn't told a soul, not even my mother or my friends or Todd, who couldn't think of anything at that time but cocaine. Bringing a child into the maelstrom of Todd's drug addiction would have made a bad situation even more terrible. I'd been almost relieved when the pregnancy ended. I wrestled with my own grief and guilt at the time, but coping with Todd had soon overshadowed everything else. Only in the last year or so had I started to feel something for that lost baby.

Emma read my face. "You don't look well. Is the morning sickness really bad? Or is there something worse going on?"

"I'm fine."

. Emma caught my arm. "Tell me the truth."

It felt oddly good to have someone else in the loop. Someone I didn't have to lie to. "I'm supposed to be

25

careful," I amended. She didn't need to know the rest. My doctor had cautioned me, however, and repeating her warnings aloud somehow felt like making a miscarriage more likely.

But Emma guessed, her smirk long gone. Her grip on my arm eased. "C'mon," she said. "I'll drive you."

"What about Libby?"

"She'll be busy for a while." Emma hooked her arm through mine and pulled. "I left her my cheesecake."

I liked to think I didn't need help anymore. That I was an adult who'd been through my share of trouble and survived. But Emma's pull felt reassuring. I let her drag me across the slushy parking lot.

"I should call Rawlins," I said. "He's supposed to pick me up."

"What, you've hired our nephew during his spring break?"

"Why not? I need a driver, and it keeps him out of trouble."

"Where's Reed?"

I had an annoying tendency to faint, which nixed a driver's license, so a driver was the only way to keep my job. Fortunately, my original employment agreement has provided the services of a part-time chauffeur at the expense of the newspaper. "Reed's in London," I said. "Semester abroad. Rawlins has been filling in."

Emma pulled her cell phone from her pocket. "I'll call him. He'll probably be glad to have an afternoon off. Where are we headed?"

"The Fitch estate. I'm meeting Delilah Fairweather there."

I allowed my little sister to boost me into her pickup—a rattletrap vehicle better suited to farm animals than my Ferragamos, but today its blasting heater felt good on my toes. With Emma multitasking behind the wheel, she spoke with our nephew as we hurtled out of the parking lot and hit the road.

"So I'm taking over," she said into her cell phone. "You can be a juvenile delinquent this afternoon."

I heard Rawlins laughing when she terminated the call.

"Don't you have to go to work?" I asked, hoping she might break down and tell me about her new job.

"Later," she said. "Much later."

Since our parents' hasty departure, Emma had turned her skills and lifelong fondness for lost causes into a sometimes successful career training show jumpers for the Grand Prix circuit. For several years she had lived frugally but well enough on the meager income she earned from work she loved, so I was suspicious about her new employment.

I said, "You're keeping secrets. And if Libby's upset, it must be something very tacky."

Emma shot me a wry glance. "Don't worry about me, Sis."

"When are you going to tell me about your job?"

"You're pregnant now," she said. "The news might be harmful."

"It's that bad, huh?"

"Not bad," she said. "Just . . . different."

Chapter Two

We roared toward the suburb of Philadelphia commonly called the Main Line, a posh yet pastoral enclave where grand houses stood behind discreet hedges planted long ago. The names that lettered brass plates on the stone pillars flanking so many driveways had been listed on the passenger manifest of the *Mayflower* and were later carved in the stone facades of Philadelphia landmarks. Their backyards included shooting ranges, tennis courts and sometimes even polo fields. They kept employees on staff to clean their floors, their guns and their tax returns.

The people here lived a way of life my sisters and I understood. We'd been brought up in the same lavish world and only lately lost the fortune required to maintain such a lifestyle.

At a crossroads marked by split-rail fences and green pastures that looked a lot like the horse farms of Kentucky, Emma hung a sharp right turn and pulled through a gate tall enough to rival the entrance to Oz. She gunned the truck through the gates and drove up a winding driveway lined with trees. Forty pristine acres rolled gracefully away from the drive, dotted with yellow and purple crocuses. Grazing on the new shoots of grass in the distance were three sheep—the remains of the purebred Shropshire flock that had roamed the estate grounds years ago and given the whole landscape the look of a Gainsborough painting.

Gradually, the manor house that most of us still called Fitch's Fancy came into view—one of the most spectacular in a spectacular neighborhood.

First we saw the crenellated battlements of the house rising above a grove of hemlocks. Then Emma's truck rounded the last curve, and the home greeted us with all the majesty of the Northumbrian castle it had been patterned on. The stone walls climbed with thick ivy, curls of smoke wafted around the chimneys, and the lancet windows winked in the sunshine. The house gave every impression that we'd entered another century, although the truth was given away by a satellite dish on the roof.

"Boy, it's a bitch, isn't it?" Emma rested her foot on the brake and peered through the dirty windshield. "This place was really something in its day."

"It still is. Sort of."

We both saw the crumbling stones in the walkway, the rampant ivy, the dislocated downspout dripping rainwater. Fitch's Fancy had been neglected.

"Why are you meeting Delilah here, of all places?"

Delilah Fairweather was the city's most popular event planner, with a schedule busier than that of Condoleezza Rice.

"It was the only way I could catch her. She has an

appointment here this afternoon. She's supposed to be organizing a museum party for Saturday night. But she's dropped the ball on a few details, and I said I'd check on things."

"That doesn't sound like Delilah."

"I know. Lexie asked me to give her a gentle reminder."

Plus I was a little worried about my friend. Delilah had dodged me twice already and missed a lunch date. She never passed up an opportunity to enjoy the seared tuna or the people watching at our favorite downtown lunch spot.

Before Emma could respond, an old white Bentley suddenly roared around a low stone wall. The antique car hurtled toward us with the accuracy of a cold-war torpedo.

Emma blew her horn and yanked her truck over to avoid a crash, and the car almost shot past us free and clear. But it was towing a small flatbed trailer—just big enough to haul two mud-spattered motocross bikes and a blue surfboard. The trailer clipped Emma's bumper and slewed sideways. Then it hit a pothole and tumbled over, dragging the Bentley off the driveway and halfway into the ditch. We heard an awful bang, and Emma cursed. I grabbed the dashboard and caught a quick glimpse of the driver—an old man with a shock of thick white hair and huge rubber goggles that gave him the look of a demented pilot who had just beaten the Red Baron in a dogfight.

Emma jerked her truck back onto the driveway

before we crashed, too. "Who the hell was that idiot?"

"Pierpoint Fitch, I think."

"Is he dead?"

Both of us popped open our doors and stepped out onto the gravel. Emma ran toward the car. I found myself trapped against the pickup by the fallen surfboard. Pierpoint Fitch, best known as "Pointy" to his friends, unfurled his storklike body from the car and stood up, looking bizarre, but uninjured.

"Hey, hot dog," Emma called. "You okay?"

"No thanks to you," he snapped, shoving his goggles to the top of his head. His hair immediately stood on end as if he'd stuck his finger in a light socket.

"Me? This is your fault!"

"Poppycock!"

Pointy Fitch, nearly eighty, had a pair of baggy shorts hanging on his bony hips—shorts that would have looked more natural on a skateboarding teenager than an elderly millionaire. His skinny, blue-veined legs disappeared into a pair of enormous sneakers, and he warded off the afternoon chill with a faded blue sweatshirt emblazoned with the name of a prep school he hadn't attended in sixty-five years.

He stomped around the Bentley to inspect his over-turned trailer. The sight of the damage prompted him to let out a string of quaintly Victorian curses. "Blast! What an infernal, confounded botch!"

"Cool your jets," said Emma. "We'll call a tow truck."

"The devil with that!" He reared back and gave the

trailer hitch an ineffectual kick. Then, "Ow!"

"What are you trying to do? Break your foot?" Emma bent and expertly pulled the pin from the hitch.

Immediately, the trailer disengaged from the car and keeled over. We heard the motorcycles crunch under the weight of the trailer.

Pointy squinted at my sister with new respect. "You're not half bad for a hoyden. You're one of those Blackbird widows, right?"

"Don't get your hopes up, old man. I only date grown-ups."

Affronted as a maiden aunt who'd just heard a naughty limerick, he blustered, "Don't be ridiculous, young lady! I am a gentleman!"

"That's what they all say. Hey, are you hurt?"

"Certainly not. I'm as tough as pemmican." He used his knobby knuckles to rap his own skull. "See? Indestructible!"

"Maybe we should take you to the hospital, just to be sure."

"I'd rather be boiled in oil by South Sea savages than set foot in a germ factory like a hospital. No, thank you, no hospitals for me!"

"Humor me, you old geezer. Let's get you checked out."

"You'll have to wrestle me to the ground," he replied. "And a little wisp like you would have your hands full."

"Who you calling a—hey, where are you going?"

He had turned away and marched back to his car. "I

32

have pressing matters to attend."

"But what about your trailer?" Emma called.

"Leave it!"

Without further exchange, Pointy climbed back into his Bentley, started the engine with a roar and drove off in a spray of gravel.

Emma walked back to me. "What the hell is a pemmican, anyway?"

"I always thought it was like beef jerky."

"What a loon. Isn't he the maniac with the Frisbees?"

Millionaire Pierpoint Fitch had not settled into a dignified retirement from his long and spotty banking career with a suitably quiet pastime like stamp collecting. No, Pointy Fitch had taken up sports and traveled around competing in everything from miniature golf to the senior badminton championship. His family thought he was eccentric. Everyone else figured he was nuts.

Eyeing the crushed motorcycles, I had to agree with them. "I thought Pointy was into tennis and archery. This looks dangerous."

Emma nodded. "Last I heard, he was shooting marbles at some coot convention in Atlantic City. Where do you suppose he's off to in such a hurry today?"

"A Mensa meeting?"

Emma laughed. Except for a few distant cousins, none of the Fitches were known for the sharpness of their wits.

"Look," I said, "thanks for bringing me, but there's

no need for you to stick around. I'll walk up to the house from here. Delilah's bound to be waiting for me."

"Forget it," said Emma. "I'll go park by the sheep barn and come find you. Don't slip and fall. This sidewalk hasn't been swept in years."

As she drove away, I hiked up the slate walkway into the geometrically perfect garden of yews, ornamental trees and delicate ground covers. If the Fitches lacked the education and God-given talent to create great beauty, at least they had enough sense to hire those who did. Although it had been ages since a gardener had properly tended the elaborate plantings, I could still see the bones of good design beneath the overgrowth.

I slowed my pace as I reached the fountain—empty today but for the marble figure of a naked woman taking aim with a bow and arrow, symbols of the Fitch family's favorite pastime. The huntress had always made me smile because her eyes were slightly crossed. I reached out and gave her bare behind a pat, then looked up at the tall windows of the ballroom.

I was too young to remember the days when bons vivants and madcap heiresses drank Prohibition liquor at glamorous Fitch parties, but I had certainly attended my share of swanky bashes in the house. My family and the Fitches went back a few generations. The spring balls were noisy and fun—fancy dress with big bands from New York and, later, with local rock groups that rattled the windows. The famous archery tournaments had been the kind of blazingly sunny summer afternoons where children played red rover on the lawn, chased everywhere by Fitch sheepdogs, while Fitch servants churned ice cream, and parents drank gallons of juleps and tried to shoot arrows at straw-stuffed targets.

But as I reached the first plateau in the garden, I suddenly saw a huge moving van parked on the lawn by the back door. The logo of Kingsley's auction house was printed on the side of the truck. The Philadelphia-based company specialized in estate sales.

It was never a good sign to see an estate sale company pull into your driveway.

Two uniformed employees struggled out of the house carrying a glass-fronted bookcase. A third Kingsley's employee leaned against the kitchen entrance by the dog door with a cigarette.

I stopped on the walk, struck by the end of a great family's story. Once moneyed and influential, the Fitches had tumbled to this—the day when all their possessions went off in a truck to be sold.

"Nora?"

I spun around to see Boykin Fitch standing in the brambles beyond the ornamental garden. In a pin-striped suit and a pair of thick rubber boots, he looked surprised and ludicrously handsome entangled in the weeds.

"You startled me, Boy." I smiled. "But I think the first time I met you, it was right here in this garden."

He grinned as he disengaged his boot from a thorny

35

trap and began to climb over the hedge to greet me. "Were we looking for champagne?"

I steadied his arm as he lost his balance. "Yes! Your grandparents chilled it in the snowbanks on New Year's Eve and forgot where all the bottles were. We used to keep those old kerosene lamps out here for searching, remember? Are you looking for some now?"

"No." He managed to get over the hedge, but cast a puzzled glance at the weeds around him. "I think I dropped my wallet." He grabbed one buttock and frowned.

"Have you looked in your other pockets?"

Amiably, he followed my suggestion and began to pat his clothes. "I know I had it earlier, but I—" When one hand struck the breast pocket of his jacket, his face cleared into a smile. "Golly, will you look at that!" He produced a worn Gucci wallet from his jacket. "I had it all along!"

Deep as a birdbath. That was Boy.

After he put his wallet into his hip pocket, I shook his hand. "It's nice to see you again after all these years."

I hadn't bumped into him in a decade, but the years had been good to Boykin Fitch. He'd grown tall and distinguished with a patrician profile and a noble gaze prone to staring pensively into the distance. Or maybe he was just trying to remember his own phone number. For all his good looks, Boy Fitch was as endearingly dim as a Labrador retriever.

I'd known him as a teenager, when he'd been held back for a few extra years at prep schools better known for their athletic fields than for their libraries. Family connections got Boy into the Ivy League school where it took tutors and well-paid friends six years to help him acquire his degree. After that, he'd gone to a law school nobody ever heard of, but departed without a diploma, his academic performance best forgotten.

Lately, though, Boy had managed to find the perfect career for someone with his particular combination of good looks, good manners and lackluster intelligence.

He found politics.

With the help of a media genius, he'd been miraculously elected to the Pennsylvania legislature, where a young and handsome scion of an old family created quite a stir. By keeping his head down and other body parts out of scandal, he attracted the attention of his party's chieftains. Some tentative fund-raising turned into an avalanche of money and now there was talk of a campaign for a US Senate seat. For those of us who remembered Boy as the kid who knocked out his own front teeth with a tennis racket, it was hard to believe.

I said, "What's going on? Why is the Kingsley's truck here?"

Boy smoothed his thick brown hair off his forehead. He wore a patriotic tie printed with little waving flags. "My uncle Zell is selling the place. And everything in it."

"Now? This minute?"

Boy nodded glumly. "He's trying to pull a fast one on the rest of the family. We got here as quickly as we could, but Kingsley's has security guards all over the house. We can't get inside."

"Boy, how awful!"

"We want nothing more than a few family keepsakes, but Zell says no. I don't mind losing the house so much. It's kind of an ugly old pile, don't you think?" He looked up at the imposing structure. "But gee, I sure wish I could have my old train set."

"The house is magnificent!" I argued, shocked that anyone would think of selling such an estate without the approval of the whole family. "And each room is a masterpiece. The library alone—with the Alfons Mucha lithographs embedded in the wallpaper! I love Art Nouveau."

"Who's Art Nouveau?" Boy asked, genuinely mystified.

In that moment, I was sure Boykin had found his calling. Suddenly, I could clearly picture him walking in the shadow of a helicopter, amiably cupping his ear and playing deaf to the cries of his constituents.

"Uhm, Art Noveau is—well, I'm just sorry about the whole situation. You must all be devastated."

"Yeah, my dad just left in a temper."

"I saw him. He looked very upset."

Boy sighed. "Frankly, I'm glad he took off. You never know when Dad might do something really crazy. He hasn't been himself lately. Did you see his motorcycles?"

"Yes, but he won't be using them in the near future. We had a little fender bender, and the bikes ended up in the ditch by the driveway."

"Well, that's a relief."

Boy's father, Pierpoint, had been raised at Fitch's Fancy along with various siblings. Due to a glitch in someone's will, the house had not passed to Pointy, but to his sister instead—and upon her death, to her second husband, best known to all of Philadelphia as "that rat bastard," Zell Orcutt, who was universally disliked and snubbed by the Old Money crowd.

Zell, it appeared, was getting his revenge now.

Boy said, "Dad's ready to murder Zell over this."

When he first rode into Philadelphia, Zell claimed to be an Oklahoma wildcatter and quickly won the affections of a rich, susceptible widow, Hannah Fitch Barnstable. After they eloped, Zell's true character started to show. First he was thrown out of the Schuylkill Club for cheating at cards. Then there was a hushed-up affair concerning missing bearer bonds. Instead of lazy, glamorous afternoon parties with longtime friends, Zell threw splashy bashes with lots of social climbers. He walked around carrying his own pint of cheap bourbon, slapping backs and nuzzling his wife's friends.

And everyone heard whispers that he'd impregnated two of his stepdaughter's high school friends.

My own unpleasant brush with Zell happened during a Christmas party at Fitch's Fancy. While whispering with a boy in the shadow of the staircase, I'd heard Zell slap his wife on the landing above us. My friend fled moments later when Zell strutted down the stairs, but I couldn't move. When Zell rounded the newel post and saw me, he came over and backed me against the paneling. He reached out and pinched my chin hard between his thumb and fingers.

"Hey, there, little lady," he crooned. "What are you doing here in the dark?"

As I pushed his hand away, his wife leaned down over the banister and said in her odd, baby voice, "Zelly, don't."

His boozy grin never wavered, but he let me go, giving my bottom a swat as if I were a heifer that needed a send-off.

As time went on, Zell humiliated his wife so regularly that she gradually found it easier to stay out of the public eye. In the last several years before her death, her daughter ran off, and Zell took over the estate. Hannah died a recluse.

That Zell ended up sole owner of Fitch's Fancy was bad enough, but selling it out from under the rest of the family was the act of a rattlesnake.

"I wish I could help, Boy. Want me to distract someone so you can run inside?"

He smiled. "Actually, my cousin Verbena just broke a basement window and sneaked in. I'm supposed to wait here in the garden. I guess I tackle the security guard if he makes a move."

"I'm so sorry about this, Boy."

"Me, too." He looked up at the imposing home and

sighed. "Gosh, this old house has a lot of memories. I fell out of that window once."

We both turned at the sound of footsteps behind us. Emma came striding up the sloping garden, looking every inch the girl who'd been expelled for seducing a high school football coach.

Boy caught sight of her and stopped breathing, completely absorbed by the tensile strength in her long-legged walk, the lean curves of her body and the knowledge of all things sexual that glowed in her eyes. I prepared to watch the Emma Phenomenon.

To me, Em said, "Who's the leaning tower of propriety?"

I gave her a stern glance. "Emma, you're probably too young to remember Boykin Fitch. Boy, this is my sister Emma Blackbird."

They shook hands firmly, and perhaps Boy flinched. Emma said, "Don't I know you from somewhere?"

I said, "Boy is our state legislator. He may be running for the Senate next year."

Boy ducked his head humbly. "Well, now, nothing's official."

Emma frowned. "I usually go for the lawbreakers, not lawmakers. Are you—?"

"Maybe you saw my picture in the newspaper."

Emma sized him up. Although she'd been burned by love, that didn't stop her from pursuing the opposite sex when she felt the urge. Her recent history with men had included an alcoholic country-western has-been and the toothy kid who drove the tow truck that

41

hauled her pickup out of a muddy horse pasture. The only characteristics they had in common were a willingness to be bossed around by Emma and plenty of stamina in bed. To me, Boy seemed an unlikely prospect.

Emma must have reached the same conclusion. She shrugged and hooked her thumb in the direction of the Kingsley's truck. "What's going on? Looks like the place is getting robbed in broad daylight."

"In a way," I said. "Zell is clearing out the house. He's selling everything."

Emma looked surprised. "No kidding? The old cowpoke is settling up his gambling debts at last?"

We heard some yelling from the direction of the house. The security guard dropped his cigarette and ran over to help one of his compatriots, who plunged out of the ballroom French doors, wrestling with a tall, rangy woman with spiked white hair.

"Uh-oh," said Boy. "Cousin Verbena."

Verbena Fitch Barnstable let out a scream that shook the tree limbs around us. It was the scream that tens of thousands of rock-and-roll fans had heard in stadiums all over the world fifteen years ago. Backed by the howling guitars and thundering drums of the rock band Harass, Verbena had belted out raunchy lyrics and spewed whiskey on mosh pits on five continents.

She shrieked again and fought her captor like a tigress.

As we ran up through the garden, I saw her twist and viciously knee the burly young man in the groin. He let out a strangled yelp and crumpled to the ground. But the second security guard reached Verbena at that moment and locked one muscled arm around her body. Her prematurely white hair flashed in the sunshine as she struggled with him.

"Let me go, you son of a bitch! Let me go!"

"Take it easy, lady!" The young man panted while his friend rolled on the wet flagstones, groaning and clutching his wounded parts.

"Verbena!" Boy cried.

"Take your hands off me," she snapped, elbows flying with lethal accuracy. The former rock-and-roll star knew her karate, and it wasn't just stage moves. Verbena squarely jammed her elbow into the young intimidator's liver.

"Release her immediately," Boy commanded unnecessarily. The guard had already dropped her, and Verbena landed on her feet. Without thinking, I reached out to steady her, but Verbena swung on me with a murderous glare in her eyes.

"Take it easy," Boy soothed, his hand light on her shoulder. "Let's not hurt anybody else."

"These anabolic idiots won't let me inside," she shouted, shaking off his touch. "There are things I own in that house!"

"I know."

"Sorry, miss—uh, ma'am—uh—" The security guard who was still standing rubbed his sore belly. "We have orders not to let anyone inside."

"My desk." Her jaw trembled with rage. "That's all

I want. It was my desk from childhood, a gift from my mother long before she married that bastard. It's not Zell's, but mine, and I want it!"

The guard shook his head so firmly that I knew he'd fought with families before. "Sorry, but our orders—"

"Let's be reasonable," Boy said, mustering the sort of persuasive bonhomie that seemed natural to politicians. "I can have a court order here in a few hours. Can you stop moving things into the truck until I get the proper paperwork?"

"Sorry, sir."

"This is ridiculous," Verbena snarled. "Boy, stop sucking up to this Neanderthal."

She was still wildly, grotesquely beautiful—skinny and arrogant with a stage presence that could rival Mick Jagger's. Her juicy red smear of a mouth was unmistakable, her solar flare of hair was white-hot, and her deep-set eyes were still as fierce as those of a feral cat. Rock fans knew her as Viper, and in many ways she lived up to her name.

A troubled wild child, Verbena had left home early and struck out into the world to make her own way. Never really a musician, she'd first been a camp follower of an Irish band, then shot to fame when their singer got sick and Viper stepped onstage in Germany. She started yelling song lyrics in her distinctive rasp, and a star was born. She bounced from band to band for a while and ended up with Harass, cutting at least one important rock-and-roll album. Fans adored her hard-bitten, working-class style and never guessed

44

she'd come from a wealthy Philadelphia family.

Viper didn't burn out like a comet or fade away into a drug-addled twilight like so many rockers. Instead, she abruptly left Harass and returned to Philadelphia. Her family paid for media silence, I'd heard, and the Old Money crowd had closed ranks to bury her past. At long last, she reappeared with a baby daughter. Lots of people in my social circle knew about her rock star days, but it was considered bad taste to bring it up. Anyone who did was promptly shunned by powerful Fitch family friends.

To reinvent herself, Verbena went to culinary school, of all choices, and she eventually opened an upscale bakery and tea shop on a leafy Philadelphia neighborhood corner where rich young socialites dropped in for occasional afternoon indulgences. Her angelic blond daughter grew up playing with a rolling pin in the window of the shop. When Verbena's decorated cupcakes became her trademark and nearly as popular as cheesesteak sandwiches in the city, Verbena had successfully made herself over on behalf of her own little girl.

But today, she was Viper all over again.

"Boy, go find Zell right now," she commanded. "Where's that chickenshit son of a bitch hiding? He was here an hour ago. Go get him!"

"I tried reasoning with him already, Verbena, but he wouldn't listen."

"Then punch him in the gut or something! Anything!"

I said, "Look, Boy, we're intruding. This is a family problem, and Emma and I are only in the way—"

Verbena finally became aware of the need to be civil. "Hello, Nora," she said shortly. "I'm sorry you had to see this. I suppose you'll print the whole story in that newspaper column of yours, won't you?"

"Nora's not going to betray anyone," Boy said. "Let's keep our anger focused where it will do the most good."

"Yeah," said Emma. "Keep your eye on the ball, cupcake." Emma had extended her hand down to the moaning security guard on the ground. He appeared to forget his injuries as she hauled him to his feet.

"Cupcake," Verbena said, narrowing her glare on my sister. "Very clever. You're Emma, aren't you? The youngest Blackbird widow?"

"That's me," Emma said. "And you're the cupcake lady."

Em was probably too young to remember Viper.

"Don't talk to me about cake today, all right?" Verbena snapped. "I've had quite enough cupcakes for a while."

"Fine, we'll get out of here. As soon as we find Delilah Fairweather. Is she around?"

"I saw her a while ago," Boy said. "She was with Zell."

"Big surprise," Verbena snapped.

"Now, now, Verbena."

"What's going on?" I asked.

"She's helping him!" Verbena sputtered. "To start

46

that disgusting restaurant of his!"

Mystified, I asked, "Restaurant? Zell's opening a restaurant?"

Boy looked uncomfortable. "It's not exactly your kind of establishment, Nora. It's—well, have you ever been to Hooters?"

"To—?"

"Zell's venture is called Cupcakes, but it's the same principle. It's pretty sordid. Tonight's the grand opening."

Verbena trembled with rage. "I should go over right now and throw a firebomb through the window."

Boy put his arm around his cousin's shoulder. "Let's find Delilah for Nora, and then we'll get out of here. There's no sense prolonging the pain."

They turned away, and I hesitated on the walk. Boykin cast a glance over his shoulder, though, and gestured for us to follow. The four of us walked around the moving van and up several steps to a smaller garden where Verbena's mother had once planted herbs and vegetables for the household kitchen.

"They're up here somewhere," Boy said, drawing his cousin by the hand.

"If I see that asshole," Verbena muttered, "I'll probably kill him."

I'm not sure which one of us spotted him first, but in just a few steps we all stopped on the flagstones, frozen by the sight in front of us. Then Boy let out a startled curse and dropped Verbena's hand. He took

47

two quick paces forward. Automatically, Emma followed him, but they both stopped again, in shock.

Verbena clapped both hands over her mouth to stifle another of her screams.

A person lay sprawled in a patch of dried lavender, as if making snow angels without the snow. An elderly man with a barrel-shaped beer gut, and wearing a fringed pony skin jacket. I could see his long grizzled hair shivering in the breeze, the only visible movement. His face was half turned away from me, but I recognized his profile.

Zell Orcutt.

Dead.

The feathered tip of an arrow stood stiffly upright on his chest, the shaft buried deep in his flesh as if shot there by the stone huntress in the fountain. With one gnarled hand, he had obviously tried to pull it out before death seized him.

Verbena gave a long, keening howl and shoved past Boy. She threw herself down next to her stepfather, and for an instant I thought she intended to strike him. She clenched her fists and drew back, but inches from hitting him, she froze again, her face a mask of shock. She opened both hands and began to sob. "You bastard," she said. "You horrible, rotten bastard!"

She sounded frightened, I thought.

"Oh, God." Boy fumbled for his cell phone. "Oh, my God."

I stepped back and felt the sky spin around us. The air began to twinkle with thousands of tiny stars.

Emma turned and saw my face. "Oh, shit," she said in a voice that sounded very far away. "Don't faint."

Chapter Three

*T*his is not a good idea," Emma said several hours later when we arrived in a suburban parking lot not far from the King of Prussia Mall. "Even the coroner said you looked bad, and that can't be good."

"I'm okay."

I wasn't okay, but the last place I wanted to be was home alone right now, with the image of Zell Orcutt's body in my head and memories of my husband's shooting death flashing back as if it had happened yesterday. Tonight's nightmare was too vivid to bear by myself. I wanted to be with people. I wanted to feel alive.

I said, "I need to find Delilah. Then I'll go home."

"And just where the hell was she?" Emma asked. "I thought she was supposed to meet you at Fitch's Fancy."

We exchanged a glance.

"Delilah must have forgotten about me, that's all. She's so busy."

"Doing what?" Emma muttered.

I said, "Let's go into Cupcakes and find out."

"I still say it's a dumb idea."

"You don't need to come."

"The hell I don't." Emma grinned suddenly. "Cupcakes may not be your kind of place, but it's certainly mine."

Cars and SUVs jammed the parking lot, and a crowd flocked toward the entrance—mostly men, mostly drunk. Rock-and-roll music roared from speakers hidden in the shrubbery. On the sidewalk, we passed a mob of teenagers held at bay by adults checking identification. Emma poked her chin at one of the doormen, and he nodded us inside.

Two blond hostesses with perky smiles and equally perky nipples greeted us. "Welcome to Cupcakes!"

"Save it for the boys," Emma said.

Cupcakes was bedlam fueled by testosterone and rock and roll. One glance told me that Cupcakes planned to lure its customers with the promise of barbecued hot wings and big-screen televisions tuned to sports, but primarily with the Cupcake Girls.

Carrying a tray of drinks over her shoulder, a very young woman in short shorts and a T-shirt snug enough to have been sprayed on her body tottered past us in spike-heeled shoes so high her ankles wobbled. Strategically printed on her shirt was the company logo—twin cupcakes that looked more like bare breasts than dessert.

Emma took one look around and said coolly, "Think I could get a burger? Or do they only wait on people with the Y chromosome?"

I almost couldn't hear her over the cacophony of

hard rock and the blare of dozens of televisions shouting various basketball games. A roar of male laughter erupted from a table where a simpering waitress brandished menus like a fan dancer. The air was heavy with the smell of fried food and beer.

Pacing in the doorway to the bar was my friend Delilah Fairweather. As usual, she had a cell phone jammed to her ear, and she was lambasting a hapless underling on the other end of the line. Her crimped hair danced in the topknot at the crown of her head.

But Delilah spotted me and snapped the phone shut in midtirade. "Girlfriend, you are a sight for sore eyes! How great you came tonight! You doing a little slumming? I don't suppose you've seen Zell Orcutt anywhere? The guest of honor at his own party, and he hasn't shown up yet!"

"Delilah—"

Revved with more than her usual energy, she cut me off. "Here I am trying to keep two hundred redblooded men away from the Cupcake Girls until he—damn, you look odd. I know this isn't exactly your scene, but—what's the matter?"

Emma said, "She's had a shock. I tried to take her home already, but she's stubborn."

"What's happened? Oh, my God!" Delilah slapped one hand to her cheek, and her eyes popped wide. "I was supposed to meet you at Fitch's Fancy! I totally forgot! Oh, Nora, I'm so sorry—"

"There's no need to apologize," I said.

"This has been such a crazy day. It's not like me to

51

forget a single detail, and I sure wish I hadn't started with you."

"Really, it's no big—"

"I mean, Zell has been a pain in my tush about this party for weeks. And now he's so late I had to start the band without him, but—"

"Don't wait for Zell." I tried to stanch her gush of words. "He's not coming."

"Not coming? That sleaze bucket better show up in the next ten minutes or I'm never running another one of his—" She caught sight of my face and realized I wasn't kidding. "What's going on?"

"He's dead," I said.

Delilah's dark eyes widened again, and for once she couldn't speak.

"Shot with an arrow on the grounds of Fitch's Fancy a few hours ago."

A cyclone of a woman, Delilah had more energy than an entire cheerleading squad and twice as much enthusiasm. She'd given up a corporate job to follow her bliss into the event-planning biz and had worked herself to the top of the game in Philadelphia. Any party worth promoting had Delilah running the show, and I wasn't surprised that Zell had hired the best to launch his restaurant, although I was puzzled why Delilah would take a job like Cupcakes. Usually, she was more discerning.

"Oh, honey!" Instantly sympathetic, Delilah took my elbow and gently guided me into an alcove out of the mayhem of the party. "No wonder you look so shaky! How did it happen? Was it an accident?"

"The cops don't think so," Emma muttered.

"It was murder? My God. Who killed the old bastard? Anybody interesting?"

Unsteadily, I shook my head. "They don't know yet."

Delilah hugged me. "Nora, I'm so sorry I forgot about you. If I hadn't been so frazzled, maybe I could have gotten you out of there before it happened."

"Make her sit down," Emma ordered. "I'll get her something to drink." She turned to me. "You've got to take care of yourself now, Sis."

Delilah's brows rose at Emma's tone. "Is there something I should know?"

"No," I said.

Emma snorted. "I'm going to the bar. What can I get you?"

"I've had enough already, thanks," Delilah said.

I noted two martini glasses on the table, one still showing a few sips. I said, "Club soda for me."

"Club soda," Emma said, "coming right up. Keep an eye on her, Delilah."

"Sure." Delilah waited until Emma had left before saying, "Nora?"

Perhaps I was waiting to get safely through the first trimester. Or maybe I wasn't ready to admit that I was inconveniently pregnant. I wasn't prepared to discuss my current condition with anyone yet. Not even with my best friends.

So I said, "Don't let me keep you from your job. You

probably have a zillion calls to make."

Delilah eased me onto a stool at the tall table where she'd been drinking. "If the guest of honor's dead, I might as well take it easy. Man, I can't believe it. I was just with him a couple of hours ago."

The room was warm, and I slid my coat off my shoulders. "What did you go to see him about?"

"Oh, you know, party stuff." She helped arrange my coat on another stool, then finally met my eye. "To be honest, we had a big fight. I don't usually scream at clients, but Zell is—was—well, I'd better keep the specifics to myself."

"Not for long. The police are going to come looking for you, Delilah. They'll be talking to everyone who spoke with Zell today."

She was nodding fast and reached for her drink. "Sure, sure. I understand. I didn't see anything, though. I mean, except Zell acting like an asshole, same as always. We were supposed to finalize details about tonight, but instead we had a squabble and I left."

She picked up her martini glass and drained the last inch of liquor in one swallow. I finally noticed that she wore only one earring, and her makeup was not as pristine as usual. Two of her beautifully manicured nails were ragged, too.

"What did you fight about?" I asked.

"Money, of course. We had a deal, but today he decided he wanted a discount." She laughed shortly, unamused. "I probably won't get paid at all now. Not good timing for me. Maybe his partner will pony up, but I doubt it."

"Zell had a partner? You mean, in Cupcakes?"

Delilah looked at her empty glass as if she wished she hadn't finished the martini. "ChaCha Reynolds. You ever meet her? She's running around here acting like one of the Cupcakes herself. To tell the truth, I don't know which of those two I hate working for most. Maybe ChaCha. She's always calling me sassy." Delilah pulled a bitter smile. "Ever notice you white women never get called sassy? Just the sistahs."

"So she isn't exactly overburdened with social graces."

"Hey, there's a name for women who put little girls in tight clothes and make them shake their booties for a bunch of drunk frat boys, and it ain't Mother Teresa." Delilah glanced around for a waitress. "She isn't going to be exactly grief stricken now that her partner's dead, either."

"Oh? Why's that?"

Delilah cast me a sideways look. "You playing detective already?"

"I can't help being curious."

"They had a big fight here yesterday. You can ask her yourself. Here comes ChaCha now."

Charging out of the kitchen came a tiny lady with the perfectly toned body of a preteen gymnast and the pinched face of a sixty-something woman who'd spent her life hustling for a buck. The gold jewelry around her wrinkled neck, wrists and fingers said she'd been successful.

Under her breath, Delilah said, "Story goes, ChaCha used to be a chorus girl in one of those Branson country-western shows."

ChaCha hurried over to us with a clipboard in hand. Her hair was a brassy red wig styled into a bouffant that added three inches to her diminutive size. Her Cupcakes T-shirt hinted at childlike breasts, and below the shirt she wore nothing but a pair of black dancer's tights and low-heeled tap shoes with a strap across the ankle. Her legs looked lean and strong. The bare skin of her arms, throat and face was a little loose, but tanned to a deep shade of mahogany, except for the white rings around her eyes, no doubt caused by the eye protection of a tanning booth.

"Look at the color on that woman," muttered Delilah. "She's darker than me."

"Delilah!" barked ChaCha, her voice raspy from years of nicotine.

"No need to shout," Delilah said. "ChaCha, this is Nora Blackbird from the *Intelligencer*."

"Oh yeah? A reporter?" Her accent definitely originated somewhere west of the Mississippi, but her sharp gaze bored into me with the intensity of a Wall Street trader.

"She writes the society column."

ChaCha gave a snort that made her sound like an asthmatic horse. "You look like you belong at a cotillion, all right. You're here to work?"

"Well, I—"

"'Cause we can use the ink. First you should jaw with a couple of the Cupcake Girls, then the chef. He's straight from Austin and makes his own barbecue sauce. It'll make your story about Cupcakes more, you know, classy."

If the queen of England walked in, she couldn't bring any class to the sordid ambiance of Cupcakes. I said, "Miss Reynolds—"

Under the table, Delilah gave my knee a silencing bump. "Nora probably wants to circulate a little first, ChaCha. Maybe she should talk with some of your VIP guests."

"Don't waste too much time with that shit. The chef didn't fall off no chuck wagon. He's going to be one of our biggest draws. Meanwhile, Delilah, where the hell is my partner? Zell was supposed to be here hours ago."

"I—"

"If he's got one of the Cupcakes in a hotel room somewhere, I'm gonna cut off his balls with a bowie knife and throw 'em in the nearest deep fryer."

"Uhm—"

There was no stopping ChaCha's rant. "If Zell spent as much attention on business as he does on those rodeo queen wannabes, we wouldn't have had so much trouble getting this dump opened." She shoved her pen into her red wig and pointed at me. "Talk to the chef. I gotta put more toilet paper in the john."

With that, she marched off in the direction of the

restrooms, a tiny figure so bowlegged she couldn't have stopped a pig in an alley.

"Boy," said Delilah. "Somebody should warn Donald Trump about ChaCha. She's a tycoon in the making."

"You didn't want her to know Zell's dead?"

"I was worried she might kill the messenger, and you don't look so hot to begin with. Besides, his granddaughter's here, and this isn't the place to learn your grampa's gone."

"You mean Clover? Verbena's daughter?" Astonished, I glanced around the crowded restaurant. "You're kidding, right?"

"No joke, honey. Not only is his grandchild here. She's working."

"Working! How? Not—"

"Yep, she's a Cupcake Girl. Zell hired her himself."

"No!" Shocked, I said, "His own granddaughter? Good heavens, how old is Clover now?"

"Still jailbait. Maybe sixteen?"

I shook my head. "Even Zell couldn't be such an idiot."

"Sixteen is plenty old enough these days." Delilah glanced around us and pointed. "And this one's older than most. There she is. On top of the bar."

I spun my stool to get a better look at the show being performed on the long bar in the middle of the restaurant. Six young women wearing not much more than big smiles were prancing in clumsy unison. Arms around each other, they bent at the waist and waggled their bottoms, then formed a kick line and bounced together in a cowboy-booted imitation of Broadway choreography. Gathered beneath them along the bar, men cheered and whistled.

Though I hadn't seen her in years, I spotted Clover easily. In the center of the line, she was the blond girl with long legs and the prodigious bounce beneath her Cupcakes T-shirt. Her gaze was alight with the fire of a girl just discovering the power of her sexuality.

A photographer crouched beneath her at the bar, snapping pictures. The flash popped like a strobe light, drawing attention to her alone amid the other girls. Likewise, Clover projected every atom of her being directly into the lens of the camera. As if the rest of the room did not exist, she beamed herself into the world of the photographer, and somehow that made her more magnetic, more clearly the center of the Cupcakes storm.

"Who's the photographer?" I asked Delilah over the music. I pointed at the drab young woman taking pictures. She also looked very young.

"Not one of the usual suspects," Delilah replied. "You know her?"

I shook my head. The young woman wasn't a journalist I recognized or one of the well-known professional photographers around town.

Still, her actions seemed to focus the whole room on Clover, who was the worst dancer but by far the most charismatic of all the girls. She was taller, livelier, more sexual than the others. Even Clover's makeup—

a lacquered-on sheen of colors dusted with sparkling powder—seemed to glow with more radiance than that of the others.

As we watched, Clover lifted her fist to her mouth and began to lip-synch to the pop song blasting from the speakers. Her dancing companions shot her glares, but Clover didn't care. She was the center of attention.

I tipped my head to get a better look. "Are those real?"

Delilah understood my meaning. "I hear it's the latest thing. Getting a boob job for your sweet sixteen. But when my little girl gets to this age, she's gonna get a computer and a chastity belt. You missed the first act of the floor show. Clover and ChaCha just had a screaming fight in the office."

"They did? About what?"

"I didn't understand, really. There was a lot of cussing going on, though." Delilah put her hand over mine. "Listen, honey, you should go home."

I rubbed my forehead, trying to dispel the headache that threatened. "I wanted to talk about Saturday night's party at the museum."

"Oh, Lord, did I forget something? I don't know what's wrong with me! Zell had me spooked, I guess."

"It's okay. I wanted to touch base with you, that's all, for my piece that will run on Saturday. The invitations went out today."

Delilah switched gears smoothly like the professional she was. "The BlackBerry cell phone thing? Honey, that invitation is so hip I can't stand it."

A few months ago, I'd been asked to make some suggestions to the art museum board to attract a new demographic of charitable donors they wanted to call the Young Collectors. The museum constantly fought the image of being a fuddy-duddy organization that catered to octogenarians who stared at old masters while sucking on their oxygen tanks. To attract new money and new energy, I had suggested an "underground" party, to be held after midnight in the museum basement, and by invitation that would go out only at the last minute via cell phone text message and by BlackBerry—the latest in high-tech gadgetry among the young, moneyed crowd. The party committee had leaped upon my ideas. But the party was only days away, and many details were still up in the air. I'd been asked to light a fire under Delilah, and I thought I could do so in the guise of asking her questions for a pre-party mention in my newspaper column. Delilah saw through my ruse.

"Don't worry," she said. "I'll get all the bases covered, honey, I promise. We'll talk tomorrow if you like, when you can concentrate better. Why don't you go home? Richard was just here. He could take you—"

I had been massaging my temples, but stopped. "Richard's here?"

"As big as life. Maybe he's chasing a big story."

"At Cupcakes?"

I was getting accustomed to Richard D'eath's commitment to his calling as a crime-stopping reporter for the city's prestigious newspaper. Unlike my somewhat precarious employment at a Philadelphia rag, his job required long, irregular hours of tracking down stories that always landed on the front page. But Cupcakes wasn't his usual territory.

Delilah slipped back onto the stool beside mine. "How are things going, by the way? With you and Richard?"

"They're going. We've been seeing a lot of each other."

But Delilah shook her head. "Lose the evasive maneuvers, honey. It's me you're talking to. That man is fine."

I laughed unsteadily. "Yes, he's good-looking."

"And you're cool as ice cream."

"Not so cool," I said. "Things have heated up a little."

"A little? Or a lot? Have you—hold on, have you fallen off your pedestal, girlfriend?"

I put my elbows on the table and rubbed my face. "I've done some stupid things in the last few months, Delilah."

She grinned. "You doin' the deed with Richard?"

I took a deep breath. "Just once."

Delilah let out a raucous laugh. "Honey, once the barn door is open, that horse is gone! Congratulations. Richard's perfect for you! Smart, sophisticated, cultured. Just right."

"Thank you, I guess."

"So," she said, "things must be officially over between you and your prince of darkness?"

"With Michael? Yes. Definitely yes. Completely over."

"Good," she declared. "Because he's here tonight."

I nearly fell off my stool.

"With some wiseguy friends on the other side of the bar. See? They've ordered half the menu, and they're smoking cigars, drinking the most expensive booze in the place and pretty much acting like Bobby De Niro is going to show up any minute to do research for his next movie."

"Oh," I said in a squeak.

"He's got some tacky girl hanging on his arm, and not one of the kiddie Cupcakes, either, but a grown woman with some dangerous curves. I'm afraid she's going to give him a lap dance before the night is over."

I followed Delilah's pointed gaze across the crowded restaurant, over the tops of many heads and through the hazy air to a large table set on the mezzanine that was prime seating to watch the Cupcakes show. Four men and their dates sat before a forest of bottles and plates of food. The women were animated, brightly dressed and vividly made-up, with plenty of long hair that curled around naked shoulders. By contrast, the men were still except for the wreaths of smoke that wafted upward from their cigars. Two of the men were wearing open-necked shirts with gold jewelry nestled in their chest hair.

I found myself staring across the restaurant and directly into the steady gaze of Michael Abruzzo.

He didn't move and neither did I. The woman beside

him had somehow entangled her entire upper body around his arm, and she was giggling into his ear. He didn't seem to notice her or the hubbub of Cupcakes around us. As for me, the rest of the room evaporated in a heartbeat and took all the oxygen with it.

"Completely over?" Delilah said from far away. "I don't think so."

I wobbled off my stool just as Emma arrived with our drinks.

"Hey," she said. "Mick's here."

"I heard."

"One of the Cupcakes told me he gave her a three-hundred-dollar tip."

"Well, well," said Delilah. "I guess crime does pay."

Emma put the drinks on the table, and I murmured that I'd be back shortly. Delilah started to apologize, but I waved it off.

"You okay?" Emma caught my elbow.

"I need a minute." I slipped her grasp and headed for the ladies' room.

It was down two steps and along a hallway decorated with autographed head shots of some Cupcake Girls along with the usual jumble of fake antiques, a dusty Western saddle and a lariat pressed into service as decor. My footsteps were quick but unsteady on the tile floor, and I finally found myself at the termination of the hallway, where it widened for two lavatories and an old-fashioned European phone booth with wooden doors and frosted glass.

In four more steps I was thankfully alone in the

ladies' room. There, I leaned against the stainless steel sink and tried to quell the new wave of queasiness that had nothing to do with morning sickness or finding dead bodies.

I had been an idiot, yes. For over two months I'd let Richard D'eath into my life in the foolish hope that he could make things better for me. He was supposed to be a plateful of healthy vegetables after months of rich and decadent chocolate mousse. But the vegetables brought only more complications, and now I felt sick.

It had felt like the right choice once. A good man instead of a bad boy.

But now it all felt wrong.

Someone flushed, startling me. In another moment, a teenage girl came out of the stall. The photographer who had been filming Clover.

"Hi," she mumbled, avoiding my gaze.

"Hello." I stepped back so she could have the sink. "Wild party, isn't it?"

"Yeah, I guess." She pumped soap into her hands and—just like my six-year-old niece—closed her eyes and began to scrub, humming "Happy Birthday" to be sure she washed for the correct amount of time.

She was of medium height with a square body concealed by a khaki vest over jeans and a frayed thermal T-shirt. Her face was very young, with freckles instead of makeup. Her lower lip had a sexy plumpness, but it was chapped. Her hands were stubby, her nails unpolished. Pinned on her camera bag was a Hello Kitty button and a press badge on which someone had scrawled *Jane* in large, loopy, childish letters.

When she finished washing her hands, she snatched a towel from the dispenser, still trying to ignore me.

I must have looked pretty scary to a kid, I realized—a grown woman on the verge of tears. I made an effort to control myself, but she jammed her used towel into the trash and bolted out of the bathroom, clearly glad to get away from me.

"Nice," I said aloud. "Now you're scaring children."

Alone again, I blotted my eye makeup and powdered my nose. I steeled myself to act normal. I had been doing it for weeks, and I could certainly do it for another few minutes. Long enough to get away from Cupcakes without speaking to Michael.

I took a deep breath and went out into the hallway.

Where Michael waited.

Tall and watchful, he leaned one shoulder against the opposite wall by the phone booth. He'd cut his hair to something respectable, and he wore a suit, but with the tie undone and his shirt collar loosened—maybe by a woman.

He looked at my stomach. "Is that mine?"

My brain blew a fuse. Then I reached to touch the makeshift belt I had fashioned for the vintage Carolina Herrera suit I'd put on that morning. I'd used a man's silk necktie to belt the jacket, which didn't quite fit me anymore. "Is the tie yours?"

He nodded. "It looks good. You look good."

"You look . . ."

"Scary?" he suggested. "Because you're trembling."

I shouldered my handbag. Above us, music wailed, and we could hear a thunder of cowgirl boots stomping on the bar. I wasn't ready for this. I hadn't decided what to say or even how I felt. So, idiotically, I said, "This isn't your kind of nightspot."

"Or yours."

"Are you having a good time?"

He shrugged. "It's just a place to do business."

"Who are your friends?"

"Not friends. Associates."

Or coconspirators, I thought.

Michael studied me a little longer, and I feared he was seeing everything I'd tried to repair with makeup. His own beaten-up face—damaged during his misspent youth—concealed many secrets, too.

He said, "Somebody's dead, right?"

"Y-yes." It shook me to know I was so transparent to him. "Emma and I were—it's a long story. The man who owns half this place—he was murdered earlier today."

"Murdered? Who did it?"

"I don't know. I'm a little afraid for my friend, though. Delilah might have been the last person to see him alive."

"Delilah? The black woman?"

I shot him a look. "Her race has nothing to do with anything."

An unamused smile crossed Michael's mouth. "You think the cops are going to be that politically correct?"

"Don't be—look, she's just the last person to talk with the dead man, that's all."

"So you're worried about her."

"I'm not worried—" I stopped, unwilling to concede his point. I forced myself to say calmly, "Delilah's not in any trouble. She's going to have to spend a lot of time answering questions, though, and she's a very busy person. It will be inconvenient for her."

"Whatever you say," he said. "Have you talked with the cops?"

"Emma and I were questioned for a couple of hours."

"That's enough to upset anyone."

"You would know," I said tartly. "Have you been arrested yet this week?"

He shrugged again. "There are a few more days left."

"When you wear a suit, it's usually because you're talking to lawyers."

"Not tonight." He slid his hands into the pockets of his trousers, a gesture I knew he used to disarm people.

Not handsome, Michael nevertheless had a certain manner that Libby once said "makes the drums in a woman's jungle pound pretty hard." When I first met him, I felt struck by libidinal lightning. We got emotionally naked together very quickly, too. The result had been the most satisfying and troubling relationship of my whole life.

He said, "Besides hanging out with the cops, what

have you been up to lately?"

"Things have been quiet."

"Still dating Clark Kent?"

"He's not—" I considered counting to ten, but said, "Richard and I have spent some time together, yes."

"I saw him here earlier. He wanted to interview me, in fact."

"To learn your opinion on global warming?"

Michael smiled at last, a smile that reached the very bluest depths of his eyes and changed everything. "I've missed you, Nora."

We heard someone laugh at the far end of the hallway, then start toward us with ponderous footfalls. A stranger coming to break us up before we'd said anything that mattered. Without thinking—because heaven knows I didn't expend a single synapse to consider my action—I stepped across the six feet of hallway that separated us and put both hands on Michael's chest.

He said my name again as I pushed him backward into the antique phone booth. He bumped his head, and I closed the door, locking us both inside a space barely big enough for one. Tilting my face up to his in the dark, I said, "I've missed you, too."

Okay, maybe it was the exploding hormones. Day and night, I'd been fighting some crazy impulses, and now here was the man who knew exactly how to light my fire, only it was already blazing and what I really needed was an entire engine company to cool me off before a whole city block went up in flames.

But I kissed him anyway. He kissed me, too, hands in my hair, something like a growl in his throat. I pushed my tongue in his mouth and my hands into places they shouldn't go. Every nerve came alive like tinder to a spark. It was the joy of being with someone who didn't need to talk, just knew me and what I needed.

In another instant he had me off my feet with my back jammed against the door. He nudged my knees apart and touched me so surely that I couldn't think, couldn't breathe. I couldn't stop the painfully delicious combustion of heat and desire inside myself. A torrent of pent-up energy and emotion swelled, and when it burst, it was with stars and noise and the sheer joy at being alive.

I gasped and held on to his shoulders, trying to catch my breath again, but it came out in a stupid sob.

"I know," he whispered against my hair, holding me close, but more gently. He smelled of rich food and smuggled cigars and his own familiar, heady scent. His mouth had tasted of expensive scotch. I could feel his heartbeat, but my pulse was twice as fast.

"It's happening again."

He slid one hand up my back, soothing away the tension that had seized me since we'd come upon Zell Orcutt's body that afternoon. He said, "I don't know why you attract so many dead men, but you do."

With my eyes closed, I put my cheek against his rough one, awash with relief and something dangerously close to love. "Are you counting Richard in that group?"

"You bet." I felt him grin. "Do the two of you do this sort of thing often?"

I hiccuped a laugh. "Does your new girlfriend?"

"She's not my girlfriend."

"Does she know that?"

I felt his smile again. "Maybe not."

I pulled away by a few centimeters and looked up into his face, so familiar and yet not anymore. I tried to find something specific that was new and decided he'd lost a few pounds. His body felt tighter. Still good, but harder. Our minds seemed to work just as before, though. He could read me, know my feelings and my fears.

For an instant, it didn't matter what had come between us.

But then it was back.

"Michael, this isn't—"

"Sex in a phone booth doesn't mean anything?"

"No. It's just—sex. If you want me to—"

He stopped my hand. "Let's not make this any messier than it already is." He touched my cheek. "Do you feel better now?"

"Yes." I sighed to dispel the tension in my chest. "And no."

"The dead guy. Is he somebody you care about?"

"He was a pretty awful person, as a matter of fact."

"I guess that's good. Maybe you'll keep your nose out of this one?"

"Yes."

"Is that a promise?"

I steeled myself. "I don't think I need to make any promises to you. We both know they're not binding."

He sighed, too, and let me pull away. "Nora. I didn't think things would go this way when we—when you and I were together."

I tried to put my clothes back where they should be. "I thought you wanted a different kind of life."

"I did. It just went the other way."

"You have choices, you know. You're making a good living. I see your gas stations everywhere now, and surely your other businesses are booming, too."

"It's not about the money."

"Then what is it? Misplaced loyalty?"

"It's complicated."

I couldn't fathom what he was doing. "Michael," I said, "I can't be with you when you're this other person. Not if you're a criminal."

He absorbed that and discarded the part he didn't need to hear again. "So you still think about us?"

"Michael—"

"Forget I asked." He closed his eyes and braced his shoulder against the opposite wall, putting dead air between us. "I know what you want. A house in the suburbs with kids and a swing set. Maybe one of those ducks on the porch—the kind you dress in doll clothes. What's up with those, anyway?"

"I don't know."

He said more gently, "I'm glad you're going to get the family you need."

"Shut up," I said. Taking a handful of his shirt, I pulled him back to me and kissed him until I felt emotion burn in the back of my throat. When I broke the kiss and looked up into his eyes, my vision blurred. "Sometimes I can't believe it's over between us."

"Believe it." He turned his head away. "It's over."

"I still have the ring you gave me."

"Sell it," he said, unable to look at me anymore. "Hock it. You can use the money, right? Fix the roof on that house of yours."

His voice had turned cold.

I turned him loose and fumbled to get the door open. He helped, and we were out in the hallway again, no need to speak anymore. He put his tie right, and I quickly went up the hall to escape the best thing that had ever happened to either one of us, if only he could change who he really was.

Something must have happened in the restaurant while we were gone. I came up the steps into the bar and found Delilah and Emma standing together looking wide-eyed and panicky.

"Hey," I said. "What's—"

"Who the hell are you?" a female voice demanded—Jersey nasal and laced with toxic sarcasm.

It was the woman who'd been sitting with Michael. Her lipstick was a shade that didn't exist in nature, and her contact lenses glowed a poisonous green. In one

73

long-taloned hand, she held the remains of a pink Cosmopolitan.

"You're her, aren't you?" she snapped. "The bitch he was sleeping with before me?"

Delilah snorted at her unintentionally comic semantics, which only fanned the flames.

"Hello," I said with extreme civility. "I'm Nora Blackbird."

She batted my hand away and shot a murderous look past my shoulder just as Michael came up the step behind me. Her face tightened with fury, and the next thing I knew she threw the Cosmopolitan in my eyes.

Michael caught my arm and spun me behind him to prevent further mayhem, saying, "Darla, wait—"

But it was Emma who flashed into action. She took a step and swung her fist. The punch connected perfectly, and we saw Darla's eyes go blank and her knees wobble once before they crumpled completely out from under her.

Which was the moment Richard came through the restaurant door. He caught his balance with his cane to better absorb the scene.

Michael handed me his handkerchief and said curtly to Richard, "Take her home."

Which was how I ended up with Richard long before I figured out what I wanted to do about him.

Chapter Four

I n Richard's car sopping up, I said, "My reflexes must be off. I never get hit with drinks."

Richard said, "You must have been distracted."

I heard his tone as I tucked the damp handkerchief into my bag. Clamping my knees together, I tried not to think about what I had just done in a phone booth with someone I truly hadn't intended to see anymore. I had disgraced myself, and I felt ashamed.

It was time to forget about Michael and focus on the new man in my life.

Except he was sulking.

"Is there something else you want to argue about, Richard?" I tried to make my tone light. "Or should we just cut directly to the big distraction himself?"

"I don't want to argue."

"Then tell me why you were at Cupcakes tonight. Did you have an urge for hot wings?"

He didn't bother trying to smile. "I went to Cupcakes to talk to Abruzzo."

"I see. So he's a story you're working on?"

"Half the city's working on his story." Richard took his eyes off the road long enough to glance at me, tension bristling from him. "He went back to the family business, so everybody assumes the Abruzzos are going to be bigger and more powerful than ever. But a guy on the desk called to tell me about the Orcutt murder and that he'd heard your name on the police scanner. So I went out to Fitch's Fancy to look for you. By the time I got there, though, they told me you'd come here, so I thought I'd ride to your rescue."

"Oh. I—I guess I should thank you."

He shrugged. "I should have been here sooner, but the local television trucks were there, setting up to watch the crime scene guys work. I stuck around."

"Did you talk to the police?"

Of course he had. Richard D'eath had come to Philadelphia from New York after a traffic accident required a stint in a respected orthopedic rehab facility. While he recovered from his broken bones, the local newspaper hired him to cover their corruption beat, and he'd seized the job with the extreme relief of a man who hated lounging around in a hospital bed. Once downgraded to an outpatient, he'd put his cane and New York street smarts to good use and driven half a dozen crooked politicians out of the mayor's office. I knew he couldn't pass a crime scene without asking questions.

"Yeah, I talked to the cops."

"What did you learn?"

"I heard all about you."

I turned to look at his profile. Unlike Michael, who looked every inch a thug, Richard was toe-curlingly handsome. Sandy hair spilled boyishly over his smooth forehead, his nose was straight and

76

inquisitive, and his body was more fit than his loose, earth-toned clothing usually showed. Women often slipped him their phone numbers, and one night I actually witnessed a professor of women's studies fall off a barstool when he arrived to meet friends for a drink.

He always smelled delicious and could argue politics late into the night. And his eyes—one blue, one hazel—were direct and observant. But he was ill at ease with emotion, and I was still trying to discover if that meant Richard lacked the capacity to be intimate with anyone other than a story source.

"The police talked about me? What does that mean?"

"You made an impression. You and Emma both. Fortunately, they don't think either one of you killed Zell Orcutt."

"Have they figured out who did?"

"Not yet." Richard was frowning. "Did you know Boykin Fitch was there? The Senate candidate?"

"He's not a candidate quite yet. Yes, we spoke. We're old friends."

"I should have guessed," he said dryly. "Is he for real? Am I supposed to believe the Forrest Gump routine?"

"Boy is a very nice person."

Richard wasn't listening. "His father showed up, too. Pierpoint Fitch, right? Waving an old badminton racquet and talking pretty crazy. Enough to get the cops interested."

"The whole family is furious with Zell for auctioning off Fitch's Fancy. None of them want to lose the estate. It's been in the family for over a century."

"Yeah, I gathered from the shouting. Boykin Fitch couldn't get his father out of there fast enough."

"Pierpoint didn't murder Zell."

"Why not? He's crazy, but not crazy enough?"

I recalled an incident from my youth when I'd visited Fitch's Fancy with a slew of birthday cake–crazed children, who, after the usual fun and games, were drawn to the sheep barns to look at new lambs. One ewe had just given birth to twins, and we were fascinated by the newborns. But the smaller of the lambs was misshapen and couldn't breathe, and its struggling throes frightened us. I remembered Pierpoint Fitch stepping in. He picked up the dying lamb, and cradling it in his arms, he told the group of children how it was sometimes kinder to end an animal's suffering. He took the lamb away, and we knew what he had gone to do. But he'd wept with us as he spoke, and his unchecked emotion lent a certain unforgettable melodrama to the whole event.

But I knew Richard would take a different view, so I said merely, "He's not a violent man."

"I thought you were going to say their blood is too blue for killing each other."

I pushed Pierpoint out of my mind and considered the victim instead. "Zell didn't have blue blood."

"No class, huh?"

"He hired his own granddaughter to be a Cupcake."

"That's pretty low," Richard agreed.

"That's Zell for you."

"I guess some guys just don't fit in your world."

I turned sideways in the seat, conscious that Michael was between us again as clearly as if he'd opened the door and climbed into the car. "Are you trying to make a point, Richard?"

Richard kept his gaze on the road. "I can't believe I still need to."

"You tried to interrogate him tonight."

In the light from the dashboard, Richard glanced at me. "Abruzzo told you that?"

"Fess up," I said. "You're working on the organized-crime story, aren't you?"

"You know I can't reveal details about my current investigation."

"Think I'm going to tell someone at my own paper who will scoop you? Or are you concerned I'll tip off the mob?"

"Nora—"

"Just tell me what's going on, please. What is Michael involved in now?"

Richard let a few seconds tick by. Then, quietly, he said, "I don't want to hurt you."

"It isn't you who's doing the hurting."

Richard contemplated his choices as he drove up the dark highway toward Blackbird Farm. I could see him weighing personal and professional matters.

At last, he said, "Remember last December? Some cops were on a special detail to catch a ring of car thieves. The bust went wrong, and somebody shot a cop."

I remembered the incident all too painfully. Although I had spent part of that fateful evening with Michael, I hadn't been completely sure of his whereabouts at the time the police officer was murdered.

"Yes," I said. "I know about the killing."

"Well, the police never caught the shooter. He's still at large."

"Do they know who it was?"

"They know who they want it to be," Richard said. "And now I hear they've got a source who's willing to talk—who's passing information to them."

"Information that's trustworthy?" I asked. "Because a petty car thief might say anything. You have to consider the source. You can't believe what you hear from—"

"Take it easy," Richard said.

I bit back my panic. If someone in the Abruzzo crime family wanted Michael out of the way for a long time, creating a false testimony was the quickest way to put him back in jail.

When he was a teenager, he had been able to survive a prison sentence. But I wasn't sure he could live through it now. He loved to go fishing. To ride his motorcycle. He laughed, ate, drank wine and made love with more abandon than anyone in my acquaintance. In fact, I'd never known a man who enjoyed his pleasures so openly. As if he might never enjoy them again.

In the quiet of the car, Richard said at last, "Am I

crazy? Thinking you and I could have something, Nora?"

I felt myself flush with remorse.

Here I was, jeopardizing my future with Richard because I couldn't make a clean break with a likely criminal. "Of course we have something, Richard. I—look, I'm sorry you doubt it. I'm sorry for a lot of things."

"You protect him even though he's a monster."

"He is not a monster."

Richard sighed.

"All right," I conceded. "Maybe he's no angel. I won't make excuses for Michael anymore. I did that for my husband, and now I know I only enabled his drug use. But, Richard, I don't believe Michael is capable of killing anyone. If you want to devote your waking hours to proving otherwise, that's your prerogative, but—"

"Has he got you hypnotized or brainwashed? Do you see what he's doing?"

"He's changed," I said. "At least, he's trying to."

"Are you sure about that?"

"I don't know. I thought he was trying to get away from that life. But deep down, he loves his father, and he wants to be loyal. Michael struggles with this—this basic instinct to outsmart the system. I can't believe he gave in to it."

"You're going to get hurt with him, Nora."

"I'm not with him," I snapped. "I'm with you."

"You mean that?"

"Yes. Absolutely."

Richard asked, "Did you tell him about the baby?"

I flushed hot, remembering what I'd done in the dark less than an hour earlier. I'd let myself go. Forgotten who I was. And here was Richard trying to help me regain the part of myself I relinquished when I was with Michael. I said, "It's none of his business. He doesn't need to know I'm pregnant."

"I'm glad to hear it." Richard sounded tired. "For one thing, he's got a new girlfriend."

"So I noticed."

"I hope she knows what she's getting into."

His sarcasm needled me. "You and I are together now, Richard. What more do you want?"

"You know what I want," he said just as harshly, and pulled into the long driveway of Blackbird Farm.

The house loomed ahead of us in the dark—a fieldstone farmhouse built during the time of William Penn and added onto in haphazard ways until the original structure was nearly consumed by more modern additions. The property had been in my family for generations, and now it was mine to preserve. Hanging on to such an old estate came with so many problems and expensive bills to pay that I was nearly overwhelmed just making sure the roof was waterproof. As the whitewashed fence posts flickered past us, I reflected that it seemed important to stay in a place where my life felt composed. Even when things were falling apart.

When Richard swung the car into the gravel circle at

the back of the house and stopped, I made no move to get out, but sat quietly for a moment and tried to piece together the thoughts I'd been fighting for several weeks.

"I'm sorry," I said at last. "I don't know why. But I'm not ready to go to bed with you again."

Richard turned toward me in the seat. He was gentleman enough to smile. "I'll admit the first time wasn't the best experience, but it got the job done."

"That's not what I—"

He said, "I can't promise that we won't have a few more mistakes the next time, either, Nora. But that's one of the great things about creating a relationship, you know. Learning to be good together."

"Do you think we can?"

"Don't you want that?"

I couldn't stop myself from touching my belly. I didn't know what I wanted. All I knew right now was that my choice was going to affect my child, and I didn't want to make any more mistakes.

Richard shut off the engine, got out of the car and came around to the passenger door. He opened it and helped me stand, which turned into an embrace.

Above me in the darkness, he said, "Let me try to convince you."

I smiled and hoped it didn't look shaky. "I'm game. But not tonight, please. It's been an awful day and—"

He tried to change my mind with a kiss.

There was no avoiding it, and I prayed he couldn't divine that I'd been kissing Michael just an hour ago.

I felt a rush of shame.

I should have enjoyed the moment. After all, Richard had all the right qualifications to make a woman's knees go weak. I closed my eyes and thought it would be a relief to feel something for another man. As Richard's arms tightened around me, I tried to make it happen. Around us, the night whispered, and Richard's gentle, nibbling kiss coaxed me to forget, to start anew.

But I found myself wondering in which pocket I put my house keys, if there might be one more can of soup in the pantry, and did I have a new book to take into the bathtub with me tonight?—all thoughts that should have been swept aside by passion. Which made me feel doubly guilty for having climaxed in Michael's arms in a phone booth.

Before Richard could sense my mind had wandered off like a bored toddler in search of excitement, a colossal snort resounded five feet away.

I yelped, and Richard cursed.

Mr. Twinkles stepped out of the darkness, his tail swishing and his ears laid flat against his long neck. Emma's horse snorted again and shook his head threateningly at Richard. The white blaze on his nose flashed in the starlight. Richard and I leaped apart.

"Dammit! This horse is an escape artist!"

Richard sagged against the car. "I think I just had a heart attack."

I made a grab for the nylon halter on the horse's head, and Mr. Twinkles graciously allowed me to do so. Then he jammed his nose against my body and gave me an affectionate shove. I held on, patting his sleek neck to settle him down. "I'm sorry, Richard. This is Emma's latest project, Mr. Twinkles. He's supposed to jump fences, and I think Emma has taught him too well."

"You keep him here at the farm?"

"Only when Emma can't afford to board him at a respectable place." I rubbed Mr. Twinkles between his now curious ears. "Which is most of the time. Now that he knows how to get out of the paddock, he spends most of his time hanging around my back porch, looking for treats."

Mr. Twinkles weighed twelve tons for all I knew, but he was surprisingly nimble on his feet. He spun around lightly, presenting his daunting hindquarters to Richard, who scrambled over the hood of the car to avoid getting kicked to the moon.

"Jesus! Is he dangerous?"

"I haven't a clue." I felt guilty for making light of the situation when Richard was clearly shaken. "I'm sorry. Would you like to pet him? Make friends?"

"No," said Richard from a safe distance. "I'm from Manhattan, Nora. I don't do horses."

"He's just an overgrown pet, really. He can be very sweet." I patted the horse's neck.

Richard reached the driver's door and opened it. "I'll pass. I'd better be going, anyway. Unless you need help—uh—putting him in the barn?"

"I can manage."

Richard promised to phone in the morning. As he drove away, Mr. Twinkles seemed very pleased to have me to himself. While I waved to Richard, the horse lovingly snuffled my pockets for a bedtime snack and hit pay dirt in my handbag. I unwrapped a peppermint as we walked over to the paddock, and when he was once again standing on the right side of the paddock fence, I presented him with the candy. Positive reinforcement. While he crunched it, I gave him a stern lecture, closed the gate and said good night.

I let myself into the kitchen and flipped the light switch, which caused a disconcerting crackle behind the walls and a flicker in the chandelier before light finally filled the cavernous old room. The refrigerator—only twenty years old—hummed with modern efficiency in the middle of an otherwise rustic kitchen that featured a collection of antique cookware hanging overhead and a stone floor that had endured the crunch of General Washington's boots.

The telephone had been ringing when I stepped inside, and the answering machine picked up.

My sister Libby's voice echoed in the kitchen. I put my handbag on the counter and unbuttoned my coat while she talked. "I thought you'd be home by now," she said, sounding wounded. "Have you thought about the calendar? Because I've made a preliminary appointment with a new photographer. His name is Jean Claude. Doesn't that sound artistic? No commitment, just a consultation. I'm told he's a master at disguising those tiny unsightlies. You'll enjoy it, I promise! Call me!"

"You're out of your mind," I said to the machine.

I didn't notice the puddle in the middle of the floor. I slipped on the stone and barely saved myself from a fall by grabbing the edge of the counter.

"Damn!"

I'd spent the morning crouched under the kitchen sink with a roll of duct tape. Obviously, my first universal solution had failed me this time. The mysterious Blackbird plumbing was erupting again for no reason.

I peered under the sink to locate the latest problem. No drips had sprung through the hunk of duct tape, but a fresh leak oozed from a new crack farther down the pipe. I sat back on my heels and sighed.

Time to phone a plumber.

But the killer nighttime rate wasn't in my reach.

"What the hell." I'd take the risk and wait until morning. Meanwhile, a well-placed bucket and an armload of towels would have to hold back the tide. I wedged a plastic bucket under the new leak and distributed the towels around the floor.

Then I opened a can of alphabet soup and poured it into a saucepan. These days, it was the only food I could tolerate besides Jiffy Pop popcorn. While it heated, I frowned at the limp Christmas cactus that stood on the windowsill.

A diamond ring hung on one prickly leaf. Catching light from the chandelier, the diamond that Emma called the Rock of Gibraltar sparkled deep inside its facets. I'd put it there New Year's Eve, minutes after Michael gave it to me before he disappeared for two months. And there it had remained.

While I tried to decide who the father of my child should be, I let the diamond hang there.

"I should sell it," I said aloud. "I could pay the plumber, at least."

My husband, Todd, had died because he couldn't give up cocaine, shot by his drug dealer on a night when I couldn't keep him at home. I had failed to protect him from himself, and he was dead.

And then Michael came along—equally driven by some inner motivation I did not understand. He loved the challenge of crime, the chesslike planning, the bluff and risk of poker for high stakes. And I could not keep him at home, either—not when he heard the call that drew him out at night.

I turned back to the stove to stir my soup. I flipped on the answering machine and listened to the rest of my messages.

"Sweetie!" shouted my friend Lexie Paine. "Can't wait for the museum party on Saturday! Hope you made contact with the elusive Delilah. We expect a cast of thousands—well, at least two hundred—and I can't manage without her!"

The second message was a mumbling female voice. "Miss Blackbird, this is Joyce from the bank, confirming next Tuesday's appointment. We're sending our home inspector to see you at two."

To the machine, I said, "How could I forget?"

The bank appraiser who was scheduled to tour the crumbling house had the power to bless my latest attempt at renegotiating my financial position. Or he could nix everything and ruin me. Just when I needed to be fixing a dozen household problems, new leaks, squeaks and broken doorknobs seemed to pop up in other parts of the house.

With the bowl of soup on the table at my elbow, I opened my laptop. First I sent an e-mail to my boss at the *Intelligencer.* My report on the Daffodil Luncheon would make a nice little item in tomorrow's edition of the society column. I took a moment to describe the menu, the clothes and the guests.

After that, I gave in to my curiosity and Googled Zell Orcutt. I found a few mentions in local newspapers for Cupcakes, his recent business venture. A group of local parents had protested the building of Cupcakes so close to a day care center—a justifiable complaint in my opinion. Old news articles mentioned his name in connection with some business deals gone bad. I noted one partner went to jail, while Zell was photographed leaving for a vacation.

Kingsley's auction house had already posted plenty of details on their Web site about Fitch's Fancy in anticipation of the upcoming sale. The information included a family history, which I skimmed. Zell was barely mentioned, clearly deemed unimportant to the provenance of the estate.

I let my imagination roll around various Fitch

family members. I had seen all of them shoot targets during the summer archery parties. I wondered which one had been angry enough to use a bow and arrow to kill Zell.

I ladled more soup into my bowl and finished it while I double-checked Lexie's earlier e-mail concerning the museum party. Museum employees would help the linen service dress up the basement space on Friday, and flowers—a gift from Lexie herself—would arrive on Saturday afternoon. But everything else—food, drink and entertainment—depended on Delilah. And for some reason, she wasn't doing her usual first-rate job.

I pushed aside the thought that Delilah had been at Fitch's Fancy before we'd discovered Zell's body. She hadn't killed Zell. She might have argued with him and needed double martinis to calm down, but she hadn't killed him.

But whether the police would dismiss her as easily as I could—that was another matter.

Chapter Five

*I*f the school nurse had simply told us the truth about morning sickness, she could have skipped the lectures on birth control. My mother could have given away our copy of *Our Bodies, Ourselves* that she kept prominently displayed on the bookshelf next to her Nora Roberts collection. The whole condom industry would whither and die, ruining the New York Stock Exchange and probably the economy of the entire nation. Maybe the world.

Like clockwork, I flung myself out of bed at seven thirty and barely made it to the bathroom for my usual hour of gut-spraining retches. Afterward, I climbed over the nearly insurmountable side of the bathtub and soaked my aching muscles for half an hour. Feeling somewhat more alive after that, I slipped into a faded satin robe I'd purchased years ago at my favorite vintage-clothing store in Paris. It was a little too big, but cut like a Victorian evening gown and beautifully hand-stitched, so I always felt pampered when I wore it. Still nauseated, but pampered.

I went downstairs to find Mr. Twinkles standing by the back porch, waiting for a handout. He was overjoyed to see me and nuzzled my robe with more familiarity than I should have allowed. To distract him, I produced some wilted celery stalks. When I went back inside, he wistfully kicked the door with one forehoof.

Back in the kitchen, I pulled a Jiffy Pop from the pantry. With the stove heating up, I picked up the phone to call the plumber only to discover my answering machine blinking again. Someone must have called while I was in the tub. I touched the button.

"Nora?" Delilah's voice sounded shaky. "Honey, I

could use your advice. Could you give me a call? It's—look, it's pretty important."

I immediately punched in her cell number, but I was put through to her voice mail. Either she had turned off her phone or she was speaking with someone else. Frustrated, I said, "Delilah, sorry I missed your call. I'm at home. Give me a buzz when you can."

Concerned, I disconnected and stood staring out my kitchen window while I shook my Jiffy Pop. "Maybe she just wants to talk about Saturday's party," I said aloud.

Mr. Twinkles looked back at me through the window and gave a conversational nicker.

"I'm not talking to a horse," I said to him.

Instead, I brewed myself some tea and called the plumber. By the time I ate enough popcorn to keep down the prenatal vitamins, Emma arrived, ominously lugging a duffel bag. She demanded, "What's Twinkles doing on the porch?"

"I threw him out of bed," I said.

While Emma went to put Mr. Twinkles back in his paddock, Libby came into the kitchen carrying a gadget in one arm.

"What in the world is that?" I asked.

"It's a food scale!" She plunked it triumphantly on my kitchen table. "You can weigh everything you eat and calculate the calories, see?"

"I thought you weren't on a diet."

"I'm not! It's for you! I've decided I'll be your diet coach! I think it could be a new career for me. I've been on every diet known to mankind, so I'm an expert. I'll take care of everything for you. Aren't you relieved?"

"That's not the first word that comes to mind."

She took a large Macy's shopping bag from over her arm and put it on the table. "I brought the Atkins book, too, see? For quick results, you can't beat it. Weight Watchers is best for the long haul, but Atkins is it for fast weight loss." From the paper bag, she pulled out a variety of books. Diet books, all with covers depicting slim women with big Stepford smiles.

"Libby—"

"And I've got my old Thighmaster in the car with a few other exercise enhancers. You'll love using it!"

"I—"

"And I brought breakfast, too! Two fresh bagels for Emma because she could use a few curves, and a lovely cup of fat-free yogurt for you, Nora. Of course, I've already had a grapefruit and a long walk this morning, so I don't need—"

"You met the photographer already, didn't you?"

"You mean Jean Claude?" Libby pinkened. "Nora, he's a genius! And so in tune with women's attitudes about their bodies! You're going to love him! And I— good Lord." She stared at the foil pan in my hand. "Why are you having popcorn for breakfast?"

Caught, I said, "It's my lunch. I've been up for hours."

While Libby consulted her watch, Emma came back inside. She rolled her eyes.

Tartly, I asked, "How are your knuckles this morning?"

She grinned, pleased with herself for decking Michael's companion. "Did you see her lights go out?"

"Yes. I assume you have a good lawyer in mind?"

"She was asking for it." Em tossed her duffel on the table and then looked down. "Do you know you have a puddle on the floor?"

"Gee, I hadn't noticed." Only a blind person would miss the lake that was creeping in all directions despite my attempts at repairs. "What's in the bag? More exercise equipment?"

"Nope. I decided to move out of my apartment."

"How interesting." I put down my breakfast and girded my loins for battle by tightening the belt of my robe. "And what does that have to do with your bag in my kitchen?"

"You need a roommate. My first paycheck doesn't kick in for another three weeks, so I'm moving in here."

"Do I get a vote in this decision?" I asked.

Libby said, "What I want to know is what kind of business doesn't pay its employees for three weeks?"

Emma ignored her. "What's to decide? I need a place to live, and you need," she said with a menacing pause, "some help around the house. This way I'll be closer to look after . . . Twinkles."

I could see she was threatening to spill the beans to Libby.

Libby's decision to become my diet coach was a cakewalk compared with the ordeal she would launch when she learned I was pregnant. In a grumble, I said, "Keeping that animal off my porch would be a good start."

"I'll do my best."

Libby said, "If you move in here to save money, Em, you can quit that job, right?"

"Don't start," Emma warned.

"Okay, that's it!" I threw caution to the wind. "Just what kind of job is this, anyway? Is it disgusting?"

"No," said Emma. "I'm a hostess. I greet people at the door. I'm using my people skills."

"A hostess?" I couldn't get my head around the mental picture. "At the Dungeon of Darkness? Why does a store that sells games need a hostess?"

"Games?" Libby laughed. "Nora, you innocent lamb, it's a *dungeon!* It has nothing to do with the troll and dragon games Rawlins used to play with his nerdy friends. It's a sex club!"

"It's not a sex club!" Emma exploded. "It's a safe environment for people who have common interests."

"Wait, you mean—?"

"Domination is the common interest," Libby said. "Women in leather, men in hoods."

"There are no hoods!"

"I saw your costume, Emma. It's a leather bathing suit with pirate boots."

"Oh, Em," I said. "What's next, for heaven's sake?"

"Nobody touches me! The first person who does

gets a broken arm, which I've made very clear. And since when," she snapped, swinging on Libby, "did you start thinking like Queen Victoria?"

"I'm as open-minded as the next person, but there are limits!"

"Look," Emma said to me, "I've got a heap of vet bills. Either I find a way to pay, or I have to sell Twinkles. But I can't sell a horse until he's fit again, can I? So I took the job, and I'll move in here for a few months. Everything will work out fine."

"You can live here for free," I said, "and quit that job immediately."

"I've got to pay the vet."

"Emma," I began.

"You don't have a vote in this. Besides," she continued with a malevolent gleam entering her eye, "you need somebody here to look after you."

Libby took the bait.

"Why does Nora need looking after?" she demanded. "I'm the one who needs support while the Erotic Yoga Society is on hiatus. Besides, you don't want to be a third wheel, do you, Emma? Nora and her lover should be alone to explore the intimacies of their new relationship. Where is he, by the way?"

She paused in the act of unpacking one bagel, three cups of coffee, a tub of cream cheese and the smallest container of yogurt I had ever seen. Libby had come outfitted in a snug exercise ensemble—lavender stretch pants and a lavender zip warm-up sweater over nothing but a peep of pink bra that quivered with enough tension to launch a javelin. Her auburn hair was caught up in an artfully disheveled do complete with wispy bangs and curls at the crown of her head. Her makeup was perfect: her earrings were tasteful. As usual, she looked as if she'd just rolled out of bed after a luxurious bout of lovemaking.

"She means Richard." Emma took one of the coffees and pried off the plastic lid.

"Is he upstairs?" Libby asked.

"No."

"Why not? Are you having bedroom trouble already? Because I'm thinking if the whole diet coach idea doesn't work, I could become a sex therapist. It's my dream actually. Maybe I should work with the two of you. It could be like an internship for me."

As Libby opened a plastic container of tomato-basil cream cheese, my stomach executed a quick barrel roll. Taking care not to draw attention to myself, I took up a position by the refrigerator—just a quick dash to the downstairs powder room if nausea struck. Emma noted my strategy with a smirk.

Fortunately, Libby didn't notice. She rooted around in a drawer to find a serrated knife and began to carefully slice a bagel. "Emma told me what happened last night, Nora. How exciting! She said you'd tell me everything else."

"What happened to Zell wasn't exactly exciting."

"I don't mean about Zell! I mean about Cupcakes! Was it very fun?"

97

"It was mostly gross, Libby. It's somebody cashing in by coercing young girls to act very foolishly because they don't know any better."

"I've seen their television commercials. I love the little dances they do." Libby gave a cowgirl shimmy. "And the pictures of cupcakes? With the single jelly bean on each one? So cute!"

"Two months ago you thought selling vibrators was cute," I said. "Then the police arrested you."

Libby stopped dancing and frowned. "If I had the money, I'd hire a lawyer to get my inventory back. I kept a few items for my personal collection—which is perfectly legal, by the way—but I wish I could get my hands on the Magic Wand again."

"Libby!"

"What? I know I'm not allowed to sell them in public places. Although I don't understand why, except that most lawmakers are prudes."

"Not all, I hope." I sent Emma a meaningful glance.

"What does that mean?" Libby asked, on alert.

Despite the glare Emma sent me to keep my mouth shut, I said, "Boy Fitch made eyes at Em yesterday."

"He did?"

"He did not!"

Libby stopped slathering cream cheese on the bagel. "I used to babysit him! Oh, he was such an adorable child!"

Emma slugged coffee. "You didn't touch him, did you, Lib? Because that's definitely illegal."

"Of course I didn't touch him. He's at least five

years younger than me. He was darling, though. Not very bright, but darling."

"I wonder about that dim-bulb routine myself," I murmured.

"He could be good for you, Emma. And it's time you had a normal relationship."

"There isn't going to be a relationship," Emma said. "The guy is dumb as dirt."

"Maybe he has hidden depths," Libby said. "All you have to do is give him a little sign, Em. Not your usual sign, of course. Don't grab his butt and drag him to the nearest Motel Six."

"I have no intention of pursuing Boykin Fitch. He's not my type."

Libby aimed the tip of her knife at Emma. "All men are your type. Especially those Dungeon ones, the submissive fellows who want to be ordered around." She looked thoughtful. "Except they never like being ordered to fix the leaky toilet, do they? The woman who figures out how to make chores sexy is going to outearn Bill Gates."

"Even Bill Gates has more sex appeal than Boy Fitch. Jeez, going to bed with him would be like hitting the sheets with—"

"It's not always about hitting the sheets!" I cried suddenly. "Is sex all anybody thinks about anymore? Whatever happened to having someone to challenge your mind? To understand you? To listen and make you feel loved and needed and appreciated? To do crossword puzzles with! Intimacy is what matters!

Emotional and intellectual intimacy! Who cares about sex? It's meaningless!"

Emma and Libby blinked at me.

"Sermon over?" Emma asked.

"Is she talking about Richard?" Libby asked. "Are you saying he likes crossword puzzles more than sex? Because that's just not normal."

"His conversation is always that egghead stuff," Emma agreed. "Sometimes I think he's going to break out a pipe and start quoting Shakespeare."

"I *like* Shakespeare!"

Libby looked concerned. "You're not sounding like yourself, Nora."

"Yeah," said Emma, evil grin starting again. "It's like your hormones are all messed up. Why don't you grab your fat-free yogurt and tell Libby the big news?"

Libby looked interested. "Big news?"

"Brace yourself," Emma advised.

"What's going on?" Libby asked.

"Rat fink," I said to Emma.

"Hey, you could have kept quiet about Boy."

The bell at my front door chimed then. Perfect timing.

"An early visitor?" Emma asked. "Your crossword soul mate, maybe?"

"It's probably the plumber." I checked the kitchen clock and wished I'd taken the time to get dressed. "I didn't expect him so soon."

"He comes running because you're his best customer." Emma headed out of the room. "I'll get the door. Don't tell Libby who the father is. Not until I get back, anyway."

Emma left, and Libby put the bagel on a plate and carried it to the table. Without thinking, she took a finger swipe of cream cheese from one of the bagels and licked it. "Whose father? What's she talking about?"

There was no sense postponing it any longer.

I retied my belt again and sat down at the table. "Libby, I can't be in your calendar photo. And I can't go on a diet right now."

She eased her bottom onto the kitchen chair beside mine, instantly sympathetic. "Of course you can, Nora! I'll help you every step of the way. You only need to drop a couple of tiny pounds—"

"I'm not losing weight for your photographer, Libby. I—"

"Two pounds!" she cried. "Five at the most! Just enough to tighten up the jiggle in your derriere."

"My derriere does not jiggle!"

"It's to be expected once you hit thirty, Nora. I find the best solution is to exercise in the nude. That way, you have no secrets from yourself." She held up one hand to stop me from speaking. "Now, don't get angry. Getting down on yourself is the worst way to start a diet. Here, I brought you a present." From the bottom of the Macy's bag, she flourished a tiny slip of pink lace.

"What's this?"

"It's a thong. The Hanky Panky, style 4911. Until you get thin, this is the answer. Honestly, Nora, all my friends swear by it. Even Monica Lewinsky looked good in the 4911!"

I suspended the tiny thong from one finger. "Are you kidding?"

"I'm totally serious. You'll thank me the instant you put this on and look in the mirror. I brought you a week's supply, all the colors. See? I bought them for myself, but they're slightly the wrong size, so I thought of your bottom immediately! They'll do wonders for the jiggle."

Before I could grab a frying pan to hit her, Emma came back into the kitchen. Followed by Boy Fitch, of all people.

"Nora," she said, holding back a big laugh. "Boy's come to see you."

I snatched the thongs off the table and stuffed them back into the Macy's bag.

Boy wore another pin-striped suit with a tie printed with tiny Uncle Sams, and he carried a newspaper under his arm as if setting out for his office. With his other hand, he held up a paper bag. "I figured if I disturbed you this early, I'd better bring breakfast. It's bagels."

I shoved the Macy's bag under the table. "Good morning, Boy."

"You'll have to slice them," he said. "Last time I tried, I cut my thumb and ended up with twelve stitches."

"Uhm, Boy, you know Emma, of course. And this is my sister Libby."

"Libby." Boy put on his politician's smile. "Of course I remember you."

Beguilingly, Libby shook his hand. "Hello, Boy. I suppose I need to call you Senator Fitch now."

"Of course not." Boy gazed down at her, oozing a fondness that looked genuine. "You were the reason I never quite learned my multiplication tables. Somehow, I could never concentrate on my home-work when you were around."

"What a lovely thing to say." Libby had stars in her eyes, and I could see Boy had another vote.

I could also sense a dangerous flicker of electricity in the air, so I said briskly, "Come sit down, Boy. Have some coffee."

"I had no idea you lived like this, Nora." Boy glanced up at the vaulted ceiling of the kitchen as if expecting to see a vampire bat hanging from the dusty rafters.

"If I let the cobwebs get carried away, Vincent Price shows up."

He frowned. "Your cleaning service?"

"No, Boy, I only meant—well, please have a seat." I took Boy's arm to guide him into a chair.

Boy hadn't shaved and suddenly I realized he seemed more dazed than usual. I handed him the take-out coffee intended for me. Emma sat across from him, and Libby and I took the other seats so that he was surrounded by expectant Blackbird faces.

He placed his copy of the morning newspaper on the table. "I don't know where to start."

"Bagel?" Libby asked.

He shook his head and put down his coffee cup. "Emma says you haven't seen today's paper yet. So you haven't heard the police arrested my father for Zell Orcutt's murder."

We all gasped.

I said, "Boy, we had no idea! I'm so sorry."

"The police came in the middle of the night. Dad lives in one of the cottages on the Fitch's Fancy property. I stay with him when I'm not in the state capital, and I—I'm sorry." His train of thought chugged away from him, and he rubbed his face. "I've been up all night. I'm not making much sense."

The Fitch cottages were more like mansions than their names implied. The four large houses were occupied by various Fitch relatives, although I'd heard they were owned by Zell and grandfathered to the relatives rent-free. Pierpoint lived in one, Verbena another. Some cousins occupied the other two, although they also had homes in warmer climates. All of the family treated the grounds of Fitch's Fancy like a huge park, one so large they rarely saw their relatives.

I said, "What do the police think happened?"

"I don't know. Dad went to reason with Zell about selling the estate, but—well, you saw Dad leave. He was angry, so I guess the discussion went badly." Boy picked up one of the diet books and frowned at the cover. "Thing is, Dad threatened Zell once before. In front of witnesses. So the police figured they had an ongoing disagreement."

"Did they?"

"Didn't everyone disagree with Zell?" Boy asked.

Emma had grabbed the newspaper and was skimming the front-page article about the murder. "The cops didn't arrest Pointy. They just call him a 'person of interest.' That's a big difference. Maybe the geezer didn't knock off Orcutt. Maybe they're just using the rubber hoses to find out what he knows."

"Em's always joking," I said, noting how Boy's face went white. "Did the police find the murder weapon?"

"Not yet," Emma replied.

Boy said, "There's a collection of bows in the billiards room at Fitch's Fancy. Chances are good whoever killed him simply took one." From his pocket, he fished a small object. "I don't know if it makes any difference, but after the police left, I found this in the garden."

We leaned forward to look.

"An earring," Libby said.

A gold hoop earring.

Boy was watching my face. "Nora? Is this yours?"

I swallowed hard. "It's Delilah's. I noticed she only had one earring on last night."

"That doesn't mean anything," Emma said. "We all know she was there. So she dropped an earring. So what?"

"The police will want to see this, though," Libby

predicted around a mouthful of cream cheese.

Boy looked dismayed. "I didn't want to give it to them if it belonged to one of you. Why confuse things? You didn't kill Zell."

"You should give that to the police," Emma said.

"Uhm, yes, I suppose so." Boy tucked the earring back in his pocket. "Listen, I probably shouldn't have come. . . ."

"But?" Emma prompted, putting the paper down on the table and folding her arms across her chest.

"Since you were at Fitch's Fancy yesterday," Boy said, "I wondered if maybe the two of you saw something. Something that might help my father?"

"We didn't see more than you did."

Boy turned to me. "You're observant, Nora. And I know you've helped people before when things like this have happened."

Emma said, "Nora's not a private detective you can hire."

"I know, but—"

"And she's got her own life."

"Em," I said.

"I'm desperate," Boy said directly to me. "My dad probably hated Zell as much as the real killer. But this—this is something he didn't do. He's been ill lately, and sometimes he gets confused, but I know he's innocent."

Boy opened the newspaper to a photo on the second page. The photographer had snapped a picture as two burly police officers hauled Pointy Fitch off to jail.

The face of a frightened old man stared up at us from the table. The wisps of white hair that floated around his balding head gave him the look of a confused homeless person, and his watery wide eyes reflected panic.

"Oh, dear," said Libby, struck to the heart by the photo.

"Nora," Boy said, "if you have any information, any impressions—anything at all that might help my dad, I'd be grateful."

"She's not for hire." Directly to me, Emma said, "It's time to think of yourself, you know. You have to stop trying to help every hopeless case that comes through your door."

I looked at the newspaper photo. Pierpoint Fitch. He wasn't a man who would kill anyone. I was sure of that. I didn't want Delilah implicated. And Boy's discovery of her earring didn't bode well. I studied his expression for signs of Machiavellian guile, but all I could see was the face that prompted his own mother to say she was afraid one good sneeze might deprive Boy of what remained of his brains.

"I'll ask around a little," I told Boy. "I'll see what I can find out."

"Thank you," said Boy.

Emma turned away.

Libby wiped her sticky fingers on a napkin. "I'll make sure she does her best, Boy. Sometimes Nora needs a little help. Please know that I'll do everything in my power—"

"Give it a rest," said Emma.

We were all on our feet by then, and a knock sounded at the back door. I opened it and found Mr. Ledbetter standing on the porch in a blaze orange parka and his patched overalls. The gruff handyman who had come to Blackbird Farm in all weather for hundreds of emergencies acknowledged me with nothing more than a grunt and strode into the kitchen with his clanking toolbox in hand.

"Good morning, Mr. Ledbetter." I forced the good cheer required to keep the handyman's spirits from plummeting to their normal depth of gloom as he surveyed my latest home disaster. "Would you care for a bagel before—? Oh, hello."

I hadn't noticed the younger man who had been lurking behind Mr. Ledbetter. But just as I began to close the door, he scooted inside, shyly ducking his head so I couldn't get a glimpse of his face beneath his grimy baseball cap.

Mr. Ledbetter said, "This is my new assistant. Not that I need one. But here he is."

"Hello," the younger man mumbled. "I'm the new assistant."

"How do you do?" I shook his hand. "Why, Mr. Ledbetter, I thought you said you'd never put up with a helper. Even your own sons—"

"Just temporary," muttered Mr. Ledbetter. He hunkered down on the floor to examine the pipes beneath the sink.

The new sidekick plunked down his own toolbox—

much newer and lighter—on the floor.

Boy suddenly said, "Rudy? Is that you?"

Perhaps as a politician he had developed the skill of recognizing faces, because he clearly guessed right. The expression on Mr. Ledbetter's assistant's face was startled. Boy put out his hand to him and said heartily, "Great to see you again. You have a new job, I see."

"Uh," said the handyman's assistant. "Hi, Mr. Fitch. Yeah, new job."

"The hours must be better," Boy said jovially. "You still in touch with your old partner? Or did Darla quit, too?"

"Uh, no," said the assistant. "Look, I'd better . . ."

"Don't let me keep you," said Boy. "You've got to make a good impression on the new boss, I suppose."

"Yeah," said Rudy, already getting down on his knees to join Mr. Ledbetter beneath the sink. "Nice seeing you."

"Nice to see you, too," Boy replied. "And say hello to Darla for me if you run into her, will you?"

I elbowed Libby aside and escorted Boy to the front door myself. He started to thank me for my help in clearing his father, but I cut him short.

I said, "Boy, how do you know the plumber's assistant? Is he an old friend?"

"Rudy? Oh, no, he did some work for a committee I serve on in the legislature."

"What committee?"

"He used to be an investigator," said Boy. "Working

in organized crime. I guess the benefits must be better working as a plumber, though, huh?"

I said, "Maybe so."

But I doubted it.

Chapter Six

*B*oykin left, and Libby—unaware she had cream cheese on her chin—announced we were late for a Yolates class. "You'll love it," she gushed. "I have your whole day planned. A little exercise, then a salad for lunch followed by an herbal enema."

"Jesus," said Emma. "Are you trying to kill her?"

"Thanks, Lib, but I have to work today."

Emma was in a hurry to pick up some liniment for Mr. Twinkles, so she dragged Libby out. I made a phone call as soon as they disappeared out the driveway.

My nephew Rawlins showed up about twenty minutes later. He came in through the back door, slugging from a plastic bottle of Mountain Dew.

"Hi, Aunt Nora. Hey, you look nice."

In Grandmama Blackbird's closet, I'd found a slimming black Saint Laurent suit with a pencil skirt that was a little snug. Underneath it, I put on an Old Navy camisole with lace trim for warmth. "Is it too tight?"

"Heck, no. You look really pretty. Kinda sexy."

I gave him a kiss as I slung my coat around my shoulders. "Rawlins, you're so sweet to help me, but I swear if you breathe a word to either of my sisters, I will recommend you be grounded until you beg for mercy."

Rawlins grinned. "No breathing, I promise."

During the last year, Rawlins had gone through a phase of wearing jewelry that required the piercing of various body parts. I was glad to see him down to two earrings and a stud through his left eyebrow. Although still a slouchy teenager with baggy jeans and a set of headphones permanently slung around his neck, he'd grown up a lot in recent months. I thought part of his transformation may have resulted from spending time in the company of Michael Abruzzo. Michael ran a tight ship at the garage where his posse hung out— ostensibly to rebuild cars, although I was pretty sure other activities took place there. To his mother's dismay, Rawlins had almost become a regular in Michael's crew. I thought the association had brought improvement. My nephew could actually look an adult in the eye and hold a comprehensible conversation now.

Rawlins said, "So whassup?"

Well, almost comprehensible. "I need to go into the city. You don't mind driving?"

"Nope. Except maybe on the way we could stop to pick up my tux for the Spring Fling."

"Sure."

"I'm driving Mom's minivan." He rolled his eyes.

"So you and I are going to look like a couple of dorks?"

He teased me right back. "Unless you'll sell me a car from Mick's lot. I could really use a nice set of wheels this weekend."

We went out onto the porch and stood looking across my driveway at Mick's Muscle Cars, the used-car lot Michael had built on the part of Blackbird Farm I had sold to him during the first wave of my financial crisis. The asphalt parking lot was still full of ridiculous cars with tail fins, racing stripes and high-performance tires, but lately I'd noticed his salesmen had stopped showing up for work. During the winter, someone had mysteriously plowed the snow from my driveway, but once the weather warmed up, nobody came around. A few neon flags fluttered forlornly in the breeze over the deserted sales lot. It appeared that whatever Michael was mixed up in elsewhere, it took all his resources.

But one of the cars had been hastily parked on the end of the line, with one wheel definitely resting on my property. It was a low blue coupe that I didn't remember seeing until this morning.

"She's a beauty," Rawlins said on a sigh.

"She is?"

"Sure. The 1968 Mustang GT, the California Special. A two-twenty-horsepower engine with a two-barrel carb, see? One of the best ever built."

"Rawlins, how much money do you have in your pocket?"

"Huh?"

"I'm serious. That car is parked on Blackbird Farm. Possession is nine-tenths of the law, right? So I can sell it. How much money do you have?"

"Maybe ten bucks after I pay for the tux rental. Aunt Nora, are you pissed at Mick or something?"

"Or something," I said. "Mostly I could really use the ten bucks. Let's go have a look at your new car."

Together, we walked across the crunchy grass of the still-frozen yard together. Rawlins knew where the secret key was hidden to the salesmen's shack, so within another few minutes he had the ignition key and was sitting behind the wheel of a Mustang with two barrels of carbohydrates, whatever that meant.

My nephew breathed deeply, as if to inhale a fine automotive fragrance. Which smelled like mildew to me.

"Sweet," said Rawlins prayerfully.

"Seems like just another car."

"You don't appreciate fine American craftsman-ship." He turned serious. "The Mustang is a classic, maybe the hottest car ever built. Unless you're a Corvette fan, which I'm not."

"You sound like Michael. You really want this thing?"

My nephew's eyes got round. "What will Mick say? This baby's worth real money!"

I got out of the car and walked around it. I kicked the tires, wiggled the side mirror and bounced the rear bumper for no reason except I'd seen people do it in the movies. "This clunker is ancient." I pointed. "There's rust inside the wheel thingies, and the motor probably needs an oil change. But it would make a very nice ride to the dance this weekend. Show me some money, kid. Let's make this official."

"Sure thing!" He fished a grubby five-dollar bill out of his pocket along with four ones and some change.

I didn't bother counting the change. "So it's yours. We'll figure out the paperwork later."

Once the decision was made by somebody who resembled a grown-up, Rawlins became enthusiastic about the plan. He helped me into the passenger side and spent some time fussing with the position of his own seat before pulling out and carefully steering us up to the road. Once on the highway, his confidence grew and we were soon sailing along with the wind whistling into the car through various gaps between the ill-fitting windows. Delighted, Rawlins let his foot rest a little heavier on the accelerator.

"Who are you taking to the Spring Fling?" I asked. "Anybody I know?"

"Shawna Greenawalt. Her dad's the director of some historical society around here."

"Is she nice?"

Rawlins might have blushed. "Real nice, yeah. She plays first base on the girls' softball team. We're in the Future Farmers club together."

I laughed. "Rawlins, you want to be a farmer?"

"Hell, no," he said. "But the club gets to go on really

cool field trips. In January we went to the state fair in Harrisburg. That's the sweet thing about going to public school now. We don't have to wear ties and go to boring old Washington all the time. How many times can one kid visit the Capitol?"

When the family resources did their about-face, Libby had pulled all her children from private institutions and sent them to the local public schools instead. The kids didn't seem to mind. In fact, I thought they were flourishing in their new, more diverse environment. Libby's income from the life insurance policies of various dead husbands was enough to keep them all in necessary clothes and gadgets, but so far they were still enjoying public school.

"Is Shawna going to be a farmer?"

He laughed. "No, she just dropped the H-bomb on her parents."

"The H-bomb?"

"She got into Harvard. She starts in September. She wants to major in international studies."

"Good for her." I couldn't help thinking such a girl would have a positive effect on her boyfriend.

Which made me think of someone else.

"Rawlins, when you went to prep school, was there a girl named Clover in your class?"

"You mean Clover Barnstable?" He shuddered. "Don't remind me."

"Oh?"

"That chick is scary."

"Scary how?"

He focused on the road in front of us—glad, I think, not to have to look at me. "She's pretty and every- thing. But she's into weird stuff."

"Drugs?"

"No. At least, not more than anybody else." Rawlins shrugged, unaware that my heart had contracted. "For her, it's guys. Guys with money especially. And—you know. Sex."

"She had sex with boys for money, you mean?"

"Not exactly. But she wanted presents, and she's not shy. She's got those fake—you know—and all the guys wanted a look, so they were all giving her junk, and pretty soon she was doing more than showing, know what I mean? I mean, okay, I get it, but those things of hers are totally bizarre. I stayed away from her as much as I could."

I thought I heard a hint. "But not completely?"

His hands suddenly fidgeted on the steering wheel. "Are you going to tell my mom?"

"No breathing, remember? It goes both ways."

"You mean it?"

"Rawlins, you do know all about safe sex, right?"

He laughed nervously. "I can't believe we're talking like this."

"You have condoms, don't you?"

"Are you kidding? My mom started giving me those when I was thirteen. I have this huge collection—all colors, all shapes."

"But do you use them?"

"I don't really have much opportunity. Shawna's not

into it. But everybody has sex now. All the high school kids."

I knew the statistics. I had heard the buzzwords. Friends with benefits. Hooking up. It all seemed so casual now for teenagers, while I was still wrestling with the emotional consequences of my hormonal urges. "But you? With Clover?"

I tried to imagine my awkward, inarticulate nephew with that sophisticated, sexy girl I'd seen dancing on the bar at Cupcakes.

Rawlins was chewing on his lower lip. "Look, it was only one time with Clover."

"Once is enough," I said. I should know.

"We didn't even take our clothes off. I just—you know, unzipped. And she—"

"You had oral sex."

"Yeah, and I gave her a ticket to a concert. I didn't feel like going anyway."

I tried to remain calm. Surely it wasn't good for kids to shrug off such an intimate act. Surely it dehumanized both of them. "You still need to protect yourself, Rawlins. Especially if your partner is promiscuous. I don't mean just physically. Emotionally, too. And waiting is still the—"

"Okay, okay, you can skip the abstinence lecture. Shawna and I are holding off. Can we stop talking about this now? I'm really weirded out."

"Okay. We can stop for now, but this conversation isn't over." My best hope was Shawna, I thought suddenly. I hoped a girl headed to Harvard had a good

117

head on her shoulders and could talk to Rawlins about sex in an adult way.

I said, "Have you seen Clover lately?"

"I told you, it was just the one time, and—"

"I don't mean 'Are you having sex with her?' Just have you seen her around?"

He shook his head. "No, I go to a different school now, and she dropped out anyway. I think she's being homeschooled."

"By her mother?" I couldn't imagine Viper teaching algebra to her daughter.

"I don't know," Rawlins said. "I guess so. Or maybe she just quit."

"Do you know a girl maybe named Jane? A friend of Clover's?"

"Jane Plain? Her real name is Parker or Planker or something. Yeah, she used to hang with Clover. Probably still does."

"Do you know anything about her?"

"Only that she's like Clover's fan club. Ever since elementary school, it's like she doesn't have a personality, so she leeches off Clover. Why do you want to know?"

"I saw her yesterday, that's all."

"She goes everywhere Clover does. Hardly says anything. Some kid beat her up on the playground once in fourth grade, and she just let him do it. Didn't fight back, didn't even cry, just let him. Real passive."

"Did Clover try to help?"

"No. I think a teacher broke it up."

We arrived in New Hope soon after that and Rawlins parked in front of a shop that rented formal wear. He left me in the car to ponder what life as a teenager had become. A few minutes later, he came back carrying a long plastic garment bag and a shoe box.

He showed me the box. "Do I have to wear rented shoes?"

"Of course not," I said. "Wear what's comfortable. Want some help putting that stuff in the trunk?"

"Yeah."

Rawlins was juggling his various bags, so I got out and popped the trunk for him. Together, we looked inside. He said, "There's a bunch of stuff in here."

I leaned closer and saw two large black nylon suitcases. "I'll move them over."

But I couldn't budge the suitcases. They were deadweight.

"Let me try." Rawlins handed his bags to me and grabbed one of the suitcases by its handles. "Whoa, really heavy."

"You can't lift it, either? What if we lighten the load?" I reached in and opened one of the suitcases.

Which was how Rawlins and I found ourselves staring at a very large amount of money. Twenty-dollar bills wrapped in rubber bands. The bills looked well used, not like new currency. I couldn't begin to guess how much cash had been packed into the suitcases.

Rawlins murmured a curse in one long, slow breath.

I leaned shakily against the rear of the car and tried to absorb what we'd just discovered.

"Somebody left all this money in the trunk." Rawlins sounded like a kid again.

"Not somebody," I replied. "Michael."

"Why? There's a ton of cash here."

I put the garment bag on top of the suitcases. I closed the trunk, and we got into the car.

"What's going on?" Rawlins didn't start the car but sat staring out the windshield in shock. "What's Mick doing?"

"He's in business, Rawlins. A lot of cash businesses."

"Why doesn't he put the money in the bank? Most businesses deposit—"

"I know what other people do, but Michael is—he's not exactly a chamber-of-commerce type."

Abruptly, Rawlins said, "He's been running around with different guys lately."

I turned to look at my nephew. "Have you met them? The people he's dealing with?"

"Not really. He kinda threw me out of the garage. He said I should get a life. I thought he was kidding around, but when I went back a couple of days later one of his guys wouldn't let me inside. Said some people were talking to Mick and I should get the hell out."

"What people?"

Rawlins shrugged again. "I don't know. One of them was a kid a little older than me. That was weird. Why do I have to get a life while that kid gets to be with Mick?"

I heard the hurt in his voice finally. "I don't know, Rawlins."

For the first time, I was confronted with the concrete evidence that Michael was up to something nefarious. I knew what kind of people carried large amounts of cash—and it wasn't upstanding citizens.

In a little while, Rawlins started the car and we drove into Philadelphia without much further conversation. He drove more slowly than before, as if concerned that the money he was transporting might be obvious to other drivers.

I tried to push aside my panicky thoughts about Michael. And although I'd planned to pay a visit to ChaCha at Cupcakes, it was clear after my condom conversation with Rawlins that taking him to Cupcakes was a bad idea. I decided a quick stop at Verbena's tea shop might be more informative. Maybe someone in her workplace had some insight into her relationship with her stepfather.

I helped find a parking space on the street and invited Rawlins to the bakery, but he felt he should stay with the car.

"I mean, what if somebody tries to steal the money?"

I pointed out that any self-respecting car thief would more likely choose the upscale vehicles parked around us, which seemed to ease my nephew's mind.

"Okay," he said. "But I'm still going to look mean at

anybody who comes along."

He showed me his threatening look, and I was honestly surprised to see my nephew could manage a pretty dangerous thousand-yard stare. With a pang, I realized he'd developed it by watching Michael.

I left him listening to his headphones and studying the display screen on his cell phone.

Verbena's quaint tea shop stood on a busy residential corner only a few blocks from the city condo where I had lived with my husband before his death. I remembered when the bakery opened. While still living in the neighborhood, I had enjoyed tea with girlfriends there when the pace of my life had been gentler.

I maneuvered through a parking lot of baby strollers on the sidewalk. A steady stream of customers swept through the distinctive blue door to reach Verbena's famous cupcakes. The sweet fragrance of baking wafted out onto the sidewalk.

Inside, I saw the crowded tea tables to my left—all covered with chintz linens and mismatched china. Groups of women—young mothers, mostly—sat sipping their green tea and chatting across tables. There were plenty of babies in laps, diaper bags on the floor. In another corner, a foursome of older men drank coffee and seemed to be arguing over something in the sports pages. A college student sat alone tapping on his computer, and two middle-aged women in bulky sweaters were bending their heads over a handful of photographs. The lush scent of fresh-ground coffee mingled with a nutmeggy smell in the air.

Although the left side of the tearoom had the atmosphere of a neighborhood gathering spot, a line of patrons inched along the display cases to the right of the door. Everyone picked up a distinctive blue-and-white box at the beginning of the line, then served themselves from the trays of goodies. People filled their boxes with the cupcakes and paid for them at the register before breezing out of the shop. The cupcakes were beautifully topped with pastel pink, yellow or blue frosting, and each sported a red jelly bean in the center. The similarity to the cupcakes depicted on the T-shirts at Cupcakes was obvious. It looked to me as if Zell Orcutt had copied his stepdaughter's signature product.

I scanned the crowd, hoping to see someone I knew.

Behind me, the door suddenly slammed on its hinges, and all the customers turned to see who had arrived.

Clover. In close proximity, she was thinner and rangier than she'd appeared while dancing on the Cupcakes bar, but her breasts looked more like devices designed to save her from drowning. Over tight jeans, she wore a dyed fur bolero jacket with a buckle-encrusted Versace bag on her shoulder and pink sunglasses on her nose. "Mother! Dammit, where are you?"

Customers turned to stare.

"Mother!"

From behind the bakery cases came Verbena. Her

white hair was still spiked, but she wore a clean white apron over tight jeans with chef's clogs on her feet. She wiped flour from her hands with a crisp tea towel. Today she looked far more composed than when she'd wept over her stepfather's body.

In front of the whole crowd, Verbena said with all the concern of any suburban mom, "Honey, what's wrong?"

Clover took off her sunglasses and fought back tears. "You won't believe it. That bitch really fired me."

"Clover! Why?"

The girl jammed her sunglasses into her bag. "She said she didn't want me in the show anymore. That I had no talent. That I ought to go back to baton class with all the other losers! Baton class!"

"Honey!"

Verbena took her daughter's arm and pulled her into a space by the bakery case. It wasn't private, but clearly sent a message to the crowd that privacy was requested. Clover swiveled one hip, though, making it obvious she wanted the limelight right where it was. Among the tea shop patrons, you could have heard a pin drop.

Clover yanked free of her mother's touch. "Who does ChaCha think she is? Doesn't she see I'm gonna *own* Cupcakes now?"

"Well," Verbena began.

"She needs a reality check! What's an old bag like her wearing the Cupcakes shirt for, anyway? What guy wants to look at her little saggy boobs? It's me they want!"

"Maybe you misunderstood—"

"I didn't," Clover snapped, dashing tears from her face. "She told me to leave and not come back. She said she'd mail my paycheck. Who does she think *signs* those checks?"

"With your grandfather gone—"

"What?" Clover blazed. "Are you taking her side? You think I'm a loser, too?"

"Of course not, honey—"

"Because you can shove it, you know. Just like ChaCha!"

"I never said—"

Clover summoned cold rage. "I'm better than all the other girls put together. I look the best, and who cares about their stupid dances? Nobody's going to ruin my career—not some two-bit, washed-up old bat like her!"

"Let me make you some hot chocolate. You can have a snack and we'll figure this out."

Clover's anger bloomed into astonished fury. "Are you kidding? You want me to get all fat and ugly? You think I'm a failure, too, don't you? Well, forget it, Mother. You can't make this day any worse than it already is!"

"What can I do to help?"

"Give me some money," Clover snapped.

"Okay." Verbena reached for the pocket of her apron. "Do you need to buy some lunch for yourself?

I have a few dollars—"

"Are you kidding? I need real money!"

"We've been over this before, Clover. If you wait for your paycheck, you'll appreciate—"

"Oh, shove it!" Clover marched to the cash register and slammed her hand down on the keys.

The money drawer popped open, and Clover began grabbing handfuls of cash and jamming them into her handbag. Verbena didn't move, and the silence in the shop made Clover's thievery all the more appalling.

When she'd emptied the drawer, Clover rammed it shut and spun around so fast that she knocked me into the display case. As I caught my balance, she slammed out the door and stalked off up the sidewalk.

Verbena's expression astounded me.

She was actually smiling as she watched her daughter storm away.

I collected myself and ventured forward. "Verbena?"

"Nora." She blinked, surprised to see me. "Are you all right?"

"Yes, fine. But Clover is so upset—"

"More angry than hurt. I value high spirits in a child, don't you? Strength of character, a powerful will. I'm never more triumphant as a mother than when I see Clover's glorious temper. Do you have children?"

"No," I said. "Not yet."

"Well, you'll understand someday." She hesitated, clearly torn between ending our conversation then and there and making amends for Clover's rough shove.

Finally, Verbena said, "Would you like some tea? And a cupcake? I was about to make a batch myself. I couldn't stay at home today. So I came to work, where I'm happiest."

"Everyone copes differently with death."

"Baking helps me cope with everything. Come into the kitchen. I have an hour before I go choose a casket."

I'd seen my fair share of peculiar responses to grief, but this one bewildered me. I followed Verbena around the display case and through a doorway to the bakery. Four white-aproned bakers bustled between the stainless steel counters and the daunting wall of ovens. As Verbena entered, they all seemed to focus more sharply on their tasks.

Verbena led me to her private corner of the kitchen. With a careless gesture, she indicated a stool, and I sat down. She pulled a crockery mixing bowl down from a shelf and set it purposefully before herself, like a potter placing raw clay on a wheel. From a refrigerator drawer, she brought eggs and milk. A glass jar of flour came down off a shelf. I could see she had created a ritual for herself.

I found myself wondering what her rock fans might think of her now.

As she gathered her ingredients, I said, "I didn't have a chance to give you my condolences last night. I'm very sorry for your loss."

"Zell was no loss," Verbena said. "Not to me, anyway."

"Still, his death must be a shock."

"For Clover more than anyone. She considered Zell her grandfather. She cried half the night."

Although she spoke of Clover's pain, I certainly hadn't seen a hint of dismay.

"It's a shame she's lost her job." Verbena frowned. "But Clover is a determined girl. And she's always wanted to be more famous than me. She'll find something even more exciting now. Something more suited to her talents. She's really going places."

I had hardly seen stellar quality in Clover's Cupcake performance, but I said, "As her mother, you must be a little relieved that she's been fired from a place like Cupcakes."

"I want whatever Clover wants," Verbena corrected. "But I never thought Cupcakes was right for her. She's destined for something bigger."

"Well, she must have enjoyed working with her grandfather."

One-handed, Verbena cracked two eggs into the bowl and tossed the shells into a nearby sink. "At least he gave her a shot—that's what's important."

"I hear your uncle Pierpoint is being questioned for Zell's murder."

"I heard that, too."

"Do you believe he killed your stepfather?"

"It's possible." Verbena began to whisk the eggs with a strong rhythm. "Uncle Pointy and Zell fought on and off for years. But Zell fought with everyone in his life, you know."

"Even Clover?"

She smiled at last. "Of course not with Clover. Everyone loves Clover."

"Did they get along?"

"I just said they did." Verbena stopped whisking. "Are you implying that Clover might have hurt her grandfather? Because that's ridiculous."

"No, I only—"

"She loved him, and he loved her in his own way. If you think you can print something about Clover and her grandfather, you'll have me to answer to."

I suddenly saw Viper standing before me. "Verbena, that's not at all what—"

"If you're wondering who killed my stepfather, you should trust the professionals."

"I do. Generally, that is."

But Michael often said murder resulted from circumstances that involved drugs, money, family or sex. Sometimes all four. The only category Pointy fitted was family.

Carefully, I said, "Pointy seemed a little irrational yesterday when I saw him. But he hardly seemed murderous. And surely Zell had more dangerous enemies than Pointy."

"Dozens," Verbena agreed, going back to her whisking. "It would be easier to find somebody who *wasn't* his enemy. He was always helping people in business."

And frequently ruined those businesses when he forced the owners to cut him in on the profits. I asked,

"What about love affairs?"

With another frown, Verbena said, "I doubt he called them love affairs. Zell went for one-night stands. Not that I would know. Once I left home, Nora, I paid as little attention to my stepfather as possible. Look." She rapped the dripping whisk against the bowl and pointed it at me. "I think the police have the right person. Or at least the right branch of the family."

I couldn't have been more surprised if she'd beaned me with a rolling pin. "I beg your pardon?"

"Who had the biggest reason to get rid of Zell Orcutt right now?" Blithely, she reached for a glass measuring cup. "Whose career would be severely damaged by a connection with a venture like Cupcakes?"

I blinked. "You're saying Boy might have wanted to kill Zell?"

She shrugged. "Politicians will do just about anything to get elected these days."

"But . . . your cousin Boy?"

"He's not as sweet as he pretends. He's ambitious, too. Maybe it's a family trait. And, of course, you don't swallow that dummy routine of his, do you? He may be clumsy, but he's not an idiot."

I almost told Verbena that Boy had asked me to look into Zell's death. He wouldn't ask for my help if he were guilty of the crime himself. Or would he?

None of it made sense.

Claiming I had to get to work, I begged off waiting for Verbena's cupcakes and said good-bye. I bought a box at the counter and went outside, still wondering about the Fitch family. They were even nuttier than I had thought.

Standing with Rawlins on the sidewalk was Clover. She had one arm draped around his shoulder, and she appeared to be sticking her tongue in his ear.

Chapter Seven

I skidded to a stop and quickly backpedaled to the bakery doorway, almost dropping the box of cupcakes in my arms. What to do? March over and humiliate Rawlins? Or break them up before their public display of affection officially got them arrested for public lewdness?

Beside Rawlins, Clover looked like a praying mantis—long, skinny legs made to look longer by the height of her heels, and arms that seemed stretched to inhuman lengths. Her pouty lips had been smeared with so much sticky lip gloss that they looked like pink flypaper. And by the way she draped her arm around Rawlins's shoulder and leaned in to lick his earlobe, she might have been a giant flesh-eating insect tranquilizing her victim before she sucked his succulent brain out of his skull.

Judging by his expression, Rawlins would have died empty-headed but happy. As he clung to a parking meter to keep his balance, his face was dazed and delirious.

Clover's hand slipped from my nephew's chest, down his quivering abdomen to linger at the belt that barely kept his corduroys on his hips.

A passerby, a young man in a yarmulke, carrying a backpack, shook his head and muttered, "Get a room."

I had to do something.

On the corner, there was a trash can and a public telephone. In a burst of inspiration, I headed for it, juggling the box of cupcakes and scrabbling one-handed through my pockets for some change. Luckily, the phone hadn't been vandalized. I dialed Rawlins's cell number and fed coins into the phone.

Thank heaven the cell phone ruled every teenager's life. Rawlins answered his automatically. "Uh, yeah?"

"Rawlins," I said sternly, "you're going to get arrested for that kind of behavior."

"Huh?"

"I'm on the corner at the pay phone."

He looked around, hastily disengaging Clover's hand from his pants. At the sight of me glaring at him, he nearly ripped the parking meter out of the pavement. "Uhm . . ."

"I'm coming over."

"Oh—okay."

By the time I had hung up the receiver and marched over to them, Rawlins had his libido sufficiently under control to pretend surprise. "Uh—uh, Aunt Nora!"

Clover took her arm away from his shoulder, tossed her head back and used her long fingers to rake her hair as if she were auditioning for a Pantene commercial. She took one look at me with my box of cupcakes and sighed with loathing.

My nephew swiped the back of his hand across his ear. "Aunt Nora, this—this is Clover."

"Hello, Clover," I said. "How nice to meet you."

She shrugged. "Yeah, whatever."

"We were just—you know, talking about stuff," Rawlins said. "Stuff about—you know, just stuff."

"How scintillating."

As if I were invisible, Clover went back to eyeing Rawlins. "You're so hot," she breathed. "I don't remember you being this hot."

Rawlins turned an alarming shade of primrose. "Uhm . . ."

"I'm having a party." She used her forefinger to trace an imaginary heart on his chest. "Friday night. It's supposed to be like my birthday, only it's not. Everybody cool is coming."

"Oh," said Rawlins. "Sounds great."

"It's in a club. Chastize, do you know it? The owners are comping the space because I bring in, you know, business."

"You do?" I couldn't imagine what business Clover might attract.

Clover ignored me and tossed her hair again. "Yeah, everybody cool wants to be with me. I'm gonna get written about in the newspapers and stuff."

"Really?" Rawlins asked. "Aunt Nora writes a column for a newspaper."

Clover gave me a longer scrutiny, but shook her

head. "Not dressed like that, she doesn't. Anyway, I just got this new purse. Nice, huh? And these earrings. I kinda liked them when a boy gave them to me, but now I think they're gross. Do you think they're gross?"

"They look nice," said Rawlins, except he wasn't looking at the earrings.

Clover toyed with the bangles on her wrist. "But these bracelets are so last week, right? I'm going to throw them away. Or maybe get some new ones for the party. So, you know, you should come, Raw."

Rawlins was too mesmerized to understand her ploy. "What?"

"To my party."

"Yeah, sure, great," he said. "I'll be there."

"I just wish I had some decent jewelry to wear."

"Rawlins," I said, "isn't Friday the night of the Spring Fling?"

"The what?"

"The school dance," I said even louder. "You know, the tuxedo, the car?"

"Oh, right!" He was nodding. "Yeah, the Spring Fling."

Clover's lip curled in teenage disgust. "You're not going to some loser fest, are you? How lame is that?"

"Well—"

"My party is way more cool than some school snooze. So you'll be there, right? I mean, you can use my name at the door and they'll let you in, even without ID."

134

"Well." Rawlins avoided my eye. "I'll try."

"You're too hot for high school kids." In full wheedle mode, Clover angled her body closer until her enormous breasts were directly beneath my nephew's nose. "Come about midnight. That's when things really start to rock."

From the street, brakes squealed. Then a black Jeep pulled to the curb, and someone dressed in a khaki vest and baseball cap cranked down the window far enough to stick a camera out, aimed at Clover.

Another hair toss and eye roll. "Will you look at those guys? Are they ever going to leave me alone?"

"Who?" Rawlins was oblivious. "What?"

"The paparazzi," she said. "They chase me everywhere. I can't escape. I gotta go, Raw. See you Friday, right? Ciao, baby."

She gave him a deep, lingering kiss on the mouth in full view of the photographer, then squeezed my nephew's behind. I thought I heard Rawlins squeak, but she released him and strutted away, swinging her hips. The eye of the clicking camera followed her up the sidewalk to a fire hydrant where she'd left a gleaming BMW parked with one tire up on the curb. She struck a quick pose for the benefit of the photographer, then climbed into the car, and made a bad business of threading it out of its illegal parking spot before finally roaring up the street. She blew her horn just in case the photographer failed to notice her departure.

We watched the Jeep make a U-turn and follow, and I saw that the driver was the same photographer I'd seen snapping the girl's picture at Cupcakes the night before, the same girl I'd met in the bathroom.

"Is that Jane?"

"Who?"

"That girl with the camera."

"I don't know. I wasn't looking at her."

"Do we actually have paparazzi in Philadelphia?" I asked.

"Huh?" Rawlins wiped Clover's lip gloss from his mouth.

"And why Clover of all people? It's not like she's an actress."

"She's hot."

"Hot? Is that the only quality worth having anymore?" I rounded on Rawlins. "And exactly what do you think you were doing with her, young man?"

He hugged himself and turned as pink as a kid who'd just been nabbed for shoplifting Trojans. "I'm really sorry, Aunt Nora."

He summoned a believably hangdog expression.

"It's not your fault," I soothed, then caught myself. "No, wait a minute. It's completely your fault!"

"What am I supposed to do?" he cried. "She's a piranha!"

"You could have told her about Shawna, for one thing!"

"I know, I know. I hate lying. Look, I'm not going to her party, that's for sure."

"Good," I snapped. Then, softening, I said, "Hungry?"

136

"I guess."

I offered him the box of cupcakes, but when he peeked into the cupcake box, Rawlins looked a little nauseated. "I'm not into sweets much. What about a pizza?"

To finance his snack, I handed over the nine dollars and change Rawlins had given me earlier. He drove me to the offices of the *Philadelphia Intelligencer* in the Pendergast Building and promised he'd be back in a couple of hours.

"Where will you go?" I asked. "Looking for Clover?"

"No." He blushed again. "Maybe I'll pick out some flowers for Shawna."

"Good idea."

I kissed him good-bye, and went into the lobby, through the security checkpoint and up the elevators to the floor I shared with the rest of the writers from the Features department.

I had inherited the social column when Kitty Keough died after twenty-five years of high-society gossip. Since then, I'd struggled to keep up her schedule and her readership. Although I knew the city's social set better than most local football fans understood the Eagles' playbook, I found I didn't have Kitty's poisoned pen when it came to tattling tales. I was struggling to keep her readers flipping to the back page every day. My editor had already begun to wonder if the society page was a dinosaur that had wandered into the tar pit.

But the other writers in the department welcomed me—never more so than when I came bearing a box from Verbena's Bakeshop.

Skip Malone, the sportswriter, lifted a cupcake out of the box the instant I stepped off the elevator. "Hey, Nora, how's the rubber-chicken circuit?"

Mary Jude Yashurick, the food writer and the occupant of the desk closest to mine, savored her first bite with a swoon that spun her swivel chair in a complete circle. "You're a lifesaver!" She sucked frosting from her fingers, then tried to keep the crumbs off her bright yellow sweater by cupping her other hand beneath her chin as she ate the rest. "I need a sugar rush."

"I was hoping to mooch some lunch from you."

Mary Jude blinked at me. "Not in the mood for cupcakes?"

"Not exactly."

"Upset stomach?"

"Nothing serious. I'm hoping for something bland."

"I probably have something." She hooked the handle of her desk drawer with the toe of her shoe and tugged it open to reveal her stash of goodies—samples sent by various food manufacturers. Under a mound of cake mixes, a freeze-dried lasagna and a lone can of macadamia nuts, she found a sleeve of organic wheat crackers. She tossed it to me. "Here you go. If it's organic, it's probably tasteless enough for you."

I hefted the crackers in my hand. "Thanks."

She unpeeled the rest of the wrapper from her cupcake. "You've been kinda scarce lately, Nora."

I heard the polite suspicion in her tone. "A touch of the flu got me down, but I'm bouncing back."

"Going out every night to cover the party scene?"

"Almost every night, yes."

"Because if I didn't know better . . ."

I pretended to read the label on the crackers and didn't dare glance at my friend.

When I didn't respond, she scooted her chair closer to my desk. "You know, Nora," she said in a lower voice, "I may look like a girl who fell off a turnip truck, but I didn't land on my head."

Mary Jude had a top-notch Ivy League education, but now a single mom, she worked hard to earn the meager salary the *Intelligencer* paid so she could have the flexible hours needed to take care of her mentally challenged son, Trevor.

She said, "If you've got a problem, you can ask me anything. I know my way around all the resources, and I'm not judgmental. I can help, no matter what you decide to do."

"Is it getting obvious?"

"That you popped up a bra size? Turn green at the thought of food? Yeah, to an observant expert in girl trouble like me, it's starting to look like you're thinking about a trip to the clinic."

I felt a rush of emotion. Afraid to speak of my pregnancy, I had missed out on the kind of support a good friend could offer. I shook my head. "I don't think I can do that, Mary Jude."

She polished off the cupcake, folded up the wrapper and tossed it into the trash can. "Me, neither. But I know your personal life is messy at the moment."

"A little."

"The mob boss is out of the picture, though, right?"

"Yes."

"And you're seeing a hunk from the *Inquirer* now?"

"Maybe I'm better off solo," I said, still not ready to tell anyone who had contributed his DNA to my science project. "You managed on your own."

"Yeah." She licked a final dab of frosting from her thumb. "The minute Trevor's father heard things weren't all hunky-dory with my pregnancy, he took off for Miami and never looked back, not even a Christmas card. So what? The asshole doesn't know what he's missing. But we're doing fine. Trevor makes me see the world like a kid all the time, and that's a gift. It wouldn't have been my first choice, though."

"Things may not work out for me in the life-partner subject, either."

"I'm sorry to hear that. But you can make it on your own if you have to."

"I'm so broke," I said with a sigh.

"So shop at the Salvation Army instead of Saks."

"It's not that. I'm getting used to poverty. But is it fair to a child to have only one parent?" Slowly, I opened the crackers. "I'm not even sure I can be a good mother. My own family definitely belongs in the remedial class when it comes to parental skills."

"Yeah, I met your sister Libby when she tried to sell me a pink vibrator."

"Sorry about that. But, M.J., what if something goes wrong? Or I have to cope with—"

"A child who's not perfect?" Mary Jude brushed cupcake crumbs from her desk. "I won't kid you—it can be tough. There are days when I can't stand leaving Trevor at home. And other days when I can't face going back to him."

"You're so strong. And lately I've been a basket case."

She nodded sympathetically. "You've been through a lot. And now you're pregnant and feeling alone, so it's scary as hell. Listen, you want to talk to somebody about adoption? I know a lawyer who specializes in the private kind."

"Thanks," I said. "But that doesn't feel right, either. This is something I really want. And yet . . ."

Mary Jude's phone began to ring, so she rolled back to her own desk. "I know, I know. Your brain feels like a pinball machine right now. Part of that problem is hormones. The best thing you can do is take care of yourself. And ask for help if you need it." She grinned.

I went to my desk, oddly elated.

Nibbling on a cracker, I reached for the phone and dialed Delilah's number.

"Hey," I said when she answered. "Long time no hear. How are you doing?"

"Nora, hey." Delilah's voice was subdued. "I can't talk right now. I'm—the police are here."

I dropped my cracker. "What can I do to help?"

"I'm okay," she said, but sounded far from it.

"Do you have a lawyer with you?"

"I don't need one," she said. "We're just talking."

"If you have any doubts, call a lawyer," I said. "Do you want me to come? I can hold your hand, if you like."

"I can handle it," she said. "But I gotta go. I'll call you later."

She disconnected before I could say more.

Slowly, I hung up my phone. Maybe the cops were simply asking Delilah standard questions.

Or were the police hedging their bets?

I extracted another cracker and took a bite. It tasted like cardboard with sawdust added for flavor. I opened a bottle of water to wash it down.

Fortunately, it all stayed in my stomach. So, nibbling crackers and sipping water, I went through the heap of my mail, comfortably glad to have Mary Jude working steadily beside me.

I received dozens of invitations every day, but because we were still in the slow weeks of the social season, I stopped into the office only three times a week to sort the envelopes. In a month, my workload would double. Soon, invitations for spring events would come flooding in. To stay ahead of the game, I made phone calls and wrote e-mails like mad, glad to focus on work and block out everything else for a while.

I took my work seriously, and my party-hopping had

a purpose. Hundreds of philanthropic groups relied on newspaper coverage to promote their causes and help raise funds. It was my job to show up and report on clothes, decor, food and people, but also how much money was raised. Patting donors on the back resulted in more donations later.

I felt I could do my part for good causes by attending as many functions as I could squeeze into my calendar. During the height of the social season, I sometimes made appearances at two or three events each night.

Across the room, someone dropped a coffee cup and cursed. The rest of us looked up from our desks. Will Wesley, the paper's political columnist, popped up from his chair to avoid getting his trousers wet. As always, he wore a stiff striped shirt, a crisp bow tie and red suspenders to keep his pants from falling off his fat-cat potbelly.

Muttering, Will grabbed a handful of tissues from the box on another desk and began to mop up the mess.

As everyone else went back to their work, I pulled a roll of paper towels from Mary Jude's stash and went over.

"Thanks," Will said with uncustomary civility. As I dabbed coffee off the newspaper he had splayed open on his desk, he said, "I was reading Maureen Dowd and the cup slipped out of my hand."

"Well, at least you weren't throwing the cup." I was pretty sure Will didn't see eye to eye with Maureen.

"I haven't finished her column yet," Will said darkly.

Although our politics clashed, Will suffered my presence after he discovered one of my ancestors had sat next to his at the Continental Congress in 1774. The rest of the *Intelligencer* staff remained beneath his contempt for their mongrel pedigrees and unenlightened views.

I picked up a stack of well-thumbed copies of *National Review* to keep it dry, but Will snatched it from my grasp. Not before I glimpsed a single copy of *Maxim* among the political digests.

I said, "I thought I might have seen you at the Lajeune party last week, Will. Aren't you friends with Jerome?"

"I have a standing Wednesday night dinner date with my mother."

"Oh. You weren't the only one who couldn't make it. Boykin Fitch didn't show, either. Do you know Boy?"

"Of course I do. A very promising young man."

I decided not to point out that Boy and Will were probably the same age. Will seemed determined to be an old fogey before his time. "Is it true?" I asked. "That Boy plans to run for Senate next year?"

Will busily rearranged his desk. "He hasn't made an official announcement yet, but I know he's fundraising. Why? Are you a supporter?"

I hated to dash Will's hopes that I might have converted. "We're friends."

"I see," Will said frostily, straightening to meet my eye. "Then you won't be asking who he's slept with like the left-wing gossips in this town?"

"Of course not," I replied, although that question was precisely the one I'd hoped to pose.

I heard my phone ringing, so I hurried back to my own desk.

"It's me!" Libby said when I picked up. "You're a journalist, right? So you know how to do research?"

"Well—"

"I just heard there's something called the Chocolate-Cake Diet! Where could I look that up?"

There was no sense trying to reason with her. I said, "Try Ask Jeeves."

"Thanks!"

She hung up.

Shaking my head, I collected the paperwork I wanted to take home. Then I put on my coat to conceal my figure from anyone who might be as observant as Mary Jude, and I stuck my head into my editor's office.

In his ancient desk chair, Stan Rosenstatz was stirring a cup of coffee with the eraser end of a number two pencil.

"Stan?"

He waved me into his office, but I saw the momentary flick of dismay in his face. He wasn't as glad to see me as he had been in the past.

But he put on a good front, tapping the wet pencil on the rim of his cup. "You're not going to ask me for travel expenses, are you? Mary Jude wants to go to a Scandinavian-food festival in Wisconsin, and George says the automotive column won't recover if he can't get to Detroit to see the concept cars next month. Do these writers think I'm made of money?"

I had brought along the box of cupcakes and offered him his choice. "Need something to take your mind off your troubles?"

"Thanks, kiddo." He accepted a cupcake and waved me into the wobbly chair in front of his desk. "What's on your mind?"

I sat down and decided to launch directly into the discussion I'd planned. "Stan, since Kitty's death, I know I haven't exactly attracted thousands of new readers with my version of the social page."

He didn't argue, but gave me an owlish look. "You're not going to quit on me, are you, Nora?"

He might be relieved if I did. But I said, "You're always saying we need to appeal to younger readers, right?"

He swiped a finger of icing. "If we don't, we'll soon be out of business."

"I've got some ideas to improve my column to make it appeal more to a younger audience."

"Okay, let's have it."

"First of all, I think it would be smart to send a photographer around to some of the high school proms."

He licked his finger and began to shake his head. "Marcie, the assistant fashion writer. She does prom clothes."

146

"I don't mean just the clothes. Proms are becoming something totally different than they used to be. My nephew's spring dance is a fund-raiser for disaster victims. And there's a high school in the city that's collecting used sporting goods for underserved children. It's a whole new movement to get kids thinking philanthropically, and I think it's a concept worth supporting. Some publicity would help them, and we'd get a feel-good story about young kids doing something worthwhile."

"Uhmm."

He hadn't said no, so I went on. "And how many college students live in our circulation area? They're always having parties to benefit good causes. I don't mean the beer blasts that make neighbors angry, but the charitable work college kids do."

"What are you proposing?"

"Photos, mostly, a little copy. I won't need to go to the events. I'm plenty busy covering the social season. But if we could send a photographer to a couple of events every week, I could do interviews by phone. The pictures and captions could go in the Thursday edition, the same day the weekend concert schedule goes in. I often don't have enough material for that day, anyway. We could make it a big deal, Stan."

The buzz around the *Intelligencer* offices was that the society page took up space that could be better used for sports coverage, which sold papers. I had been trying to figure more ways to keep my job, and I thought I'd finally come up with a good solution. But

Stan still looked unimpressed.

"Here's the next part," I went on, trying to stay enthusiastic. "I think I should start contributing to our online edition. Kids may not read newspapers yet, but they definitely surf the Internet. If I cover some of the school charity events—maybe even send a video camera—we could corner the market on events that young people really want to read about. Once we hook them online, we can reel them over to the print edition."

"I don't have anything to do with our online stuff, you know."

"But you could put in a good word. I think this is a great idea, Stan. I think we'd really attract young readers with this."

He frowned at the cupcake without touching it, as if his mind was elsewhere. For a moment, I thought he was trying to find the words to let me down gently.

But he said, "How much space are we talking for the high school and college stuff?"

I took a breath. "Half a page once a week."

"Quarter page to start." He lifted his head to meet my eye. "In the Thursday edition. When can you get the first one ready?"

"You think it's a good idea?" I couldn't keep the surprise out of my voice.

"It's worth a try."

"Great! I'll need a couple of weeks to lay the groundwork, make some calls, talk to some people."

"Okay, go for it," he said. "Meanwhile, I'll take the

148

online editor to lunch and see what he thinks about you contributing to that, too."

"Stan, you're terrific! Thanks so much! You won't regret it, I promise." I leaped to my feet and bounded for the door.

"Nora?"

I paused in the doorway.

He leaned back in his chair and beckoned me closer. "Let's talk another minute."

How had he figured it out? Was my pregnant stomach already bulging with a job-jeopardizing baby? I gripped the doorjamb for courage, sure I was headed for the unemployment line.

Then Stan said, "We got a call from a jeweler, said he was a friend of yours."

"Jeweler?"

"Martin Jaworski. You know him?"

Philadelphia's "King of Bling" was an old family friend who had lavished lots of attention on my mother before she maxed out her credit cards. I stepped back into Stan's office. "Yes, of course I know Marty."

"He's been a big advertiser in the *Intelligencer* for something like fifty years. Now he wants to make a change. And when a whale of an advertiser like Jaworski says he wants a change, even the publisher gets nervous."

"What kind of change does he want?"

"For years, his ads have run in Local News alongside the carpet-cleaning company and some dentist who makes your teeth look like Farrah Fawcett's."

"You're showing your age, Stan."

He allowed a grin. "Yeah, well, Jaworski's phone call made everybody in the sales department age about twenty years. He wants to put his ads on your page, right beside the social column."

"Really? Isn't Marty a sweetheart!"

Stan did not share my pleasure. "He said his customers all read your page, and that he had friends who felt the same way. He gave us the names of some other businesses to try—some upscale caterer and a furniture store who want to reach your readers. The sales guys are knocking each other over to get to the phones."

"That sounds good. Isn't it good?"

"You seem surprised."

Abruptly feeling as if I were standing on the carpet of the principal's office, I said, "I am."

"That's good. Nora, we don't want our writers going after advertising. It's a conflict, you see?"

"I've never spoken with Marty about advertising."

"I checked just to be sure," Stan acknowledged, "and you haven't. But the editor over in Local News is giving me grief. Which I don't need from outside my own department."

"Sorry, Stan."

"Just don't go trading boldfaced type in your column for advertising, okay?"

"I have a feeling I should be insulted you're even suggesting such a thing."

"Good. Grief from you, I can live with." Stan smiled a little. "You're a good kid, Nora."

Which of course made me feel guilty for not admitting I would be needing at least an afternoon off to deliver my child. Torn about giving up my secret on the spot, I said, "Thanks, Stan."

"Okay, get back to work." He picked up his cupcake. "I'm sure you've got places to go."

Chapter Eight

I met Rawlins on the street fifteen minutes later. His expression was not that of a boy with a clear conscience.

"How was the pizza?" I asked, wondering if my nephew had a tryst with Clover while I was working.

"Not bad." He handed me into the passenger seat with suspiciously good manners.

With my guilt radar at work, I gave him the address of my next stop. But Rawlins made conversation while he drove across town in the gathering darkness. He agreed to wait again while I made a quick stop at a party. By now, he seemed comfortable with the knowledge that he had two suitcases full of cash in the trunk of his car. I marveled at the adaptability of teenagers.

In Rittenhouse Square, I dashed past a man who had been loitering on the sidewalk. He wasn't fooling anybody in his pink miniskirt, slingback heels and fluffy sweater. He opened the bookstore door for me.

With a polite smile, I went into Barnes & Noble, where a publisher was launching a book by a local author who had written a children's story about the history of the city. The bookstore manager had wisely invited kids from a local day care center and a lot of city dignitaries who would read aloud to them. Fruit punch and Liberty Bell–shaped cookies were served by a costumed Ben Franklin.

I wasn't a dozen steps inside the door when I heard an unladylike bellow from across the room.

"Nora!"

My best friend, Lexie Paine, vaulted a three-year-old to give me an exuberant hug. She was dagger sharp in a short-skirted Marc Jacobs business suit buttoned to her throat. Tonight her sleek black hair fell from a simple silver clip at the back of her head, and her subtle makeup was nearly invisible on her fair skin. Diamond earrings the size of shark teeth gleamed in her ears.

She linked her arm through mine and gave me a noisy kiss. "Half the mayor's staff is here, sweetie, and we're going out for a drink later—no doubt so they can pump me for help on their latest fiscal fiasco. Want to join us?"

"Tempting," I said on a laugh. "But reading a phone book promises more thrills than talking city budgets."

If an American city could have royalty, Lexie would be Philadelphia's answer to every descendant of

Queen Victoria. She came from the oldest of Old Money, ran a brokerage firm with the single-minded devotion of a samurai warrior and, in her spare time, supported dozens of charitable organizations around the city. Plus she remembered birthdays, sent presents for no reason and loved a good party.

"I must take my thrills where I can get them, sweetie. You look all gussied up for a night on the town. I was hoping we could gossip about the Fitch family afterwards."

"Has there been a news bulletin I haven't heard?"

"So I was right!" Her expression glowed with interest. "You are mixed up in the murder."

"Not mixed up," I said.

"I can guess what that means." Lexie grasped my elbow and guided me into the bookstore's vacant poetry section for a tête-à-tête. She lowered her voice. "Please don't tell me you're emotionally involved in this thing. Zell Orcutt wasn't worth your time when he was alive."

"Nobody's weeping for him in the financial district?"

"Darling, we had dancing on tabletops all over the city today. Zell was universally disliked. What's your interest?"

I didn't want to suggest Delilah might be involved in Zell's murder, so I said, "I don't think Pointy Fitch killed him, do you?"

"Seems unlikely," Lexie agreed. "But maybe Pointy got conned just like half the other millionaires in

153

town. You wait—scads of scandals will come to light now that Zell's dead. He had plenty of real enemies."

"Do you know of anyone in particular?"

"A dozen," she said. "But I'm supposed to be discreet. Let me make a list and check it twice so I don't give away any state secrets. I'll call you tomorrow, okay?"

"Not at home," I cautioned. "I'll get in touch with you."

Lexie looked intrigued. "Someone's bugging your phone again?"

"I'm not sure."

"I thought the whole world knew you broke up with the Abruzzo family. It's scary to think the last to learn are the boys in blue."

I sighed. "They must be hoping I'll spill some beans."

"Watch what you broadcast," Lexie advised. "Or you'll find yourself testifying someday."

"So far, the only one who's spoken into the microphone is Boykin Fitch." I told Lexie about Boy's morning visit to my kitchen.

Her eyebrows lifted. "Boy was trying to cover for his daddy, huh? Seems a little late."

"What do you mean?"

Lexie had her ear to the ground most of the time, and she didn't disappoint. "Do you know Kirby Donovan?"

"The guy who drives around with a Great Dane sticking its head out the sunroof of his car?"

Lexie nodded. "Kirby, the political fix-it man. Boy's office just hired him, and you know what that means. There's a tempest brewing, and the powers that be hope to keep it safely in Boy's teacup."

"Boy has a political problem?"

"He must. Kirby is only hired when there's a mess to clean up. Nobody sweeps dirt under a rug any better."

"Have you heard anything specific about Boy?"

"Not yet. It must be something ugly, though, if Kirby's on the case. A guy of his caliber doesn't just fix a few parking tickets."

"So Boy has something to hide," I murmured, thinking Cupcakes wasn't enough of a scandal to keep him from being elected. Unless there was more to the story. "What do you think it could be, Lex?"

"Money? Corruption? Sex? Could be anything."

"Enough to kill for?"

"People have been killed for much less."

Zell's murder was getting more and more complicated. The possibilities began to swim in my head. Or maybe I just needed some food to settle my stomach.

Lexie gave me a closer examination. "You don't look so hot, sweetie. What's up?"

I hesitated. I wanted to confide in my best friend about the coming addition to the Blackbird family, but tonight was the wrong time and place. "I'm just tired."

"You need a vacation," Lexie said. "Is the party circuit getting you down?"

"Things are quiet at the moment, thank heaven. I'll

hit the ground running again once the flower show is over."

Lexie continued to study my face. "In that case, what about a getaway? Isn't there somebody with a Palm Beach house you could borrow for a few days? My mother's place in San Francisco is available at the moment, if you don't mind the plane ride. Or I could check—maybe somebody's taking their own jet to California this weekend, and you could hitch a ride."

"I can't miss Saturday night's museum bash, can I? No, I'm just a little tired. It's time to go home."

A frown still puckered my friend's forehead. "Stay at my place tonight. I can have you tucked into my guest room in twenty minutes."

I managed a smile. "You're a darling. No, Rawlins is waiting outside to drive me home. But, Lex, I really will call you. There's something I'd like to talk about."

"You mean the museum party? I just heard that Delilah forgot to confirm the band! What's next?"

I knew Delilah had been busy with the police today, but I didn't say so. "Things will work out," I promised. "The party will be terrific."

"I hope you're right." My friend gave me a quick hug. "I'll see if I can find out anything juicy about the Fitch clan. See you soon, sweetie."

For my column, I made a quick circuit of the crowd, making mental notes about who was there. Then I grabbed a press kit from the bookstore manager and complimented her on a job well-done. She thanked me for coming and told Ben Franklin to get more cookies from the back room.

I was out on the street five minutes later and found Rawlins parked near the bookstore, talking on his cell phone. I climbed into the Mustang, yawning. Rawlins clicked his phone shut, and we headed for home. In the seat beside him, I fell asleep before we passed city hall.

I might have even started dreaming. But I awoke with a start when the car decelerated and hit a bump in the road. Thinking we had arrived at Blackbird Farm, I sat up, groggy and disoriented. A quick glance out the window told me that Rawlins had pulled over on the side of a dark stretch of empty road. My voice was scratchy with sleep. "What's up?"

"Sorry, Aunt Nora. We—uh—ran out of gas."

I straightened up, thoroughly awake then. "What?"

"I should have filled the tank, I guess."

"You're joking." I tried to get a look at the gauges on the dashboard.

But Rawlins blocked my view by leaning forward to set the parking brake. "Honest mistake," he said. "Hey, this is kinda like *Night of the Living Dead*, huh?"

We were on a deserted stretch of two-lane road I didn't recognize. At once, I began to imagine worse than marauding zombies. With a trunkload of money, we were sitting ducks.

"Rawlins, this is—" I stopped myself from lecturing

him at the wrong time. "Well, at least we have your cell phone. Who can we call? Triple A?"

"Uh, yeah, sure."

In that moment, the headlights of another vehicle flashed through the rear window. Like a bolt of lightning, the glare lit up the interior around us.

"Let's hope this is a Good Samaritan," I said. "Not a serial killer with a hook for a hand."

Rawlins laughed nervously.

"Maybe it's a police car?"

"I'll check." Rawlins popped his door and slid out of the car. "Stay here."

"Rawlins! Get back inside!" I made a grab for his shirttail, but missed. No longer trying to stay calm for his benefit, I cried, "Get in here and lock your door! Are you crazy?"

But my nephew disobeyed. As I fumbled to unfasten my seat belt, I craned around to see the tall figure of another man get out of the other vehicle. I gasped. "Rawlins!"

They met halfway between the cars and exchanged a handshake and low-voiced greetings. A moment later, Rawlins came back to the passenger door just as I managed to thrust it open.

But it was Michael who leaned down and put his hand out to me. "Need a lift?"

The pounding of my heart turned into palpitations. "What are you doing here?"

"Coming to your rescue."

Although I doubted I was going to be safe, I took his

hand and got out of the car. "Why does it feel like kid-napping?"

"Keep your voice down. Kidnapping's a felony, and I sent my lawyers home for the night."

He looked tall and dangerous in his leather jacket and jeans, but he was smiling. Beside him, Rawlins scuffed the toe of his shoe in the dirt and didn't meet my eye.

"Rawlins, did you really run out of gas?"

Michael went around to the rear of the car and popped the trunk.

"Rawlins?" I said sharply.

"Don't blame the kid," Michael said. "I've been tracking down this car all day. Believe me, it was a relief to figure out who had it."

Rawlins said, "He told me to stop on this road. He said he'll take you home."

I shivered in the cold. "I'd rather call a taxi."

"You'll never get one out here," Michael called from behind the car. He hefted one suitcase out of the Mustang's trunk and dropped it on the ground, then the other. "Have you had dinner yet?"

"What about the car?" Rawlins asked him. "Should I take it back to the lot?"

I said, "It belongs to you, Rawlins. Bought and paid for."

Michael looked amused. "Can I ask how much he paid for it?"

"No."

"I'll give it back," said Rawlins.

"No, you won't," I snapped. "That car was abandoned on my property, so I had the right to sell it."

Michael said, "Kid, it's yours. Just let me have the cargo."

"You mean the unmarked bills?" I asked tartly.

To escape the coming storm, Rawlins grabbed the handles of one of the suitcases and dragged it in a series of breathless yanks over to Michael's vehicle— a large van with a crooked front bumper and a cockeyed headlight. Michael carried the other bag and tossed it through the van's open back doors. Then he and Rawlins exchanged low murmurs and I heard Michael laugh.

Rawlins came back to me, still with downcast eyes. "G'night, Aunt Nora."

"Hmph." I grabbed his shirt and pulled him close for a rough kiss on his cheek. "You scared the hell out of me."

"Sorry," he mumbled. "Really."

Rawlins got back into his new car. It started without a problem, and he departed with a scatter of gravel and a flash of taillights.

Adrenaline was still seething inside me, but it wasn't enough to make me brave. I was tired. Maybe too tired to cope with Michael alone on a dark night.

"You okay?" he asked.

"No," I said. "I hate it when you pull this kind of trick."

"It wasn't a trick. I just figured the less you know, the better for everyone."

The rusting van featured the faded logo of a flower shop peeling off the side panels. Michael opened the passenger door with a shriek of ungreased hinges. "Your chariot awaits, Cinderella."

"More of a pumpkin, wouldn't you say? Did you steal it?"

"If I were in a stealing mood, wouldn't I choose something classier?"

Against my better judgment, I let Michael boost me into the front seat, which was tricky in my pencil skirt. I felt Michael's helping hand linger on my behind, and quickly sat down on the seat. The van smelled vaguely of gladiolas. Michael closed the door, went around to get in behind the wheel and started the engine. The van coughed and trembled like a sick rhinoceros.

"Come on," Michael coaxed, and the engine grudgingly sputtered to life.

While it struggled to find a smooth rhythm, I said, "You've gone to a lot of trouble to find your lost luggage. How much is in those suitcases?"

"Eight hundred thousand dollars."

For some reason, his prompt and truthful answer only made me angrier. "And you left it parked on my driveway all night?"

"I didn't park it there. And the guy who did isn't working for me anymore."

"Is he at the bottom of a river now?"

"Nora." Michael reached for my hand.

"What do you expect me to believe?" I slid across the ripped vinyl upholstery until I was jammed against the door and out of his reach. "The only people who keep that kind of cash handy are drug dealers."

"You know I don't deal drugs. Hell, I don't even take aspirin."

"Then what's going on?"

"My piggy bank broke."

"I'm not joking, Michael. And what about Rawlins? Do you know what he thinks now?"

"He's known the score for a long time."

"We don't want him mixed up with your illegal activities. He's only a boy."

"You know I'd never intentionally get you or your family in any trouble." Michael's voice rose, too. "Last night was a mistake, and nobody's sorrier than I am. But I can't undo what's happened, can I? So if the car will keep Rawlins quiet, then—"

"Keep him quiet?" I cried. "Do you hear yourself?"

Michael sighed. "Can we get some dinner?"

"I'm not hungry."

"I'm starving. Is fast food okay? Because I don't want to be seen with you in a restaurant, and going to your place means bumping into Clark Kent."

Not to mention the plumber's assistant, the under-cover organized-crime investigator or whoever it was who had probably installed a microphone under my sink this morning. Tartly, I said, "Are you afraid of seeing Richard?"

"I figure he doesn't need to know we've been together."

"I'm not going to lie to him."

"Oh? So you told him what we did in the phone booth at Cupcakes last night?"

I swallowed hard and didn't answer.

"I didn't think so," Michael said. "That's more honesty than any relationship can stand."

"You prefer a relationship with secrets, don't you? A few lies to keep things exciting?"

"They keep things safe," he replied and put the van in gear. "Is a burger okay?"

In a tense silence, he drove a few more miles up the road to the neon-lit parking lot of a chain restaurant I had never patronized except to treat my niece and nephews. At the drive-up window, Michael ordered a couple of sandwiches and coffee for himself before turning to me. "What's your pleasure? Now that I've got my money back, I can afford to buy."

"I'm not hungry."

"Order something anyway."

"No, thank you," I insisted.

"Emma says you've quit eating."

"She's your spy now?" But another thought popped into my head and suddenly I couldn't breathe. "What else has she told you?"

"That you're not taking care of yourself. That you're getting mixed up in another murder. That you need somebody to talk some sense into you. Just order dinner, dammit."

"Maybe a baked potato," I said uneasily, not completely sure I could actually consume anything more complicated than crackers, popcorn and soup. Fortunately, the slightly rotting smell of flowers wasn't as powerful with the window cranked down.

"A potato," Michael repeated, sounding blank.

"Yes, a potato."

"Okay, okay. Coming right up."

The food came in lots of paper bags and plastic, which I juggled on my lap until Michael drove another half mile and found a place to park the car in the back lot of an abandoned bowling alley. The yellow light of a single streetlamp cast a glow inside the car. Michael had become an expert in pinpointing and avoiding surveillance, so I was sure no security cameras watched us.

I pried the lid off the coffee cup and handed it to him. "Does the money in the suitcases have anything to do with those men you were with at Cupcakes last night?"

"You don't want to know."

"Am I allowed to know who they were?" I handed him a wrapped sandwich.

"One was my uncle Lou. And Danny Pescara's uncle Carmine and his son, Little Carm. It was a diplomatic mission, that's all. Nothing too exciting."

Whatever he was up to, he wasn't going to tell me, so I asked, "How old is Little Carm?"

"I dunno. Eighteen, maybe."

I decided not to try lecturing him further about corrupting teenagers. "And the women? Who were they?"

"Scenery."

I hesitated. Then found myself asking, "How well do you know your friend Darla?"

He bit into a messy hamburger and spoke around the mouthful. "You mean in the biblical sense? How many times we've done it? What positions?"

I knew what he was trying to do. I clenched my teeth, steeling myself to press on. "I just wonder who she is. Does she have a job, for example?"

"Why do you want to know?"

"Is she the one you slept with last summer? The psychologist friend?"

"No, that's Kathy. Kathy Sweeney."

"So Darla is someone totally new? Someone you just met?"

"I didn't expect this." Michael turned his shoulder against the seat to look at me at last. His gaze was heavy-lidded, but intensely blue. "You're interested in the women I date now? That's some kind of important step, isn't it?"

"Stop it. That's not why I—"

"She's sorry, by the way. For throwing the drink. She said she'd pay to have your clothes cleaned."

"That won't be necessary." I took the lid off my baked potato and took a tentative sniff. I still wasn't sure I could manage to swallow even a bite, and the thought of arguing further made my stomach even more unsteady. Or maybe what made me woozy was the knowledge that Michael had definitely crossed the line into something illegal. Until now, I'd held out hope that he was only pretending. But the vast amount of money in the suitcases proved to me that his dark side had won at last.

Softer, I said, "I'm wondering, Michael, if Darla might be someone you should avoid."

As if his stomach had suddenly turned, too, Michael abruptly wrapped up the remains of his burger in the foil it had come in. "I remember this stuff tasting better when I was a kid. Do you think low-fat ingredients ruined the fast-food industry?"

"You're ignoring me."

"No, I'm not. Darla should be the least of your worries. Carmine Pescara, on the other hand, may have killed as many as thirteen people in his long and illustrious career. Darla may throw drinks, but she doesn't collect old bedspreads for the wet work."

The wave of nausea that rolled up from inside me had nothing to do with food. "You're hanging around with a murderer?"

"Yeah, well, he tells great jokes. He can be the life of the party when he feels like it."

"Why are you doing this?" I asked.

He knew what I meant. He said, "It's who I am, Nora."

I put the lid back onto my potato.

Michael noticed and frowned. "Is Emma right? Is there something wrong?"

I summoned some composure. "Only that she moved in with me. Emma, that is. She wants to live at the farm now."

Michael found the shrink-wrapped plastic silverware and squeezed the fork out. He handed it to me. "That's good. The two of you can look after each other. Is she drinking again?"

"I don't think so."

He shot me a cautious look. "Have you heard about her new job?"

"The Dungeon of Darkness?"

"I hear she carries a whip and wears a spiked collar."

I noticed Michael was smiling. "You think it's funny?"

"A little. Somehow Emma working as a dominatrix makes sense. It's like her calling." He caught my expression. "Nobody really gets hurt in those places, Nora."

"Are you speaking from experience?"

He shrugged. "It's not my thing, and you know it. It's all pretend, at least where she is. More silly than sexy. A bunch of accountants looking for excitement."

"I should be relieved?"

"You seem to be handling it all right. I always marvel at your ability to handle Emma. And what's Libby into these days? Not to mention her psychopathic kids. Does the baby have a name yet?"

"Max. Maximus Charles."

Michael laughed. "He'll need a name like that to stay alive in your family."

"You should talk," I cracked.

He sobered at once. "Okay, I deserve that. Let me see you take a bite."

"I'm not hungry."

"One bite."

"Why are you so concerned about—"

"Just eat something, will you?"

To prove I wasn't suffering from an eating disorder Emma must have dreamed up, I took a forkful of baked potato and ate it. Michael waited, so I swallowed two more mouthfuls while he watched from across the seat.

"Happy now?"

"It's a start," he said. "Now tell me about the murdered guy."

Chapter Nine

O f course, Michael was qualified to discuss all manner of crimes, and he clearly enjoyed doing so. He liked to read the newspaper and dissect the handiwork of his peers—frequently poking fun at their ineptitude. At first I thought it allowed him to indulge his own criminal instincts in a way that didn't result in jail time.

But I didn't really want to discuss crime with him tonight.

On the other hand, it kept other subjects from popping up.

So Michael sipped his coffee while I told him about Zell Orcutt and the Fitch family.

"You think the politician did it?" he asked when I concluded my list of suspects.

I shook my head. "Why would Boy want me to investigate if he killed Zell?"

"News flash: Politicians can be devious."

"He's not that bright."

"You sure?"

"No," I admitted. "Maybe he's smarter than he pretends."

Michael nodded. "What do you think he was doing in the garden when you arrived?"

"He said he was looking for his wallet."

"Think he was contaminating the crime scene?"

"I thought of that." I told him about Delilah's earring.

Michael put his coffee cup on the dashboard and got more comfortable in the seat. "So the police will zero in on the black woman now. That was a smart move on the politician's part."

"You don't really think Delilah will be arrested? Why?"

"It's the way the world works, Nora. She's the one person who doesn't fit into the picture of rich white lunatics."

Companionably quiet, Michael let the possibilities roll around in his head for a while. Then he said, "The killer couldn't be the rock-and-roll stepdaughter, could it?"

"Verbena? She seems to hate Zell with a passion that's more than the standard kid's dislike of the man

169

who married her widowed mother. Did you ever listen to her music?"

Michael shook his head. "I think I was inside then."

Inside a prison, he meant. I nodded. "Well, she sang angry songs."

"About what?"

I frowned and tried to think. "The usual things, I suppose. Drugs. Lost love. Abusive men. I guess I need to learn more about her."

"Hm. And her kid? What's she like?"

I told him, then added, "Clover is apparently the only person who actually liked Zell. At least, she was happy to be working at Cupcakes. I don't see her as his killer. Besides, she's only a child."

"Is she going to inherit now that's Grandpa's dead?"

"I'm not sure. She certainly thinks so."

"Is she strong enough to handle the murder weapon? And have the expertise to use it? A bow is a tricky thing to manage."

"You've done it?"

"My uncle Lou likes to hunt. Took my brothers and me out a few times when we were kids. Until I tripped over a root and—well, see?" He ducked his head and ran his thumb along the scar that grazed his hairline.

I had let my own fingers touch the small scar many times. "You could have put your eye out."

He gave me a smile. "I wish I had a nickel for every time my stepmother said that. I was eight years old. Anyway, my point is, you have to be strong to pull the arrow back. Especially if you want to get it deep enough to kill something."

"Archery is a favorite sport among the whole Fitch family. There's a huge collection of bows in the house, and they're all good at using them. That's primarily why I doubt the murderer could have been somebody from outside the family."

He looked amused. "Do you have any friends with ordinary hobbies?"

"Your family has unique interests, too."

"Burying our enemies in landfills?" Michael ruminated a while longer, his coffee getting cold. "What about the woman at Cupcakes, the dead guy's business partner?"

"You always say to follow the money. In this case, that means ChaCha, who owns half of Cupcakes. I haven't learned much about her yet. I've got to figure out a way." I thought about ChaCha for a minute. What motive could she have had to kill her partner?

At last, Michael said, "So you're going to help your friend stay out of jail."

"Delilah didn't murder Zell." I glanced at him. "Why are you smiling?"

He shook his head. "Just admiring your consistency. You always protect the lost causes."

He made it sound insulting, so I said automatically, "I do not!"

"Sure, you do. It's like you'll finally save your husband from cocaine if you can help the rest of us."

"The rest of you?"

"Me. Emma. Now Delilah. If you rescue us from self-destruction, you're finally rescuing him, too."

"That's ridiculous," I said, but without heat. He was right, of course. I knew it. But I couldn't stop myself, could I? Trying to jest, I said, "You're beyond rescue, anyway, aren't you?"

He looked out the windshield at nothing, his face suddenly going blank.

After a moment, he said, "My money's on the politician."

I sighed and shook my head. "Boykin manages to cover his shortcomings with good looks and charm, but unless he's a fabulous actor, I really don't think he has the brains to plan a murder and get away with it, let alone ask me for help afterwards."

"There's more to the story."

"Most certainly," I agreed.

Michael reached for his coffee and slurped. He grimaced at the taste, then rolled down his window to pour it away. "The politician sounds like an acquaintance of mine, a guy with the same ability to charm people. He could find a way to flatter anyone, get them on his side, you know? Acting stupid, but really watching for his chance. A con man. Easy to get along with, though, as long as you didn't push his buttons."

"Did you? Push his buttons?"

"There are two ways to stay alive in jail." Michael rolled up his window again. "One is to be the last man standing. The other is to avoid pushing any buttons

172

whatsoever. After a while, you learn the second option is best."

Sometimes Michael said things that swamped me with sadness.

"What was his crime? Your con-man friend?"

Michael shrugged. "He killed both of his parents during the Super Bowl. Used a chain saw he'd bought to cut firewood. He put their pieces in the freezer alongside his stash of Klondike bars. Crazy, but he was actually pretty good company once you got to know him. He liked to read dictionaries."

It was too much. The stench of gladiolas and the talk of Carmine Pescara and his bloody bedspreads had been awful, and the thought of plunging an arrow deep enough into a living creature to kill it was almost as bad. But this tidbit of jailhouse confidence was the end. Michael had spent time with such a person. And liked him. Joking with murderers was more normal for him than a life with me. I dumped the remains of our meal into his lap and made a grab for the door handle.

"Hey—"

"Stay here," I commanded, bailing out as fast as I could. The cold night air hit me in the face, but didn't stop the tsunami of nausea that surged inside me. I slammed the door shut and groped my way to the rear of the van before I became reacquainted with the baked potato.

Half a minute later Michael got out of the van and came around to the back, where I leaned weakly against the rear bumper. "Are you all right?"

"Keep your distance," I ordered. "Or you'll regret it."

"You're sick!"

Any number of sarcastic comebacks occurred to me, but I managed to choke them down along with another rush of nausea.

Michael handed me a wad of unused paper napkins. They smelled distinctly of fried food, so I waved them off.

"I'm sorry," he said. "I shouldn't have told you about the chain saw."

I put one hand out to stop him from coming closer. "Keep your distance."

"I want to hold you," he said.

"Not at the moment you don't."

I took a deep breath and turned around to sit on the rear bumper. I sagged there, hands on my knees, waiting for my stomach to settle. When that didn't work, I straightened up and rested the back of my head on the cool metal of the van.

Michael stayed where he was. A shaft of light caught the edge of his cheekbone and melted across his breadth of his shoulders. I couldn't quite see his expression, but I tried.

"Is this working?" he said, genuinely asking. "Being apart like this?"

I knew what he meant.

"I'm with somebody else now," I said steadily. "And so are you. Let's just—please, Michael, don't do this tonight. I want to go home."

"I'm sorry. I didn't mean to make you sick."

"It wasn't—it's a bug, that's all."

"The flu?" He looked doubtful. "Emma says—"

"Since when did you start phoning Emma all the time, anyway? And do you think that's smart? You're paranoid about making phone calls, but you dial my sister's number at the drop of a hat?"

"Nora—"

"You and your stupid obsession with secrecy goes right out the window when you feel like gossiping with my sister?"

"You're worried about me and Emma?"

"I'm always worried about you and Emma. Not together, but yes, as you so insightfully pointed out, I worry about both of you. Is that so bizarre?"

"Are you okay?" he asked, squinting. "You sound—"

"Tired!" I cried.

"I was going to say *nuts*."

"I'll tell you what's nuts. You keeping nearly a million dollars in suitcases on my property!"

"Are we back to that?"

"Did we ever leave it?"

"Nora, you've known how I operate for a long time, and—"

"And it makes me crazy, yes," I snapped. "So how come I can't put you out of my head?"

"What?"

"I can't help it," I said. "I'm possessed or some-

175

thing. When I'm with you, I don't recognize the person I am."

"That doesn't sound good."

"It's terrifying! I like myself! I've been me all my life—until I met you. And now . . ."

"Now?"

For an awful second I realized I was going to cry. I didn't know what I was trying to say.

But then a flash of headlights suddenly swept over us as another vehicle pulled into the parking lot. We both froze until the driver gave a friendly horn toot. I recognized the truck and groaned. The evening was only getting worse.

"Em?" Michael asked.

My sister killed the headlights and got out of her truck. She was wearing a pair of spike-heeled patent leather boots that disappeared up into the folds of a ragged Burberry coat that had been our father's. I recognized the frayed pockets. The coat concealed everything else on her body except a snug black necklace around her .throat. She managed to look stunning, while I could still taste vomit in the back of my throat. Great.

Michael wasn't surprised to see her. "Hey, Emma."

"Hey," she said.

"Is that your uniform under the coat?"

She strolled over with the gleam of mischief in her eye. "You want to see my Mistress of the Dungeon duds?"

"Of course." He was smiling. "I bet you look great."

The necklace wasn't a necklace, I finally realized, but a leather dog collar spiked with pointed silver studs.

Emma flicked it playfully. "You making fun of me?"

"Hell, no. I just want to know if you keep a defibrillator handy in case of heart attacks among the customers."

She strolled provocatively closer. "How about if I just pound your chest myself?"

He laughed. "Can you make it hurt really good?"

Emma reached through the open zipper of his jacket and gave his flannel shirt a friendly tug. "You like the kinky stuff, big guy? I haven't seen you in the Dungeon yet, but I bet you're quite the lady-killer."

"No indictments."

They were both grinning at each other.

I said, "If I wasn't sick already, I'd be throwing up right now."

Emma said, "She doesn't approve of my new employment."

"I wonder why."

Emma let go of his shirt and turned to me. "She likes to pretend she hasn't tiptoed over to the wild side herself now and then. Right, Sis? You spent your formative adolescence with Jill Mascione as your best friend. Tell me you didn't dabble with Sappho, the gay caterer."

Michael turned to me, intrigued. "Dabbling? How come you haven't told me about dabbling?"

"And you," Emma said to Michael, "I know the

kinds of places you've been and can guess what you've done. It doesn't seem to have caused any harm. Shall we all confess our sins and see who blushes first?"

"Point taken." Michael put his hands into his pockets and looked contrite. "Your job is your business, Em."

"Let's not encourage my little sister to play with matches, shall we?" I said, not ready to give up yet. "She's going to get burned."

"I'm sure she's thought about why she's doing it," Michael said.

Emma narrowed her eyes on him. "Playing shrink?"

He shrugged.

I said, "You're doing everything possible to keep real relationships at a distance. But at least you're not drinking, so I guess we should count our blessings."

"Ouch." Emma laughed shortly. "What's wrong with her?"

Michael said, "I've been trying to find out."

"Did you two have some kind of fight?"

"I dunno. She's very touchy tonight."

They both looked at me, and Emma said, "Did you tell him anything interesting yet?"

"Only that I want to go home."

Michael said, "Rawlins and I figured Emma should take you back to the farm."

"In case the cops are waiting to nab the Love Machine there." Emma jerked her head at Michael. "Then I gotta punch the time clock, unless you puritans have further objections, so can we get going?"

"What are we waiting for?" I asked.

"I thought you might have something to tell Mick first."

"About playing Barbie dolls with Jill?"

Emma snorted. "That wasn't all of it, I'm sure. Jill had a crush on you from the time you put on a training bra. No, I meant—"

"I know what you meant," I said. "Are you black-mailing me?"

"I'm just thinking you and Mick might want—"

"No, thanks."

"What's going on?" Michael asked.

"Nothing," I said.

"Something," said Emma.

I staggered away from them. Unsteadily, I walked out into the middle of the highway and put out my thumb, fully prepared to hitchhike home rather than reveal anything before I was good and ready, no matter how much pressure from my sister.

"Hey," Emma called. "Chill. I'll take you home."

"I'll get there myself." I backed up the road with my thumb in the wind. "Unless you think I can't handle the federal investigators who are hiding under my porch with their headphones, wondering if I dabble with the kingpin of New Jersey's underworld."

"Future kingpin," Michael corrected. "I got a lot of concrete to pour before I move up."

"That's not funny, dammit!"

"Come back here," Emma yelled. "You're too hor-monal to be out alone."

"Screw you!"

"See? Insanely hormonal. Wait up!"

"Nora," Michael called. He started to jog after me.

Fortunately, a large, somewhat rattletrap pickup truck came around the bend and caught me in its headlights. I waved both hands over my head in the universal language of get-me-the-hell-out-of-here. It slowed down. The driver leaned over and rolled down the passenger window.

I was astonished to recognize the man behind the wheel. "Mr. Ledbetter?"

"Miss Blackbird?"

Our family handyman was equally surprised to find me in the middle of a road in the dark of night. Normally, he and I had our conversations in my kitchen, where he delivered bad news about house repairs.

"Nora—" Michael had almost caught up with me.

But I opened the passenger door of Mr. Ledbetter's truck and climbed in without bothering to ask. Mr. Ledbetter grasped the situation with complete clarity and accelerated even before I could wrestle the door closed.

"Nora!" Michael made a grab for the door handle.

But we left him in our dust as I fastened my seat belt and sat back to enjoy the ride home.

Chapter Ten

I grabbed a key from under a flowerpot to let myself into the house, then went directly upstairs to bed and didn't wake until nine the next morning. If Emma came back to the farm that night after her evening in the Dungeon, I never heard her.

Naturally, I spent the first hour fighting morning sickness, alternately retching or lying on the cool bathroom floor, wondering if it was too late for a sex change operation. Being a man never sounded so good. When I could finally manage it, I took a hot shower to soothe my aching muscles and to decide what to do next. At last, I dressed and staggered downstairs, still feeling wan, but determined to make some changes in my life.

On the kitchen table sat my handbag. Emma must have brought it home from Michael's vehicle.

I pulled my last Jiffy Pop from the pantry and while shaking it over the stove, I noticed Emma's truck sitting in the driveway. After munching a few handfuls of popcorn, I slipped on my jacket and went out onto the back porch. I spotted my sister in the paddock, working Mr. Twinkles on a lunge line. The huge chestnut snorted and bucked with every graceful stride, his high spirits in play. Emma effortlessly commanded him with the smallest twitch of the line. Watching, I thought that if she could handle a wild horse with such ease, she could probably handle just about anything that walked into her Dungeon.

On the top rail of the fence perched our six-year-old niece, Libby's daughter, Lucy. She clutched the fence with both hands, as if to keep herself from leaping off to join Emma in the paddock. Lucy caught sight of me and waved, her face pink with delight, her blond braids teased by the breeze.

I waved back. Then, when Emma turned to look, I stuck my tongue out, put my thumbs in my ears and waggled my fingers at her. She laughed and gave me a one-handed rude gesture behind Lucy's turned head, so all was forgiven.

The breeze smelled like spring—and a little bit of horse—and the sun felt warm and uplifting. In a few weeks I could start putting in bedding plants and thinning out my perennials. Next spring I'd have my own child. The thought made me throw my head back and laugh at the sky.

But celebratory digging in the garden would have to wait. With the bank's home inspector coming in just a matter of days, there were dozens of household projects that required my attention.

I had turned to go back into the house when a car arrived in my driveway, a snazzy station wagon with another little girl waving from the passenger window.

The driver got out first.

"Delilah!"

My friend went around to help her passenger unbuckle her seat belt and get out.

Then little Keesa Fairweather bounded across the lawn in her red rubber boots. "Nora! Hi!"

I gave Keesa a hug. She was leggy for a ten-year-old, with a curvy face that somehow emphasized her toothy smile as well as the shy shadow in her dark eyes.

"Delilah says I can pet the horse if he's not dangerous."

"He's not dangerous, but he's big, so be careful. That's my niece, Lucy. Go introduce yourself."

Keesa ran off.

After her, I called, "Don't let Lucy boss you around!"

Keesa laughed and kept running.

I turned to Delilah. Her hair, usually neatly crimped and tied up with ribbon, had nappy edges this morning, and she had neglected to put on lipstick or mascara. Her face looked washed-out and drawn. I gave her a hug.

"Thanks," she said, lacking her usual fire. "I hope you don't mind a visit from Keesa."

"You know I love Keesa. She's welcome anytime."

"You mean that?"

"Delilah, what's wrong?"

She shoved her hands into the pockets of her jacket and watched Keesa climb the paddock fence. "She's a nice kid. She's smart. She only deserves the best. And I haven't given her the best life, have I?"

Delilah had grown up in a tough section of the city until her mother and half a dozen aunts moved the family to a suburb, where they focused on education and church and music to keep Delilah and her siblings out of trouble. But despite their best efforts to protect Delilah, my friend had given birth to Keesa while still in high school. Instead of raising the child as her own, though, Delilah had qualified for scholarships that took her to college and launched a busy career that had her rubbing elbows with the top social echelons of the city. She left her baby behind to be raised by her own mother. Even now, I wasn't sure if Keesa knew who had given birth to her. Keesa and Delilah treated each other like sisters.

I said, "Keesa's wonderful, Delilah. You should be very proud of her."

"We are," Delilah agreed, but her lower lip quivered.

"Are you okay? I'm sorry we didn't get a chance to talk yesterday, but—"

She shook her head to stem my concern. "Don't worry about it. What are you doing? Am I interrupting?"

"I was just going to take an inventory of various household problems. An appraiser for the bank is coming, and I have lots of things to fix or disguise. There's a crack in my foundation, for instance. See? I need to find a way to hide it."

"Why don't you just fill the crack?"

"It's a big crack." I led her around the side of the

house and pointed. "The Grand Canyon of cracks. I need a stonemason, and I can't afford one."

"Get a couple of mules, and you could lead tourists down that canyon." Delilah mustered a grin. "Honey, where I started out, we'd just pile up some old newspapers and junk."

I touched her arm. "Tell me what's wrong, Delilah."

We returned to the porch and sat on the steps, where we could see the children petting Mr. Twinkles's head and chattering together while Emma kept a firm grip on the horse's halter.

Delilah said, "My mama's sick, Nora. She's been feeling bad for a couple of months, but she was afraid to go to the doctor."

"Oh, no."

"She fought the breast cancer off a few years ago, remember? But now it's back."

"I'm so sorry, Delilah. Can I help?"

"Thing is," said my friend, "if she's sick, and I'm in trouble with the police, things are going to get bad."

Although I couldn't imagine anything worse, I reached for Delilah's hand. "What's wrong?"

"You know my sister Jasmine? You met her once a couple of years ago. The one with—well, the drug problem and a few other things."

I knew all about the trouble a drug-addicted family member could bring into a household. My husband, Todd, had nearly ruined more lives than his own before he was shot over a cocaine deal that went awry.

Delilah continued. "Because of Jasmine, Social Services visits Mama from time to time. And I'm afraid, Nora. If I'm in trouble and can't support my family, they could take Keesa. Social Services may take away my little girl."

"No! That's impossible!"

Delilah squeezed back tears. "Nora, I'm feeling like one of the brothers from my old neighborhood. Like the police aren't my friends anymore. Like I could be in a hell of a lot of trouble."

I put my arm around her shoulders. "Tell me what happened."

"Yesterday, the cops came to my office. They wanted to know all about my—my relationship with Zell Orcutt."

"Relationship?" I asked. "Delilah, don't tell me you and Zell—"

She tried to laugh. "Girl, you better have more respect for me than that! I was way too old for that pervert anyway. He only liked teenyboppers."

"Sorry. You meant your business relationship with Zell."

"Right. The cops came to talk to me, and they spent the whole day asking questions. I had to send my assistant out for coffee and sandwiches. At my expense, by the way."

"What did the police want to know?"

"Where I was the day he was killed, what I was wearing, who I saw."

"Why do they suspect you? Because you argued with Zell the day he died?"

"That, yes, and—look, when I started my business, I didn't have a lot of assets."

Delilah had always been closemouthed about her business affairs, so her explanation came slowly. "I borrowed from a bank to get off the ground, but I needed more money. I met Zell at one of my parties, and we got to talking. He seemed normal—a jerk with a big mouth, maybe, but he was rich, and I figured I could trust him."

"So he became your partner?"

"He was supposed to be a silent partner. But a couple of months ago he started pushing for a cut of my business. I said I'd repay him the original loan, but he didn't want that. He wanted a percentage. Nora, I get by on a low percentage anyway, and I couldn't pay him what he wanted."

"So you argued with him."

She nodded. "It was nasty, I admit. But I didn't kill him."

"I know you didn't. And the police will figure it out, too. For one thing, you've never used a bow and arrow, have you?"

Her expression told me something different. "That's part of my problem. I was camp champ at Kittanaway Lake three years running. Which the police somehow found out."

"Sheesh," I said. "Those detectives sure walk the mean streets, huh?"

"I know," she said glumly. "Somebody drove all the way up to a nursing home in the Poconos to talk to my old summer-camp director. Thing is, Nora, I don't think the cops are looking at anybody else. You won't believe it, but they got a tip about me. Some nut phoned saying I was the one who shot that old man!"

"You mean an anonymous tip? But—Delilah, that's not real evidence."

"Besides the whole stupid camp thing, the cops also have an earring of mine. I knew I'd lost it, but how it got down by that statue at Fitch's Fancy, I have no idea."

"An earring?" I said quietly.

Boykin had turned in the evidence he'd found.

"I could have dropped it in the garden," Delilah said. "But I never went down to the statue. I don't know how it got there."

Boy had indeed contaminated the crime scene by planting evidence. He had set out to incriminate Delilah from the beginning. Suddenly, his asking me to investigate the murder made sense. He intended for me to help convict Delilah.

I asked, "Was Boy the only one who saw you with Zell? Did Verbena? Anybody else?"

Delilah shrugged. "There was a moving van from the auction house at first. Then the whole Fitch family showed up. Boy, then Verbena. And Pointy, of course. Oh, and the granddaughter with the boob job, and her little friend—"

"Clover was there?"

"Sure. With that mousy little tagalong of hers."

"Jane."

"I never heard her name."

"What about ChaCha? Was she at Fitch's Fancy, too?"

"I didn't see her, but she could have been. The place was crawling with people."

"What about the anonymous tipster?" I said. "Did the police say if the caller was male or female?"

"They didn't tell me." Delilah turned to me with her face slack. "Nora, this is a crazy idea, but I think somebody's trying to frame me."

"It sounds that way," I agreed.

"I don't know why I came to you." Delilah hugged herself. "I'm so worried about Mama, and now Keesa—"

"Don't get upset," I soothed. "Let's try to keep our heads cool."

"I—I don't know what to do if Social Services takes her. I've seen it happen. If she gets into that system, I might never see her again. Nora, she'll never know who her real mama is."

"Don't worry," I said. "I'll help, I promise."

A huge tear tracked down Delilah's cheek. "Can I leave Keesa here for a little while? I'm supposed to take Mama for her first chemo today."

"Keesa can stay with us as long as you like," I said, very glad to have something helpful to do. "I have to go to work soon, but Emma is here, and Lucy would enjoy having a friend around. Look—they're getting along really well. We'll keep her with us as long as you like."

"Thanks." Delilah hugged me.

We walked over to the paddock together. Emma had begun to brush Mr. Twinkles, and the little girls sat on the fence, braiding his mane. Except that Lucy appeared to be trying to thread a single hair up her nose.

"Only thing, though," I warned. "It's possible Keesa might pick up one or two bad habits from Lucy."

Delilah smiled, clearly under the impression I was kidding. Then she offered to drive me into the city for my afternoon appointments. They all stayed by the paddock while I ran inside to change my clothes.

I rummaged through several outfits before settling on a sensible gray fine-tweed Armani jacket over a ruffled blush pink blouse that concealed my waist. A pair of black peg-legged trousers I had never been able to wear before were now forgivingly comfortable.

Just as I started down the staircase, I heard a "Woohoo!" from the back door.

Libby.

Short of faking my own death or disappearing to Antarctica, there seemed to be no escape.

When I arrived in the kitchen, Libby was speed-walking around the table. In addition to a pink track-suit and a T-shirt printed with the words I'VE GOT A CUTIE PATOOTIE, she wore leg weights around her ankles and two more bulky wristbands Velcroed to her forearms. Her cheeks were flaming, her eyes unnaturally bright. A pedometer ticked at her belt.

"Look! I brought you a bottle of extra-oxygenated water! Are you ready for a power walk?"

I barely caught the flying bottle in midair. "Libby, aren't you taking this diet too far?"

"No!" With more energy than a hummingbird, she made another lap around the kitchen table. "Not a bit. Not one bit. Not a tiny little bit. I'm fine, just fine! I took a food supplement an hour ago, and I've never felt so rejuvenated!"

"Oh, my God," I said. "You're taking pills now?"

"They're not pills! They're like vitamins!"

I grabbed her arm to slow her down. "What kind of vitamins? The pupils of your eyes are spinning."

"They are?" She rushed to the mirror hanging by the back door. "You're right! The vitamins must be working!"

"Libby, you can't take speed to lose weight."

"I'm not losing weight! I'm reinventing my body! And we'll do the same for you!"

"I think you should slow down the reinvention."

"Are you kidding? Now that it's going so well? I'm having a lime sauna mud wrap in an hour! It's guaranteed to take three inches off each thigh—can you believe it? They spray you with lime juice and mud and wrap you in plastic sheets and turn up the heat until you're thin! It's only two hundred dollars! Why don't I make an appointment for you?"

"Two—! Libby, as soon as you drink a glass of water, you'll look just the same as before, only pinker—and two hundred dollars poorer!"

"I love pink! It's so flattering! Here!" From her handbag, my sister yanked a jar, one with a label printed in Japanese characters. "I brought you another present!"

I accepted the jar from her and tried to read the label. "What in the world . . . ?"

"It's a ginger, sea urchin, watermelon-seed-based cream that smooths cellulite! Nora, it's the best thing I ever tried! So I've decided to share with you, although it's horribly expensive—even more than the lime thingie. You can pay me back when your next paycheck comes. It's just fabulous! I've been using it on my stomach, see?"

She hauled up her T-shirt to show me the soft flesh of her belly. "Looks great, don't you think?"

"Sit down," I told her. "I'm going to make you a glass of warm milk."

"Skim!" she cried.

She plunked into a chair, but leaped up again by the time I reached the refrigerator. I poured milk into a saucepan while she circled the kitchen, babbling about the various potions and products she had acquired. Around her floated the scents of perfumed herbs. My sister talked feverishly nonstop for five frantic minutes while I warmed the milk and poured it into a coffee cup for her.

She drank it in one gulping slug and blinked at me. "Do you think hot milk has fewer calories than cold milk?"

I pulled her into the library and managed to pin her

down on the sofa there. With my hands firm on her shoulders, I said, "Libby, this has gone too far. You need to get a grip."

"But I'm setting an example for you!" she objected. "Together we can conquer anything. A few pounds of stubborn flab are no match for the power of our combined karmic energy! Add a few ginger sea urchins and we're invincible! Besides, the three of us have to do everything possible to get into shape by Friday. We're meeting with Jean Claude! Except for a tiny body odor, he's every bit as yummy as Gérard Depardieu!"

"Good grief, Lib, where did you come up with this one?"

"Larry introduced us! Jean Claude is an artiste! He has brilliant theories about the female body!"

"You didn't show him yours, did you?"

"No, but I told him all about you and Emma. We had a bottle of wine to discuss our photographs. He can hardly wait to get the three of us together in his studio."

"I'll bet. Look, Libby, I don't know how many times I have to say it. Emma and I aren't doing the photo with you, and no amount of wine will change our minds."

"But—"

"If you feel strongly about it, you should go ahead and be photographed by Jean Claude. But Emma and I are absolutely not going with you."

Libby grabbed my hands and forced me to sit beside her on the sofa. "Nora, I know what you're thinking," she said. "And it's all my fault. I made you feel self-conscious about your body. I'm sorry for that, really I am. But we can compensate!"

"No, Lib."

"Or I'll try to postpone Jean Claude for two more weeks. You use my cream and just one lime sauna—my treat!—and you'll be perfect!"

I shook my head. "I won't be perfect in two weeks or four weeks or six weeks."

"Eight weeks?" she whimpered.

"No, Lib. In fact, things will only be worse by then."

"But—"

"I'm pregnant."

Libby sat up on the sofa, her pinpoint eyes turning even brighter and more glassy. Her mouth opened into a perfect O as my words penetrated the whirling hurricane of her speeding brain. "You're . . . ?"

"Expecting a baby."

"Now?" Her voice climbed the register of hysteria.

"Yes."

"*Now,* when I need you to be thin and beautiful for Jean Claude?" She leaped to her feet and stared at me as if I had just ratted out the whole French Resistance to the Nazis.

"That's not exactly the response I was expecting, since you've been pestering me for years to have a baby, but—"

"How can you do this to me?" she shrieked.

"Believe me, I'm not happy about the timing, either, but—"

"Maxine and her fat twin can't be the centerfold *and* the best picture of the whole year!"

"Libby—"

"And what about Jean Claude? He says I have a special quality! A certain je ne sais quoi!"

"Lib, you don't need Emma and me to snag Jean Claude."

"Of course I do! He wants all three of us! A little ménage, he said! Don't you see? If you and Emma are slim and beautiful, maybe he won't notice me until he's had a chance to see the beauty of my mind and spirit! It's a perfect plan! But now you choose to ruin everything by—by getting knocked up!"

"Libby, you're beautiful just the way you are. I'm sure Jean Claude already—"

"He's a man! Of course he'll see how f-fat I am and never mind my beautiful personality!" She burst into tears and began to fling herself around the room in a snit of melodrama worthy of Bette Davis. "You're so—so inconsiderate, Nora! I need you now! If I can't count on my sisters when I'm facing a crisis, who can I trust? *I can't believe you're doing this to me!*"

"Let's keep your crisis in perspective, shall we? I'm the unwed mother here."

"What's one little baby? I have *five!*" she screamed. "And they grow up, for heaven's sake! One minute they're small and hardly taking up any space at all, and pretty soon they leave! It's a snap! But a photograph is—is *forever!*"

"Now wait a minute—"

In my situation, I thought I had a lock on sympathy, but Libby burst into tears and trumped me. She had just enough breath to wail, "You've abandoned me in my time of need!"

While she sobbed, I tucked her into the sofa and covered her with a cashmere throw, hoping she might be able to sleep off her vitamins. For Libby, hysterics were an MGM Technicolor production in Dolby Sound and Sensurround. She wept with wild abandon, gushing woe and betrayal. Gradually, though, her drugs seemed to wear off and she sobbed in diminishing tones until she finally hiccoughed and began to doze.

As I tiptoed out of the library, she gave a full-throated snore.

Chapter Eleven

*D*elilah met me at the back door. Her wide-eyed expression told me she had heard Libby's shrieking. "Ready?"

"Get me out of here fast." I grabbed my handbag. "Small family emergency."

"I think you got another one now. Look who just showed up."

Pierpoint Fitch, out of police custody, stood in the backyard talking earnestly to Emma. He still wore his shapeless shorts and tennis shoes, but today he had completed his fashion statement by sporting a hat with a small umbrella attached to the top. He looked like a mad scientist hoping to hear a few alien transmissions before lunch.

Lucy and Keesa stood in Emma's shadow, staring up at Pointy as if he might sprout a spaceship and fly away.

I charged up the sidewalk, Delilah right behind me.

"I've been thinking," I heard Pointy say to Emma, "the whole time I was incarcerated, that perhaps you, young lady, are just the person I need."

Emma lit a cigarette. "Don't you think I'm out of your age bracket?"

"Age has very little to do with anything," he replied. "It's determination that counts. And hard training."

"Mister," said Lucy, "are you going to make animal shapes out of balloons? I saw a clown once who had a hat like yours."

"Emma?" I called. "Anything wrong?"

My sister squinted her eyes against the cigarette smoke as she gave Pointy a suspicious once-over. "Nothing's wrong," she said. "Except look who's out of jail."

"That was an unfortunate misunderstanding," Pointy said testily. "The gendarmes were most apologetic and released me early this morning. So I'm eager to resume my training."

Emma blew more smoke. "Training for what? Finding your marbles?"

"I feel ready to take on a real challenge, so I've

signed up for a triathlon."

"A what?" Delilah asked.

Keesa said, "I like animal balloons."

"A triathlon is a supreme test of athletic skills. Running, biking and swimming. I intend to start competing in October. That gives me eight months to prepare my mind and body."

"The mind's going to be the tough part," said Emma.

"Young lady," he said, "if we're going to work together, we need to address your adder tongue."

"I knew we'd get to my tongue sooner or later."

Pointy turned purple. "Now, see here—"

"And who said anything about being together?" Emma demanded. "If you've got some weird fantasy going, Grampa—"

Before the children heard something they shouldn't, I said, "May I ask why the police turned you loose? Not that I'm not pleased to see—well, have they arrested someone else for Zell Orcutt's murder?"

"No," he said, prim as a schoolmarm. "But I understand they are gathering evidence that implicates someone other than myself. Which was a ridiculous accusation in the first place. Heaven knows, I disliked that insufferable man, but I never lifted a finger against him. I have more important things to do with my physical skills."

"What kind of evidence?" Delilah asked. "DNA or something?"

"I gather," Pointy replied decorously, "they have

198

found the murder weapon."

"Kids," said Emma, "why don't you go into the kitchen and look for some carrots for Mr. Twinkles?"

"The bow?" I said when the children had scampered out of earshot. "How did they find it? Where was it?"

"In the garden. Hidden under some bushes. The *caprifoliaceae* viburnum, I believe. Whoever put it there, the oaf knew nothing of pruning. Even a rank amateur horticulturist knows better than to cut a woody stalk in spring. The bush was badly damaged."

"Are the police testing the bow?" I asked. "For fingerprints?"

"Yes," Pointy said.

"Good," said Delilah. "Then I'll be off the hook."

"Where's Boy Wonder?" Emma asked suddenly. "Did your son get you out of jail? Or is he too busy kissing babies somewhere?"

"Certainly not. Boykin's very busy. He's in the legislature, you know."

"Think he can get reelected?" Emma asked. "I wonder if he's as above reproach as he pretends."

Pointy flushed. "I don't know what you're suggesting."

"Nothing at all," Emma drawled. "Good thing he doesn't have to step out of any closets, that's all."

"What are you talking about? What closet?"

"It's hard to get yourself elected dogcatcher if you're anything but straight, white and conservative. And if Boy's got something on the side—"

Pointy roared, "My son is not gay!"

"Nobody would care if he is," Emma said.

"He's not!"

"So what is he?" Emma asked. "A klepto? Wino? Dope dealer? Gun smuggler? There's got to be something wrong with him."

"Nothing! Nothing's wrong!" Pointy glared at us. "At least, nothing he'll tell me about."

Emma winked at me, which I took as my cue to leave.

If anyone could suss out useful information from a man, it was Emma. Delilah and I said good-bye to the little girls, checked on Libby one last time and departed for the city.

Delilah drove, most of the time taking cell phone calls from her staff, who seemed relieved to have Delilah back in the game. While she conducted business, I sat quietly in the passenger seat and thought about who could be framing Delilah for Zell's murder.

When we reached Philadelphia, I asked her to drop me at Kingsley's. I walked through the bronze doors in time for the afternoon preview.

Twice monthly, the prestigious auction house conducted sales of the fine-arts and household items they accumulated from small estates or individuals who didn't have enough quality goods to merit a sale of their own. I slipped in with the usual crowd of buyers and perennial looky-lookers to stroll the gymnasium-sized room that was packed with furniture, old books, assorted paintings and tables groaning with housewares.

By the bright light gleaming from three exquisite chandeliers, I could see an acre of goods spread out for the admiration of the hushed crowd. To heighten the suggestion that all the items were extremely valuable, not just dear Aunt Goldie's old kitchen gadgets, the preview room walls were painted the same muted sand color as a museum's. Soft strains of recorded Beethoven played from hidden speakers.

The Kingsley's security guards who kept watch over the merchandise were dressed in uniforms suitable for Buckingham Palace, white gloves and all. A young woman in a black dress and pearls served tea from a silver samovar.

I accepted one of the delicate china cups, which contained a thimbleful of tea. "Are the Fitch estate items on display today?"

"Just a few things, since it only came in yesterday," the young woman told me. "Furniture mostly. We're still cataloging the smalls."

I thanked her and wandered into the preview room, sipping tea. I was immediately confronted by an easel displaying an oil painting of a voluptuous odalisque sprawled on a bed of seashells—definitely not the kind of thing any ultraconservative Fitch might have collected.

I prowled down an aisle of dishes and silver, looking for familiar items. A ponytailed young woman with a baby in a knapsack carefully examined a set of monogrammed silverware. Two antiques dealers I recognized were whispering over a pair of Chinese vases, no doubt hoping they'd discovered a steal. Farther along, I came upon a threesome of sixtyish women who clearly patronized the same cosmetic surgeon. They all looked at me with the same Easy Lift and distinctively pointed chin implant. A dense cloud of Chanel No. 5 hung around them.

"Nora!" said one, the woman with the blondest of the blond hair. "You're just the person we need."

It was Alexis Bliss, the president of her family's charitable foundation, who introduced me to Linda Jane Todbender, whom I had never met, but knew to be an expert bridge player with an oil fortune behind her cards, and Rose Lipkin, the titanium golf club heiress and therefore the newest of money and best known for her need to drop names into the most innocuous conversations. The three very wealthy women looked bizarrely alike, not just because of their faces, but in their expensive black pants suits individualized by the scarves knotted loosely around their shoulders in the French fashion. Rose's scarf was Hermès, Alexis wore very fine cashmere, and Linda Jane's pink one looked familiar to me—vintage Chanel, perhaps.

They peered carefully at a set of Limoges luncheon plates, checking for flaws.

"We want a gift for Bunny Wellsom," Alexis explained. "She's such a dear."

"She drove me to every single one of my hydrotherapy treatments with Dr. Ben Hardy last year," Rose volunteered.

"And organizes two book clubs," Linda Jane added. "Plus all her charity work."

"But now she's had a car accident, poor thing, and broke both arms."

"The accident wasn't her fault," Rose interjected. "She's an excellent driver, taught by Salvatore Ricci, who used to compete at Le Mans."

They spoke rapidly, overlapping one another's sentences like true old friends.

"We thought we'd cheer her up," Alexis said. "What do you think? Limoges or the Wodehouse first editions?"

Linda Jane pointed to a group of leather-bound volumes sealed in Ziploc bags to prevent anyone from damaging the books.

"I'm biased," I said. "I always go for books."

Alexis looked as disappointed as her brow lift would allow. "We're having a little tea for Bunny on Saturday. I thought the cupcakes would look so adorable on the Limoges."

Rose sighed with irritation. "I told you, Alexis, cupcakes are going out of style. Especially now with that revolting restaurant changing the whole idea of cupcakes. Who wants to eat such things?"

"Nobody actually eats cupcakes," argued Alexis. "They're just decorative. And the ones Verbena makes are so pretty."

"Sushi!" Rose cried. "It's just as pretty, plus South Beach friendly."

"We can't get sushi from Verbena. And I'd feel

guilty canceling her at this late date."

Rose already had her cell phone out of her petite handbag. "Let's call her and ask if she can make something other than cupcakes."

Alexis smiled at me. "Rose has the private cell phone numbers of all the best caterers."

Rose's call connected. "Verbena, dear? Rose Lipkin."

While Rose took care of the catering crisis, Alexis said to me, "Nora, darling, my grandson tells me he's been invited to a party at the museum on Saturday night. What do you know about it?"

"I believe it's meant to attract new members," I said, sensing ruffled feathers.

"But why wasn't I invited? I always support museum events. My grandson says he heard about it on his computer or something. Not a proper invitation, is it? That hardly seems sensible to me, but what do I know? I've only attended fund-raisers in this city for decades!"

I didn't dare tell her that the party was intended for a younger generation, so I said, "It starts very late at night, Alexis."

"Oh." She hesitated. "How late?"

"Midnight. And I imagine the music will be very loud."

"I hate loud parties," Linda Jane said.

"Hm." Alexis eyed me to determine if I was trying to outsmart her. "Late and loud. Well, that kind of event doesn't have success written all over it."

"It's an experiment," I acknowledged, wondering what subject might deflect her indignation. Then I realized I could kill two birds. "Alexis, did you associate with Hannah Fitch Orcutt before she died?"

Alexis didn't miss a step. "Not Hannah, but her mother. Who was devastated when Hannah married that awful man, by the way. She'd be delighted to know he's dead now."

"Her mother confided in you about Zell?"

"Cried on my shoulder," Alexis corrected.

"My daughter actually dated Zell," Linda Jane offered. "When he first came to town, before he married Hannah."

"Your daughter?" Alexis was aghast. "How old was she then?"

"Barely seventeen. Fortunately, she met a nice boy from Princeton in the knick of time, but Zell chased after all her friends. You must have heard the rumors, Alexis. Zell Orcutt was always seducing very young girls."

She sniffed. "I don't listen to rumors, Linda Jane. Men like Zell Orcutt have been around since the beginning of time. It's up to the girls to fend them off."

I started to disagree that children could hardly be expected to act like adults in the face of a serial child molester when Rose snapped her phone shut. "What luck! Verbena's on her way here right now. We can discuss the luncheon in person!"

"Why is she coming here?" I asked.

205

"Oh, something about wanting to see the Fitch furniture one last time. Now, have we decided in favor of the Limoges?"

With Verbena due to arrive soon, I excused myself and went looking for the furniture aisle. Another young woman in the black-dress-and-pearls uniform of Kingsley's came along. She relieved me of my teacup and pointed the way. I found a display of matching silk upholstered chairs that looked like the pieces I remembered from one of the small family rooms at Fitch's Fancy.

Farther along, I recognized a settee from the ballroom and saw several headboards, too. At last I reached a desk—painted white with pink flowers twining down the legs. A little girl's desk. Perhaps the one Verbena had been so determined to find at the house.

I opened the center drawer. Some childish hand had scribbled on the wood inside—squiggles and scratches, nothing more. I crouched beside the desk and proceeded to open all the lower drawers like any prospective buyer. They were empty, of course.

I don't know what made me do it. Perhaps my own teenage habits kicked in. Instinctively, I reached into each drawer and flipped my hand over to feel its underside, then around the interior cabinetry of the desk where Kingsley's employees might not have checked.

And I found it wedged into a place near the dovetailing.

An unsealed, oversized envelope with a cellophane window and a yellowed document inside, folded into threes. Perhaps the very item Verbena had wanted to retrieve so badly from Fitch's Fancy. I unfolded the paper.

It was a document bordered with elaborate, curlicued decoration. A birth certificate. Written in careful penmanship on the top line: *Clover Hannah Barnstable.*

Beneath that:

Mother: Verbena Fitch Barnstable
Father: Zellman Orcutt

In my hand, the birth certificate trembled like a leaf in a high wind. No wonder Verbena had wanted to get inside her former home before Kingsley's removed her old desk.

Hastily, I refolded the paper and stuffed it back into the envelope. I dropped it into the open desk drawer.

I don't remember leaving Kingsley's. Or how long it took me to get outside. I just know I found myself on the sidewalk, still reeling from the discovery of the secret Verbena had wanted to keep.

A cab pulled up to the curb, and I tottered forward to claim it. As I climbed into the rear seat, another cab pulled up. The passenger door opened and Verbena herself stepped out onto the sidewalk in front of Kingsley's. As my cab departed, she turned to look and caught sight of me through the window. I'm not sure I controlled my expression.

She watched me leave.

My heart kicked, and I felt the prickle of fear at the back of my neck.

I gave the driver directions to Lexie Paine's office building. There, I passed through security quickly—I was a familiar face—and went up the elevator to Lexie's office suite. Her new assistant brought me a glass of mineral water and said Lexie might be free in a few minutes. I thanked him and sat in a rigid, but comfortable, Danish armchair while trying to steady the pounding of my heart.

Lexie's great-great-something-grandfather had started a bank back before the invention of electricity, and the institution had grown into a giant financial firm that Lexie, well-educated, wise beyond her years and with nerves of steel, took over when her father died and her uncles—whom Lexie referred to as "the silverbacks"—decided it was time to go golfing for good. She had quickly remodeled the firm to reflect her own taste. And not just the mission statement. A cheerful Alexander Calder mobile hung from the skylight thirty feet above her assistant's desk, and a complex Robert Rauschenberg collage commanded the large wall opposite the elevators where portraits of Paine ancestors had once glowered. The faces of the staff now reflected a greater diversity, too, and investments reflected a certain moral and political viewpoint the silverbacks had not shared.

Lexie's office door swung open and a small pack of

business-suited people rushed out, clutching assorted electronic devices and scuttling headlong for the elevator. Lexie came to her door and stood there, arms folded across her chest like Cleopatra sending slaves off to do her bidding.

When the elevator closed behind her minions, Lexie said, "I hate losing money."

"You're losing money?"

"Not yet, but this economy requires vigilance. That crew actually wanted to take the weekend off!"

"Heaven forbid."

She grinned. "Well, I was going to give them Sunday morning."

"You old softy." I gave her a kiss. "I don't want to interrupt if you're separating the bulls from the bears, but do you have five minutes?"

"Ten for you, sweetie."

She slipped her arm through mine to draw me into her inner sanctum. The view from Lexie's tall windows clearly suggested she owned the city below. Thick Oriental carpets and fine upholstery provided a hush in the air. On her antique desk stood a delicate piece of Roman antiquity on a small pedestal—a sculpted fragment of a human face, no doubt from her extensive private collection, or that of her mother, a double heiress with good taste and a bank account to indulge it.

Alongside the desk, an array of busy computer screens blinked in several languages, the only hint that the room was something more than the luxurious apartment of a very wealthy connoisseur.

Lexie asked, "Did Marcus get you a drink? Oh, good. What about some fruit? Or we could send out for real food, if you like." ·

"Nothing for me, thanks."

Lexie peered more closely at my face. "Are you okay?"

"Yes. And no."

She closed her office door.

I said, "I've got some big news, Lex."

My friend stopped smiling. "Should I sit down?"

"You guessed?"

Abruptly, Lexie plunked into one of the ornate chairs that stood around a coffee table artistically fashioned from the lid of a grand piano. "Tell me anyway."

I perched on the opposite chair. "Okay, I'm pregnant."

"Nora," she said on a breath.

"I know. It's bad timing. But I—I'm happy. Really. I want this child, Lex. Very much."

Lexie leaned forward and grasped both my hands in hers. "I know you do, sweetie. Big families are a Blackbird tradition. And it's all going to turn out great for you, too, I'm sure, but—good Lord."

Her eyes filled with tears—happy or sad, I couldn't discern. In a moment, we were both crying. We'd been friends since childhood, and nobody knew me the way she did. I'd told her all my secrets, and she'd confided in me the traumas of her young life, too—and there had been a lot. Through Lexie, I learned that even respected families harbored their share of mean drunks and rapists. Life could be messy even if you had money to burn. But she had survived all of it, and if I had half her courage I could surely muddle through my own problems.

"I'll help," she said after coming back from her desk with a handful of Kleenex. "I'll do whatever you need."

"I know. Thanks." I mopped my eyes.

Lexie did, too, and mustered a teary smile. "So let's see. Are you showing yet?"

I pulled my jacket aside and flattened the ruffles to reveal my lost waistline. "Enough so my clothes don't fit very well."

"How far along are you?"

"A couple of months."

"Now, look." Lexie turned decisive again. "I don't want to be called Aunt Lexie, all right? I need a cool name. Lala or Money Belt or something. And we should set up some investments right away. Get this kid some financial security established as soon as possible. That is—I mean—I assume you're going to do this alone?"

"Well, I'm not sure yet."

Lexie sat back down to absorb that information. "Should I ask? I know you've been seeing Richard D'eath, but—oh, sweetie, I can't stand not knowing. Will you tell me? Who's the father?"

"Richard's been supportive."

She noted my evasion. "You haven't decided yet, have you?"

"No."

"You've got two roosters in the barnyard, but you want the best one to be father to your chick."

I felt the tears start again. "Right. I haven't decided."

"What does Michael say?"

Carefully, I said, "He doesn't know."

"Is that wise? Not telling him?" Quickly, she tried to take back her question. "No, of course it's wise. Even if the baby isn't his, you're afraid he'll pull a Corleone, aren't you?"

Lexie knew Michael better than anyone, except perhaps Emma. Michael liked listening to Lexie's lectures on economic theory, and she often lambasted him about his old-fashioned views on money. They had sparred, and the result was good-humored respect, if not exactly affection. It wouldn't surprise her to hear he'd been keeping cash in suitcases.

"What's he doing now?" she asked. "Call me crazy, but I thought he'd given up his life of crime. The papers say he's making a play to take over his father's business. But why would he do that if he's making a fortune with the gas stations?"

"I don't know. He won't tell me. Whatever it is, though, Lex, it's different from what it appears to be. Michael thinks like a chess player. He doesn't use a ruse unless he can use two or three at the same time, and he's always got a plan."

"And his current plan started last winter when he broke up with you and moved out."

"Probably before that."

"Pretty heartless," Lexie observed.

Yes, I thought. Heartless or part of a strategy I still didn't understand.

Lexie said firmly, "Nora, I like Michael. You know I do. But, sweetie, I care more about you. If you've got a biscotti in the oven that you want to keep secret, you're going to need help. The kind of help I can give you."

"I'm not ready to run off to Aspen or Switzerland or wherever you've got houses these days, Lex. I have a job, and I have to stay here. I'll tell Michael when the time is right."

"If you want me by your side when you do it, just whistle."

"Thanks. Look, I did come this afternoon for help. Not about this, though."

Briskly, she nodded. We were both aware of her busy afternoon schedule. "You want info about Zell Orcutt, right?"

I probably had the most explosive information about Zell already—that he was the father of his step-daughter's child. Distasteful as that was, it wasn't illegal and didn't seem immediate enough to have caused his death. But learning who Clover's father was opened a whole new way of thinking about Zell.

Lexie was already on her feet again and headed for her desk. "I made some notes. I don't know what's relevant or not. For one thing, Zell hadn't been reporting all his income. He was under investigation for non-payment of taxes."

"Isn't everyone?" I asked dryly.

Lexie grinned. "Funny girl."

"Did you learn anything else?"

She waved her papers. "Hold on to your hat. ChaCha's got an interesting past."

"Besides dancing in Branson, you mean?"

"ChaCha Reynolds has a very bad credit rating. The only way she could possibly start a business is with the help of someone with enough assets to cover for her. Without Zell, she'd be eating in a soup kitchen. But get this. She shot someone."

"Who? When?"

"A guy who owned the club where she danced. Not a nice joint, either."

"Oh, dear. A strip club?"

"Yep. Twenty years ago. She went by the name of Baby CooCoo, believe it or not. She had a disagreement with her boss and plugged him."

"Did he die?"

"Flesh wound only. But some very important flesh. Let's just say he pees sitting down now."

"Ouch. Did she go to jail?"

"Nope." Lexie smiled. "Somebody bought her a good lawyer and paid her fine, too."

"Zell," I guessed.

"Yep."

"And now that he's dead? Does she own Cupcakes

free and clear? Or will she share with his heirs?"

"In other words, did she have a motive to kill him? The will hasn't been read yet, but my sources in the legal community tell me she gets Cupcakes."

So Clover wasn't going to inherit the saloon from her grandfather. I wondered if she and Verbena knew that yet. From their conversation at the tea shop, I knew Clover expected Cupcakes to be hers. "Some family members will be very disappointed."

I considered my options. How could I learn more?

Lexie watched me frown. "Sweetie," she said finally, "now that you've got someone else to consider, do you really think you should be chasing a murderer?"

"I'm not chasing anyone," I said. "Not really. I'll just ask some questions. I'm very worried about Delilah."

Lexie's perfect brows shot up. "Delilah Fairweather? What's she got to do with this?"

"She had some business with Zell that got ugly. They argued publicly minutes before he died. Boykin Fitch gave the police some evidence that he found—an earring of Delilah's. And somebody phoned in an anonymous tip that implicates her."

"And," Lexie said, connecting the same dots Michael had, "she's the only suspect who's not from a fine Philadelphia family."

"Exactly. But Delilah is innocent. An arrest for murder would do her terrible harm, Lex."

Lexie nodded. "So unless somebody else managed

215

to be on the scene without being noticed, you're thinking the killer has to be a Fitch, right? Either Verbena or Boykin or Pointy murdered Zell? Boy's got the most to lose, doesn't he, especially if he's running for the Senate seat?"

"His father suggested there's something Boy needs to hide. Emma's going to try to find out what. Can you get me a few minutes with Boy's political adviser? Mr. Fix-It?"

"Sure."

Lexie could arrange an audience with the pope if she put her mind to it.

"Thanks," I said. "But look, Boykin may not be the only Fitch with a secret he wants to keep undercover."

"Oh?"

I told her about finding Clover's birth certificate.

Lexie's face hardened. "So the son of a bitch raped his stepdaughter?"

"He had a history of seducing young girls. I've heard lots of similar stories."

Lexie turned away to glare out the windows, but I knew she wasn't looking at the view.

Gently, I put my hand on her arm. "Do the math, Lex. Verbena is over forty now. And Clover is sixteen. Verbena was an adult when Clover was conceived."

Lexie's jaw was tight as I watched her remember her own early teens when a cousin first assaulted her, then a handsome uncle turned into a crafty sexual predator. Her voice was low. "I'll bet the abuse started when she was a kid. Verbena ran away from home when she was still a teenager."

"But why would she come back?" I asked. "Why would she seek out a sexual relationship with Zell later?"

Lexie's eyes blurred with tears. "Sex abuse is a weird thing. For a kid, it—the touching, I mean. You get to—I know this is awful—but it's true, you get to like it. Then to learn it's wrong is . . . hard. It's confusing. And humiliating, but also terrifying. It can warp everything."

I wanted to hug her. Lexie had grown into an intelligent and powerful woman. But even now she avoided relationships with men. Her behavior wasn't healthy, I felt sure, but it was a logical response. She had compensated in a way that worked for her.

"She probably went back to Zell when she was feeling vulnerable. And he took advantage of her again." Quietly, Lexie said, "I wonder what Verbena sees when she looks at her daughter."

"The joy of her life," I said automatically. "Her own child—"

"I doubt it. No." Lexie rested her fists on the windowsill and then her forehead against the cool glass of the window. "Nora, you've got stars in your eyes over your own pregnancy. It's not that way for everyone."

"Lex—"

"I'm okay, sweetie." She turned to me and pulled the mask over her emotions. "I've had years of head shrinking, so don't worry about me. It's you we've got

217

to coddle, isn't it? Are you really happy about this baby?"

So she didn't want to talk about it anymore. "Very happy, yes. On my way to being overjoyed."

She hugged me again. "I'm glad. Just watch your step, sweetie, promise?"

Chapter Twelve

Back on the job, I walked over to one of the city's premier hotels to a party for a local young man who'd won a million dollars in a reality television series. For a week, the city had been in a fever of excitement over the local boy who'd made good by ratting out his friends on national TV. Cabs darted in and out of the hotel's covered entrance, and a squealing crowd surged inside to meet the new celebrity.

The television network had festooned the lobby with banners advertising the program. On the marble floor, a throng of animated young people milled around a shiny new car—one of the prizes the winner received in addition to his cool million.

The hotel's fine restaurant—a favorite dining spot of the financial district—lay on one side of the lobby. In the doorway stood Pico Pinolini, the snooty maître d'. Pico worked seven days a week and dictated where everyone was placed in the dining room, according to their social standing. Only the rich, the powerful or the marvelously disgraced got good tables from Pico, who had knowledge of scandals sometimes long before the participants did. It was said that he once seated a notable CEO at an undesirable table near the kitchen for a lunch two hours prior to his surprise afternoon firing by his board of directors.

From his position at the restaurant doorway, Pico caught my eye and bowed slightly from the waist.

I decided it was only prudent to speak to him and went over to say hello.

"You look lovely, as always, Miss Blackbird," he said smoothly, giving me an air kiss.

He liked to seat attractive people at tables near the doorway, but only if their clothing set off the thick velvet draperies that swagged the tall dining room windows. From the gleam in his darting eyes, I gathered he approved of my Armani and ruffles. "Thank you, Pico."

"Surely you're not here for the party upstairs?" he sniffed.

"I have to make a living," I said with a smile.

He glared at the crowd in the lobby and clucked disapprovingly. "I'm certainly glad none of them wants dinner here. I would have to claim we're fully booked."

"Aren't you?" I asked. "Fully booked?"

He permitted a smile that showed no teeth, just a thinning of his lips. "Not for you, Miss Blackbird. Would you care for a table?"

"Some other night," I promised. "Soon, I hope."

He slipped me a plain business card, printed only with numbers. "My private line," he murmured. "Use it anytime."

I thanked him and headed across the lobby.

To my surprise, I saw Richard D'eath come out of the hotel bar. He looked professorial in a sport coat with leather patches on the elbows. Very Clark Kent, I thought at once. He carried his pager in one hand and used the other to manage his cane. He was intent on the pager and didn't notice me until we nearly collided beside a potted palm tree.

He looked surprised, but happy, to see me. "I should have known you'd be here."

He didn't kiss me, didn't touch me. Richard was always professional in public during working hours.

"What about you?" I risked slipping my hand into the crook of his elbow and squeezing. "Here to cover the reality survivor?"

"Are you kidding?" He laughed as if I'd said something hilarious, and tucked the pager into the inside pocket of his jacket. "I met my editors for a drink."

"Who bought?"

"They did." He grinned. "They had a proposition for me."

"A—? You mean a new job?"

Richard seemed pleased. "They've given me something to think about. Something challenging as well as lucrative."

"No wonder you look happy. Can we have dinner

later to talk about it?"

"Sorry, no." He touched his pocket to remind me of the pager. "There's a story breaking. I've got to run."

"What's the story?"

He hesitated, smile fading. "A kid has disappeared."

My heart contracted. "Oh, Richard, how horrible."

"It's Little Carm. Carmine Pescara Jr."

The boy I'd seen with Michael at Cupcakes.

With my chest turning cold inside, I said, "What's happened?"

Richard watched my face. "I don't know yet. Do you?"

"What does that mean?" I snapped, pulling away from him.

He reached for my hand. "Sorry. I—sorry. Look, I've got to go, and I don't know how long this will take. How about if I call you at home tonight? If it's not too late when I finish? I do want to talk to you."

"All right."

Richard released me, anxious to get going, I could see. But he hesitated again, as if forming an apology. If so, however, he discarded the idea. "I'll phone later. Have fun at your little party."

And he was off. His cane clacked on the marble floor as he rushed for the front door, anxious to learn the fate of Little Carm Pescara.

My little party?

I stood still, feeling as if he'd slapped my cheek.

My face stung. And I knew Pico was watching from

the restaurant, taking in our exchange and probably making an accurate guess about what had transpired. I turned away and headed up the staircase to the ball-room.

There, I needed a crowbar to get through the crowd. It was wall-to-wall people. Drumbeats and pseudo-African chanting throbbed in the air. Set dressers had decorated the room with wooden crates, coils of rope and camouflaged jeeps to suggest a thriving Third World shipping port. Fog machines generated billows of primordial steam from behind a jungle of fake plants. I squeezed into the mob, noting the short skirts and flimsy tops worn by dozens of young women who clearly hoped for an introduction to the new million-aire.

Two young professionals pushed past me without apology. Someone thrust a colorful bandanna into my hand. It was garishly printed with the title of the tele-vision program. Everyone else in the ballroom had fashioned theirs into headbands, necklaces or belts. With my bandanna in hand, I pressed through the crowd.

The reality show winner stood knee-deep in a lake of balloons also printed with the show's logo. He was tall and charmingly awkward, with an expensive haircut gelled to perfection. Network publicists sur-rounded him to maintain a makeshift receiving line. Every few minutes they allowed a few gushing fans to approach the winner while they hustled the previous group away. The man of the hour obligingly put his arm around the prettiest ones as cameras flashed. Everyone in the room beamed adoring smiles in his direction.

I made a slow lap of the room, taking mental notes. In that whole crowd, I didn't know a soul.

Until Clover Barnstable arrived.

She made an entrance followed by a camera crew of her very own. One rangy young man hoisted a light over his head and focused it on Clover for the whole room to see. A videographer followed. Clover's friend Jane hovered with her own camera, too, crouching to catch unusual angles.

Clover paused, hand on outthrust hip, to give the crowd a disdainful stare. Then the seas parted for her, and she catwalked across the ballroom. She wore a skirt short enough to require a bikini wax and a gauzy shirt that showed she was braless.

Behind me, a young man cursed and said, "That chick's just about naked!"

A hubbub followed while the publicists cleared a path for Clover to reach their millionaire. The air sparkled with more camera flashes as Clover snuggled the winner's arm.

"Nora? Long time, no see."

I turned to recognize the face of an acquaintance, Elizabeth Lammell, primary partner in her own publicity firm. Long ago in her almost forgotten past, Elizabeth had lost a television weather girl job because she had bad hair. Her dark brown mop was prone to lopsided frizz, and if there was one appearance flaw that spelled doom for television talent, it was hair that couldn't be tamed into a sleek, face-flattering shape.

Since then, however, she'd turned to promoting everything from adulterous baseball players in need of image repair to models, a few singers and at least one very successful painter who required publicity to succeed in their chosen fields. At improving public personas, she was the best in the city.

Unfortunately, Elizabeth's rough treatment of her own staff and clients had earned her the nickname of Elizabitch, which was universally known. She even used it herself.

Tonight she wore her hair pulled back in a tiny bun. Her youthful clothes were the latest fashion—French jeans, strappy Manolo sandals, a simple Hanes T-shirt and a real Chanel jacket that bespoke how well her firm was succeeding. But her huge red eyeglass frames made her eyes appear even smaller and meaner than ever, and no amount of good publicity could fix that.

"Hi, Elizab-beth."

She checked out my clothes, and gave an "I'm impressed" eyebrow. Then, "What brings you here? It's not exactly your scene." With a jerk of her head, she indicated the noisy party.

"The *Intelligencer* is going after a younger audience."

"It's about time." Elizabeth continued to scan the crowd, noting details for her mental files, perhaps.

"Also, I thought there was a philanthropic angle to this event."

She snorted. "Only to put a little lipstick on the pig. No charity is going to benefit from this cattle call except for a few dollars tossed into the pot by the TV network."

"I was afraid of that. Is the new millionaire your client?"

She blew a raspberry. "Hell, no, he's going straight to video, if you know what I mean. Until he gets a speaking coach, he's doomed. He can't put two sentences together without saying 'uh' sixteen times."

"Oh, then you're working for the television network."

"Nope." Elizabitch pulled me to a corner where we weren't so badly jostled by the people around us, but she could continue to watch the action. "This whole event is a big promo for the reality show. The network plans to come back to Philly to audition people for the next season."

"Judging by the crowd, I guess they'll have plenty of contestants."

"Yeah, ninety-nine percent of the people here are dying to compromise their values for fame and fortune. Are you a fan of the show?"

"I've never seen it."

"You're not missing much. When did reality shows become more real than reality? I'd like to see if anyone in this room could survive my job." She folded a stick of gum into her mouth.

"So who are you working for here?"

"Nobody yet. I'm checking out a potential client. Clover Barnstable. You know her? She comes from your neck of the woods, doesn't she?"

"You're working for Clover?" I couldn't keep the surprise out of my voice.

Elizabitch shook her head. "Not yet. But maybe. She hired a stylist I know. And she's asking around about me. So I thought I'd check her out. What do you think?"

Elizabitch and I watched Clover for another minute as she insinuated her body against the millionaire so that his arm was around her shoulders and his hand dangled provocatively near her huge left breast. The glare of television lights cast them both in dazzling white light.

"I don't get it," I said. "Why does Clover need you? Is she going to model?"

"I doubt she can do much of anything. But watch. People can't stop themselves from staring at her. She knows how to stand, how to look into a camera. She's got charisma. If I can get her a record deal, she'll be the American dream!"

"Can she sing?"

"Who cares? We'll hire a voice teacher and get her to practice with some of those microphones that automatically correct your sharps and flats."

"So," I said, still struggling to understand, "that camera crew that came in with Clover? Are they yours?"

"Are you kidding? Would I hire such doofuses?" She laughed shortly. "No, they're hired actors."

"Actors?" For an instant, I thought I misunderstood the industry lingo.

But Elizabitch put me straight. "They're out-of-work actors she hired to pretend to photograph her. Look, that video camera isn't even turned on!"

"Why would anyone hire actors to—?"

"It's pretty common, actually. Big celebs do it all the time to draw a crowd or get themselves into columns like yours. Making it by faking it, Nora. That's the name of the game right now."

I stared at Clover and tried to understand what Elizabitch saw. A pretty face, yes, but that absurdly inflated bosom and her long, long legs hardly added up to stardom. I watched her playfully remove the bandanna from the neck of the millionaire. She used it to pretend to wipe his nose. The crowd laughed. A few people applauded.

"She has it," Elizabitch said, more to herself than to me. "That magic. And this is her demographic—men and women, ages eighteen to thirty, the advertiser's G-spot. I could make her a fortune."

I shook my head, disbelieving.

"Who is she fucking?" Elizabitch asked. "If she's already slept with a few B-listers, I could move her up pretty fast."

"She's only sixteen!"

"Good. She won't show any wrinkles for a few more years. Yeah, if we put her in the right clothes, and she takes them off for the right people, she's got it made. Or maybe she could get herself a stalker. Or a kidnapping. That would help a lot."

A wash of nausea rushed up inside me, and I turned away.

Only to be confronted by two more publicists with eager faces. They were the same two people who had shoved me out of their way to get into the ballroom.

"You're Nora Blackbird, aren't you?" The male member of the duo shoved a glossy paper brochure into my hand. "I didn't recognize you. I'm Jared from the Rothman Agency. You took over Kitty Keough's column, didn't you?"

"Hi, I'm Grace," said the young woman, nudging her way closer to me. "Somebody just pointed you out to us. I represent Charlie Allen, the rock singer?"

Elizabitch snorted again. "Rock singer? That kid is barely out of diapers, Gracie. You can't do anything with him until he passes the third grade."

Grace frowned and ignored Elizabitch. She handed me an autographed head shot of a child with pudgy cheeks who had struck a pose straight out of *Saturday Night Fever.* She said, "Maybe you could mention Charlie in your next column? He's doing a benefit concert at his elementary school on Saturday. To raise money for AIDS awareness."

"And I represent Mia Trotter, the hip-hop sensation. We're giving a party for her next week. She's definitely material for your column, Nora. May I call you Nora?"

I was spared further soliciting when someone yelled into a microphone for quiet and then made a rambling introduction of the television winner. The young man disengaged himself from Clover and bounded onto the stage to enough thunderous shrieks, whistles and applause to satisfy a major-league record holder.

When he was finally able to speak, the winner babbled a series of malapropisms. "Dudes. To win, you have to make your alliances and play the game. Uh— I stepped up to my fate and proved my medal when it was do-or-die time, so, uh, you know, take the risk, and—hey, you can win, too."

Under her breath beside me, Elizabitch said, "Not exactly Winston Churchill. But he has potential. Unless that's a sock he's got stuffed in his pants. Wonder if he does naked pictures yet?"

I needed fresh air fast.

"Hey, Nora." Elizabitch caught my elbow as I turned away. "Let's have lunch soon. I could tell you about some of my clients."

I pretended the room was too noisy to understand her words and waved. When last I saw her, Elizabitch was making a beeline for Clover.

On the way out of the ballroom, I dropped the hip-hop singer and the third-grade rocker into a potted palm.

Five minutes later, I was outside the hotel and one of the doormen hailed me a cab.

I decided to crash a party.

On a leafy city street paved with cobblestones, lit by gas lamps and lined with majestic town houses built long ago, I knocked on the oaken door of Paddy Abernethy, the last remaining son of an old, respected family. His butler opened the door to me, took my coat and handbag and asked me to wait. A hired waiter whisked past with an empty tray, headed for the kitchen. I could hear the muffled conversation of guests in the next room. The scent of cocktail munchies floated in the air.

The vestibule of Paddy's home, heavy with oak trim, was decorated with paintings by his mother, a portraitist. As I waited, I gazed at the framed faces of a slightly cross-eyed old man, a small child with a dog, and Paddy when he was a teenager, holding the bridle of a polo pony.

Paddy arrived, wearing velvet slippers and carrying a glass of sherry. He was a short, unattractive man with a weak chin and burly shoulders, but the kindness in his expression outweighed everything else. Tonight, however, he looked surprised. "Nora," he said.

"I'm sorry, Paddy," I said at once. "I shouldn't have come without an invitation."

"No, no," he said, belatedly mustering some enthusiasm. "You're welcome here at any time. But—"

"I know what you're doing tonight is very hush-hush."

"How did you—? Well, it doesn't matter, does it?" He took my hand and drew me to the doorway of the salon, where we could see fewer than a dozen guests, all quietly engaged in conversations around the candlelit room. The furniture was faded but elegant. Bookshelves with leather-bound volumes lined the walls. A baby grand piano graced one corner.

The guests had gathered knowing their mission would be kept secret, but their voices were subdued as if they might be overheard.

Paddy also kept his voice low as he pointed out his guests. "You know Darren Flock, don't you? And that's Cozy Costain beside the piano. Between them, they're donating a million dollars to the after-school foundation. My mother always dreamed of doing something like this. And now her friends are making it happen."

"You must be so happy." I smiled. "It's a wonderful program, Paddy."

He laughed. "Mom hated kids, you know. Hired a nanny for me as soon as I was out of the womb. Maybe that's why she loved the idea of keeping children busy after school. So they wouldn't come home too soon every day!"

Paddy had gone to medical school with my husband and worked at the same transplant research project, too. As Todd's obsession with cocaine grew, Paddy covered for Todd at first and later insisted he go into rehab. When Todd died, Paddy was one of the first to come to my aid. He even hired a truck and helped carry my furniture out of our town house when I moved to Blackbird Farm. He was living proof that there was often more to a man than the monogram on his pocket.

He said, "How's life in the country?"

"I like it. I'll be planting flowers in a few weeks."

"How's Emma?"

"Available."

Paddy laughed. "Is she? I'll take that under advisement."

"Paddy, I know this party of yours is private. But I was hoping to convince you to let me write about it. If you're raising a significant amount of money, you ought to—"

"Publicize ourselves?" He shook his head. "That's not why we're doing this, Nora. I'm sorry."

"If people knew about your foundation, you might get more donations."

"Maybe so," he agreed. "But we just don't do things that way. I'm sure you understand."

"I do," I admitted. In my own heart, giving money in order to get your name in the newspaper tainted the altruism. But in recent years the practice had rescued many a philanthropic organization. I knew I couldn't press Paddy, however. He'd made his decision. And, like everyone else in the room, I was bound by social custom to never mention it again.

"Come in, anyway," he said. "Have a drink. Darcy Plattenberg is going to play the violin later."

I mingled with Paddy's guests, most of whom I knew very well indeed. Cozy Costain had been a good friend of my grandmother's, and I teased her about her

232

newfound love of poker. I spoke with Judge Hargrave Potter as he picked over a tray of tapas, looking for something spicy.

"These old folks don't like any fire in their food," the retired judge confided to me. "But me, I like pizzazz. How are you doing these days, Nora? You look a little peaked."

"I'm okay, Harry."

"Busy?"

"Yes. And I've been trying to help a friend."

Hargrave eased his bulk into a wing chair. He was an old lion—grizzled and ponderous but still full of potent strength. As crumbs of food tumbled down the front of his charcoal suit, he eyed me with a discerning glare. "What friend is that?"

"A friend," I repeated, unwilling to say more. I perched on the footstool by his knee. "Actually, she's in trouble with the police."

Harry stilled for an instant, on the alert. "Aha. Is she guilty?"

"No," I said sharply. "But one reason she's a suspect is because she's black. Or do you prefer *African-American?*"

"Either one," he said, frowning. "Surely the police have some evidence that she committed a crime."

"Not much," I said, perhaps allowing my frustration to show too obviously.

Harry's bushy brows rose, then descended sternly over his eyes. "I can't say as it's happened to me lately, but in my youth I might have been mistaken for a ruffian by the police now and then. And to tell the truth, I might have given them reason to think I was a troublemaker. We have to trust the system, Nora."

Looking at him, it was hard to imagine the judge as anything but a dignified scholar who presided over his courtroom like an all-powerful potentate who tolerated no nonsense. I knew lawyers who dared not stand up in front of him without spending many hours of preparation in their law libraries.

"This particular situation is very unfair, Harry."

He took a healthy bite out of a crust of bread spread with olive paste, and chewed thoughtfully before saying, "The racial divide is still great, isn't it?"

"Yes. My friend is in trouble. And I don't know what to do for her."

"Does your friend have a lawyer?"

"She thinks she doesn't need one."

Harry used a napkin to wipe his fingers before reaching into his breast pocket for a pen and a notepad. Carefully, he wrote down a name, then tore the page from his pad and passed it to me. "She should call this gentleman. I have a high regard for his abilities in this kind of matter."

I accepted the paper. I did not recognize the lawyer's name.

"Nora," said the judge, "there are two sides to racial profiling. It's universally condemned, yet universally practiced. But I've always felt that social change comes from people like you—young wives and mothers who want to raise their children in a better world."

"I'm trying to figure out how to do that, Harry."

"A little bit at a time." Deepening his voice, Harry said, "A great man has said that racism is the biggest cancer of his lifetime. But just because he can't cure that cancer didn't mean he shouldn't attack it in small ways."

"Martin Luther King?" I asked.

Judge Potter shook his head. "Charles Barkley."

I smiled.

"I never read much philosophy," Harry said, "but I do love basketball."

Chapter Thirteen

When I returned home that evening, there was a note from Emma on the kitchen table and a phone message from Libby. Emma reported that Keesa was happily spending the night with Lucy.

On the answering machine, still sounding wounded or perhaps hungover, Libby said, "Call me."

After another beep, Richard's voice came on. "It's Richard," he said in case I didn't recognize his voice. "Listen, I'm sorry about earlier. Can we have dinner tomorrow night? I made an early reservation."

He named a restaurant I didn't care for. I wondered

if I'd be able to swallow their food.

Without returning either call, I went to bed.

During my usual hour of upchucking the following morning, I wondered if any television network might consider giving a million dollars to the woman who survived the worst morning sickness. If so, I was definitely going to make the final four.

Emma pounded on the bathroom door and yelled something annoyingly cheerful.

My day was made complete when I saw Libby's minivan pull into my driveway an hour later. I groaned. I carried my bowl of Jiffy Pop onto the back porch. Emma was in the paddock with Mr. Twinkles, and they both ignored Libby, leaving me to cope on my own.

"I'm over my shock," Libby announced when she climbed out of her vehicle. "I forgive you for getting pregnant at the wrong time."

"Thank you, Libby." I met her on the sidewalk and gave her a kiss.

"Keesa's still at my house. Rawlins is in charge. The twins think she's the best thing since formaldehyde. For some reason, she knows everything about autopsies."

The thirteen-year-old twins, Harcourt and Hilton, had already signed up for Forensic Summer Camp, three weeks of stomach-turning adventure in the lab of a local community college.

Except for an enormous pair of sunglasses and the slight wince when I kissed her, Libby seemed back to normal after yesterday's episode of speed demonism. I asked, "How are you feeling?"

"A little hungover," she admitted. She removed her sunglasses and revealed a remarkably dewy complexion. "But much better today."

She wore a pair of powder blue stretch pants with racing stripes down the legs and a matching jacket, which was unzipped just enough to show today's T-shirt, which read HOTTIE in sequins. The pedometer still clipped to one pocket confirmed she hadn't given up on her diet yet. Cheerfully, she held up two fingers. "Nora, I have two words I want you to consider seriously."

"Just two?"

"Demi Moore."

"What?"

"What would you think about a calendar photograph of just you and your stomach?"

"Libby—"

My sister grabbed my arm and pulled me off the porch to her minivan. "Demi Moore was on the cover of a magazine when she was something like eighteen months pregnant—absolutely *huge.* You and your belly might be just the thing for our calendar!"

"Libby, I'm hardly showing at all—"

"We'll wait a few months! The bigger the better. You'll be gigantic in no time!" Libby flung open the side door of the van and dragged out two bulging cardboard boxes. "See what I brought for you? Books, some videotapes and—look—my favorite maternity clothes!"

I swallowed a moan. It was starting already, and I had nearly seven long months of sisterly advice to endure.

"I won't need these clothes," Libby said, "at least not for a while. Just make sure they're laundered before you return them."

"Libby, with five children already, don't you think you could safely give these things to the Goodwill now?"

"You never know what fate may bestow. Here! My favorite shirt! Isn't it adorable?"

Against her body, she held up a pink tent printed with a huge arrow pointing down and block letters that announced the word EXIT.

"Never in a million years am I going to wear that," I said.

"You wait," she predicted. "Someday this will be the only thing that fits and you'll be desperate."

"I'll have to be desperate and brain-dead."

"Here." She handed me a stack of videotapes to carry. "You can look through these while I carry everything inside. You shouldn't strain yourself, you know."

I should have guessed my sister's collection of informational materials might include a tape entitled *Zen Mama's Workout.* Beneath that classic I found *War Cry: The Victory of Vaginal Delivery* and *The Natural Eroticism of Breast-Feeding.*

"Don't you have anything normal?" I asked when we had taken everything but the exercise contraptions into the kitchen. "What about Dr. Spock? Or a nice, sensible nutrition chart?"

She waved airily. "That stuff's common sense. What you need is enlightenment!"

I read the title of the next videotape. "What did you find enlightening about *Making a Myth or a Mister*?"

"It has some excellent information about choosing the gender of your baby, depending upon your sexual position at the time of conception. I have so much knowledge and experience to share with my sister! Have you thought about a midwife? An underwater delivery? Maybe some meditation techniques to enhance your childbirth experience? And what about foods to plump up your placenta! I can't wait to see you get rounder!"

I stacked the videos on the table. "Look, Lib, I've got to tell you the truth. The doctor warned me to be careful."

"Don't worry! Getting a big stomach is natural!"

"No, I mean this pregnancy is delicate." I summoned the courage to speak the truth and said, "That's why I haven't told many people yet. I want to be sure I can hang on to this baby."

"Oh, honey!" All sympathy, Libby made a grab for my hand. "I know you had a miscarriage once before. It happens. I had two."

"I know, but—"

"So it's not uncommon in our family. Mama lost three. But honey, you have to think positively! Visualize!"

"I have been, believe me. But I—look, I'm not ready for all this." I indicated her videos, magazines and books, and an item of equipment that involved two rubber balls and a length of string that I didn't dare ask about. "I know you're being kind. But I—I don't want to jinx it. And I don't think I can stand the onslaught of your crackpot—I mean, enlightened advice for the next six or seven months."

"Six months? Nora, I plan to be right at your side until this child goes off to college!"

I choked back a scream. "Libby—"

"For starters," she said, shaking her finger at me, "you have to eat more than just popcorn! I have lots of recipes for healthy food that you'll be able to swallow, I promise. And you must increase your daily Kegel repetitions immediately. Promise me you won't neglect your inner muscle tone!"

"I—"

"Your lover will thank you someday. Where is Richard, by the way?"

"I—he's not here at the moment."

A long silence ticked by while Libby studied me with suspicion. At last, she said, "Richard *is* the father of your baby, isn't he, Nora?"

I still didn't know who was listening to the microphone that was undoubtedly planted in my kitchen. So I said, "I need your help, Libby."

"Anything!"

"I need to go to the Cupcakes Saloon."

Her eyes got round as if she'd just heard she was on

her way to meet Mickey Mouse for the first time. "You're not toying with me, are you, Nora?"

"No, I need a ride to Cupcakes."

Libby shrieked with glee. "You're kidding! Cupcakes! With the dancing girls and down-home hot wings? Why didn't you call me before I left my house? I have to change my clothes! I look like an Avon lady on my way to Curves!"

"You look fine. Besides, Cupcakes won't be open for business yet. I'm going to talk to ChaCha Reynolds. I just thought you might like to look around a little."

Her eyes alight, my sister grabbed my coat and hustled me into it. "Well, hurry up, for heaven's sake! Let's get going!"

During the whole trip, she babbled like a kid on her way to her first birthday party.

By the time we arrived at Cupcakes, I felt sorry for ChaCha. Libby was going to give her a truckload of ideas on how to improve business.

"Don't you think the dancers would like to see my exercise tape for pole dancing?"

"Pole dancing?" I asked, and immediately regretted my mistake.

"For strippers! It's the latest thing in exercise. Even Jude Law recommends it! But it's really artistic, too!"

As I'd guessed, the restaurant wasn't open when we parked in the lot, but we saw a couple of young girls dash through a side door. Libby and I bailed out of the minivan and ducked into the cool darkness of the club on the heels of the early-arriving employees.

Thrilled to find herself inside the infamous saloon, Libby choked back a squeal. "I'm getting goose bumps!"

She didn't notice the janitor sweeping the floors or smell the disinfectant being used to scrub down the bar. The chairs stacked on top of tables didn't diminish her enthusiasm. And the forlornly empty air hockey table, home to a bucket of water catching drips from the ceiling, did not dim the glamour for her.

It was the Cupcakes who drew Libby across the floor like a hungry fish to a juicy bug. The girls were stretching their limbs, sipping from plastic water bottles, dressed in sweatpants and sports bras with their hair in ponytails. Two stood side by side practicing a dance step over and over. They all oozed the healthy, limber athleticism of racehorses, but seemed bored by their surroundings.

"Hi, girls!" Libby called, and bounced across to them.

I let her go.

"Hey," said one of the Cupcakes. "Are you the new dance captain?"

"I do have a few suggestions," Libby said. "Have you girls heard of the stripper's two-step?"

I went along a dark hallway and found a door marked with ChaCha's name. The door stood partially open and I heard noise inside. I knocked softly and pushed the door open without waiting for a response. "ChaCha?"

To my surprise, I found her huddled in her chair and wheezing into a paper napkin. Elbows on the desk, face planted in the napkin, she was crying. Not just a soft, ladylike kind of cry, but a full-blown bawling jag.

"ChaCha?"

She snorted and spun around in her chair, teary eyes wide, nose red, face blotchy. After a loud hiccough, she said, "What the hell are you doing here?"

"I'm sorry to disturb you. Are you all right?"

"Do I look all right?" She blew her nose with a honk.

"I'm Nora Blackbird. Delilah Fairweather introduced us. Can I help?"

"Can you raise the dead?" she snapped. Then, as I apologized and began to withdraw, she said gruffly, "No, no, come in. I'm having an old-fashioned blubber, that's all."

She heaved a sigh and pulled herself together with the air of a woman whose luck never changed. On the desk lay Zell Orcutt's obituary, clipped from the newspaper. His outdated photograph glared up at both of us. Looking down at him, ChaCha said, "I'm the only one who's going to miss the old bastard, aren't I?"

When I didn't answer, she said, "Nobody gives a damn that he's gone—not his family, nobody. I'm the last person on this earth who cared about him."

"Uhm . . ."

"He loved me, you know. In his own way. He told

me all his secrets, and that has to count for something, right?"

Around us, her office was crammed with account books, reams of computer printouts and office supplies, plus mementos of her stage career. I saw a stack of old theater programs, a dusty ukulele with *Nashville* painted on its neck and several pairs of black tap shoes in various states of wear lined up on a shelf.

ChaCha shook a cigarette from a pack of Marlboros and thumbed a dime-store lighter. She wore a bulky oversized sweater that reached her midthighs over panty hose with woolly leg warmers on her lower legs. But *Flashdance* looked more like *The Golden Girls* now. She had taken off her shoes to reveal swollen bunions through the reinforced toes of her support hosiery.

She sucked hard on her cigarette, then burst into a hacking cough that quickly got out of control. As she struggled to suppress it, I noted that the fine wrinkles around her eyes, which hadn't been so visible at night, were now a spiderweb of lines.

I reached across the desk for an opened can of Dr Pepper. It was still cold to the touch. Handing it to her, I said, "Try this."

"Thanks," she croaked, and took a swig, which quelled the cough. Setting down the can, she eyed me. "You're not half bad."

I perched on the edge of her desk. "I'm sorry for your loss. You must have been very good friends."

She shrugged and took a more cautious drag on her cigarette. "Sure, friends. We checked into a hotel every Wednesday afternoon, but if that's what you mean by friends, that's what we were." Her eyes filled with tears again. "I'm gonna miss that randy goat!"

I tried to come up with a sympathetic response and failed. The mental picture of ChaCha and Zell in a hotel room temporarily overwhelmed me.

ChaCha rubbed tears away with her knuckle. "I was the only living person who bothered to be nice to him. Even his stupid granddaughter saw him as nothing but a meal ticket."

"You must have known him . . . differently."

"Those hoity-toity Fitches never understood him." With more venom, ChaCha said, "He hated the opera and didn't play their stupid country-club sports. A trip to Atlantic City to hit the tables once in a while—that was Zell's style. And mine. We used to go to the Lime-lighter Lounge to dance. Man, he could rumba!"

"He enjoyed spending time with you."

"Yeah, we had some good times." She started to go misty again.

"And if he chose you for a business partner, he obviously had a lot of respect for you, too."

She nodded. "Zell and me—we were good together."

Gently, I kept going. "Will you keep Cupcakes open now that he's gone?"

"I only own half of this place." She allowed a grumpy sort of grin. "He didn't always like what I had to say about the way things should run around here, but he let me try being the boss. I suppose I'll have to fight with those Fitch bitches now."

"I heard one of you fired Clover."

ChaCha laughed shortly. "It was me. Zell never shoulda let the kid bully him into hiring her as a Cupcake in the first place. No talent, two left feet, can't get a drink order straight to save her life—plus she walked in and right away started acting like one of those bubblegum divas on MTV. And she whined to Zell whenever I chewed her ass."

"So you fired her the night he died."

"Hell, I fired her the day before! But she thought I was kidding or something, because she came back. I didn't want her in the show at all, but she turned up here on opening night. She performed with the Cupcakes before I knew she was here."

"She wasn't supposed to be in the show?"

"Hell, no. She was a whiner. She went running to Zell every time she got a blister on her toe. Plus she couldn't dance to save her life."

"So you fired her because she couldn't dance? Or was there something else?"

ChaCha hesitated.

I said, "ChaCha, I know Zell was drawn to younger women."

"Not women." The fire blew out of her, and she said with resignation, "Girls. Look, I know he had his weaknesses. Hell, maybe that's why he and I first got together. I've always been kinda petite and flat-chested and—well, he wasn't perfect."

Of course I had already noticed the physical resemblance between Zell's wife, Hannah, and ChaCha. Both were small, childlike women.

"And his relationship with Clover?" I asked.

ChaCha shook her head vehemently. "It was never anything like that. Nothing sexy. It's the other one, the girl who's always following Clover."

"Jane?" I said, startled.

ChaCha toyed with her cigarette. "I caught Zell with girls before. Half the time, it was them who started it. He was a good-lookin' man. I found him with that Jane girl a couple of times and told her to get out. But she was always back the next day because of Clover."

"What do you mean?"

"She's some kind of paid groupie for Clover. Tags along everywhere or Clover has one of her hissy fits. I threw Jane out of here half a dozen times while we were getting ready to open this place, but Clover always made her come back."

"And then Jane and Zell—?"

"Zell couldn't keep his hands off her. And the only way I could permanently get rid of Jane was to fire Clover. Of course, that was no great loss. Except . . . Zell was awful mad at me. Last time I saw him, he was—he was awful unkind."

"He wanted Clover in the show?"

"No, he knew she was bad and was causing trouble with the other girls, too. He said good riddance. But he didn't want Clover thinking it was his idea. He told me I shoulda taken full responsibility for firing her because she and her mom were gonna make his life miserable and it was all my fault."

ChaCha started to weep again. She opened her desk drawer and pulled out half a dozen old photographs, all of them creased and faded, with edges bent as if they had been handled thousands of times. "Zell," she said, looking down at the pictures. "He wasn't a prince, but I loved him."

I put my hand on her shoulder. ChaCha traced a face in one of the photographs with her finger, then laid all the pictures onto the desk and gathered them into a neat stack, like a deck of cards. She dropped them back into the drawer.

She took one last look at the photos, then inhaled a deep breath, closed the drawer and checked her watch. "I gotta get back to rehearsal. We need to go over tonight's show before the cops come to interview me."

"The police are coming?"

"Yeah, to ask a bunch of questions. I told them I don't know nothing about who killed Zell, but they want to talk anyway."

"Perhaps you observed something without realizing its significance," I suggested. "They probably want to hear your impressions."

She grunted as she bent to buckle her right shoe. "Maybe it was that nephew, Boy. He came in here a few weeks ago with some hotshot. They talked to Zell about turning Cupcakes over to me before the place opened, which no way in hell was Zell gonna do. They

248

said it would screw up Boy's campaign to be connected with a place like this."

"Boy said that?"

"The other man did the talking. Then Boy got into it with Zell. I heard them arguing right here in this office. Boy left looking hotter than a chili pepper."

As she bent to struggle into her second shoe, I leaned over to peer at the framed photo tacked up on the wall over the desk. A young Zell Orcutt in jeans and a Western shirt with a dusty bandanna around his neck smiled as he held the reins of a pinto cow pony. A tiny girl in a cheap blouse and flounced skirt sat on the spotted horse. She wore a tiara and a sash printed with the words RODEO QUEEN.

The face of the rodeo queen was that of a very young ChaCha Reynolds. She looked like a child.

One of the Cupcakes knocked on the door then and poked her head in to say there was someone to see ChaCha in the bar.

I followed them down the hallway. The rest of the Cupcakes lounged in the restaurant, picking lazily at their fingernails and yawning. Most of them, anyway. Up on the bar, two more intrepid girls appeared to be coaching my sister Libby in the steps of their Cupcake dance. Libby waved to me, waggling her hips with gusto, but she didn't miss a beat. She looked great.

Standing beneath the bar was Verbena Barnstable. She was dressed in the uniform of a Main Line matron—expensive navy blue blazer over light wool slacks and flat shoes. She looked as if she'd put on a costume. Her white hair was unmistakable, however. And her Viper persona still glowed in her radioactive gaze.

In both hands, she balanced a bakery box. I hesitated in the shadows, sure I shouldn't let her see me.

ChaCha had no such qualms and strode over to the bar, tap shoes clicking on the floor. "Who invited you?"

Verbena dropped the bakery box on the bar. "I brought you something."

They faced each other as if across the dusty expanse of the OK Corral. ChaCha seemed to gather strength from the half-dressed Cupcake girls who lazed around her. I couldn't see her face, but her wiry body bristled with dislike. "What for?"

"Considering your relationship with my—with Zell, I thought we should try to be friends."

"Friends?" ChaCha sounded surprised. "You knew about us? Zell and me?"

"Of course," Verbena said. "He bragged about you. He said you were the only person who really knew him. The only one he could talk to. Is that true?"

"Sure, I guess so. Zell told me just about everything."

"Pillow talk," Verbena said.

"You could call it that," ChaCha drawled.

"Have the police been here to ask what you know?"

"They're coming this afternoon." She leaned close and popped the lid on the box. "You brought me some cupcakes! That's real cute."

Verbena stood stiffly still in her dress-up clothes, towering over little ChaCha. She could have squished the smaller woman with one fist, but she kept her voice low and measured. "I thought we might talk a little business, too."

ChaCha backed up a step. "What kind of business?"

"Shall we speak in private?"

"There's no need for privacy, Miss Priss. You gonna tell me to close down? Turn off the lights and lock the door so we don't embarrass anybody in your hoity-toity family?"

"On the contrary, I hope you'll stay in business. At least a little longer."

ChaCha gave a short, barking laugh. "Well, lasso me and tie me to a fence post! Do I have a new partner?"

Verbena didn't answer. Instead, she said, "I hope you'll reconsider an earlier decision about Clover."

Enlightened at last, ChaCha said, "You want me to hire the kid back."

Surprised that Verbena had changed her mind, I listened from the shadows.

"Working here was important to Clover. And she thinks she needs this job to get her career started."

"What do you think?"

"Doesn't matter," Verbena said curtly. "I'm here to make my daughter happy."

"You gotta have some talent to have a career. And you gotta get along with your coworkers. This is a team effort around here, not a showcase for a wannabe." ChaCha put her back against the bar and leaned there, spreading her arms with confidence. Around her, the Cupcakes stirred in agreement.

"She'd like to try again," Verbena said, still controlled, yet not. I could see Viper's fire building. "She'll do better this time."

"And Mama brought me cupcakes to sweeten the deal?" ChaCha laughed again, apparently unaware of Verbena's mounting temper.

"It's not bribery. Someday Clover is going to be a big star. You'll be able to say you got her started. Surely that has some appeal for you?"

"If your kid wants to be a star, Mama, you're gonna need more than cupcakes."

"It takes vision to see the truth sometimes."

I thought Verbena was going to try again. Surely she had more ammunition. Physically, she could have squashed ChaCha like a bug. And Viper could have cleared the room with one of her screaming stage tantrums. But Verbena lifted her chin and turned around.

She made a silent, angry exit. The gunfight was over without a shot fired.

ChaCha laughed, and the Cupcakes joined in. But I stood still and thought that the woman known as Viper could not have given up so easily.

Unless getting Clover's job back hadn't been her purpose at all.

I wondered if she had come for information.

"Damn!" ChaCha said when the laughter died down. "She left her cupcakes behind. Doesn't she know dancers don't eat junk food?"

Libby stepped forward on the bar. "I'll take them! For my kids, of course. I'm making a lifestyle change, but my children might enjoy the treat."

ChaCha slid the box across the bar until it came to rest against the toe of Libby's sneaker. "Take 'em."

Chapter Fourteen

*I*n the afternoon, I stopped at a mother-and-daughter tea party in Bryn Mawr to benefit a program that supplied teddy bears for firemen to give to children displaced by fires. Libby happily tagged along, bubbling with enthusiasm for Cupcakes. "I bet those girls just dance their calories away!"

"Libby," I said as we mingled among dozens of perfect little children—all in extravagant ruffles and bows—who squeezed around the small tables to sip their sweetened tea, "how far would you go to get something one of your kids wanted?"

My sister stopped gazing hungrily at the pretty displays of pastel petits fours. "Oh, heavens, have the twins gotten to you? I'm not buying them scalpels for their birthday, and that's final."

"Good thinking," I said. Harcourt and Hilton gave me the willies sometimes. They'd recently given up their obsession with making splatter films in favor of much more grisly pastimes. "They might start amputating each other's toes. No, I'm thinking about Verbena."

"What about her?" Libby popped a finger sandwich into her mouth.

I said, "I don't think Verbena wanted Clover's job back. But there she was, begging ChaCha because she knows that's what her daughter wants most."

"What my kids want," Libby said, showing more spine than usual, "they don't always get. So far, it hasn't done them any harm."

I spoke with a few mothers and a couple of nannies who had brought little girls to the party. We talked of trivialities, but I could not shake Verbena from my mind. Whatever she was up to, it seemed strangely similar to the parents who gussied up their darlings in lavish dresses for the party. Each one looked more adorable than the next. An air of competition seemed to sizzle over the elaborately coiffed hair of eight-year-olds. The children, however, were fortunately more taken with the friendly Dalmatian visiting from the local firehouse.

Money had been raised for a good cause, I told myself as I wrote up my notes in Libby's minivan.

She drove me into Center City—traveling against evening rush hour traffic—and dropped me on Walnut Street. I waved good-bye and went into the restaurant to meet Richard for dinner.

It was not my favorite dining spot. Although it was well respected and usually booked full, the fare was a somewhat outdated French menu with heavy creamy sauces, and I'd always found the host stuffy and dismissive.

I was early and thought I could slip downstairs to the bar to gather myself before Richard arrived.

Bone tired again, I really just wanted to go home.

Once, I might have called Michael to pick me up in the city. At Blackbird Farm, he might have cooked supper or joined me in the bathtub to talk lazily about our respective days. Then we'd read in bed, sharing a glass of wine before turning out the lights. For an instant I closed my eyes and longed for just such an evening, contentedly snuggled against him and absorbed in a book while anticipating a final, delicious rush of exertion before we fell deeply asleep together.

Startled, I shook myself back to reality. Not tonight. Not with Michael.

The restaurant's maître d' surprised me when he said Richard was already seated. His tone indicated how inconsiderate he thought I'd been to keep my date waiting.

I left my coat at the counter and followed the maître d' into the hushed and elegant restaurant. The crystal chandelier cast a warm luster on the room, decorated to recall a Parisian salon. Mirrors glinted on the gold silk wallpaper. The waiters swooped with silver trays. Despite the early hour, the tables were already crowded. Symphony goers had come for an early seating.

Richard had managed to reserve the best table in the

house in a private corner beneath a glowing sconce.

One look at the table, and I caught my breath.

"Richard," I said.

He stood quickly—then took care to catch his balance on his good leg—and kissed my cheek. "Hi."

He had brought white roses—dozens of them. The table lay covered in fragrant blooms with wisps of baby's breath hovering over the flowers like delicate summer moths. A bottle of champagne stood in a silver bucket alongside the table, the ice gleaming.

His smile melted my heart. I felt guilty for dreaming of someone else.

"What are we celebrating?" I asked.

"I hope a lot of things." He took my hand.

Stretching up on tiptoe, I gave him a real kiss on the mouth, one intended to put the past behind us and start our relationship anew. Swiftly, he gathered me up in his arms, uncharacteristically warm and eager. "I should bring you flowers more often."

I smiled up at him. "We're causing a commotion."

He glanced around to see a few diners smiling in our direction. "How about some champagne?"

"This really is a celebration!"

He pulled out my chair. A moment later, we were sitting across from each other.

He reached for the champagne with one hand and my glass with the other. "Busy day?"

"Obviously not as busy as yours. What's up? Did the editors offer you the new job?"

With a grin, he poured an inch of champagne into

the flute and passed it to me. "The paper wants me to become the city desk editor."

"Richard, that's wonderful!" I could see the glow of ambition achieved in his face. He had worked hard for his accolade, and now it was time to enjoy the victory.

"I had mixed feelings at first," he admitted, pouring for himself. "I like the street. But my leg, the time I've spent here in Philadelphia—things have added up for me. I've changed. Mellowed, I guess. It's time for something new."

"So you'll take the new job?"

He touched his glass to mine and met my gaze. "I was hoping you'd help me decide."

The untimely waiter appeared at my elbow and offered to put the roses in water. We allowed him to clear the table, and he promised he'd return with menus.

I drank a tiny swallow of champagne and put the flute down.

Richard drank more deeply from his glass, then watched the bubbles rise in the wine while he gathered his words. Slowly, he said, "I didn't accept the job yet, Nora. Because you're part of the equation."

Unconsciously, my hands tightened until my knuckles turned white. I took a breath and unclenched my fingers.

"Becoming an editor means settling down, staying in one place for a few years. It's not just building a career. It's building a whole life. You know I always planned to go back to New York, and my job there is still waiting for me. But my priorities have changed. I've come to some important conclusions."

I couldn't find any words.

"You've made a difference in me, Nora." He put down his glass and met my gaze steadily. "I want to stay here in Philadelphia with you. In fact, I want to marry you. I know we've got things to work out, but I'm ready to do that. We'd make a hell of a team, darling."

"Richard—"

"Will you marry me?" he asked. "I want to be with you."

"And," I asked softly, "my baby?"

He reached for my hand and held it on the table. "I know you're carrying someone else's child. I won't deny it bothers me. Hell, for a while I thought it was a deal breaker. I thought about convincing you to give it up for adoption or . . . something. But now I realize how important kids are to you. If I need to be the father to your children, I'm willing to do that. I don't care whose DNA is involved."

"But—"

"It could be our baby." He caressed my fingers. "I'd like to try, Nora."

The waiter returned. He brought menus. I doubted I could eat a mouthful, but I accepted the leather-bound folder and felt oddly glad to get my hands on it. Unconsciously, I held the menu between Richard and me and tried to steady my heartbeat. The waiter told us the chef's specials, but I didn't hear them. Things were happening way too fast. Perhaps sensing our discomfort, the waiter promised to return later and went away.

When we were alone again, Richard reached over and pushed my menu to the table so he could see me. "I love you, Nora," he said. "We'll keep the baby's paternity a secret. We'll make it work."

I wanted to believe him. Richard was offering me a way out, a way to have a normal life. For an instant, I felt a warm rush for his kindness. But I said, "Michael will find out. Someday he will."

Through pure dumb luck or some kind of alchemy, Michael was going to learn he had fathered my child. I knew it, and I dreaded it. I could imagine his reaction—part joy, part bottomless rage at being kept in the dark and denied what was his. He took nothing lightly—nothing of importance, that is. His emotions would be titanic.

Richard tried to read my expression. "Would it be easier if I did it for you? If I told him now?"

"No!"

Shaken by the suggestion, I could only imagine what Michael might do if Richard told him the truth. "Please don't do that, Richard. Promise me you won't. He'll be so upset."

At that, Richard abruptly slugged his champagne and set the glass down sharply. He planted one forefinger on the tablecloth. "Look, Nora, I've put my heart on this table. I think I deserve something besides some misplaced concern for the feelings of a thug."

"He's not a—"

"Goddammit, I'm trying to propose, and just like always we end up talking about him."

"I'm sorry. I want you to understand—"

"It's you who doesn't understand." Heads turned toward us, so Richard lowered his voice. "He's an evil son of a bitch, and the sooner you realize that, the better."

"Richard—"

"The shit hit the fan today. And this time Abruzzo's going down."

"What are you talking about?"

"Little Carmine Pescara? Poof, he's gone! And the kid hasn't run off to join the marines, Nora. Word is, he's been whacked. Probably by your old boyfriend to cover up the cop killing. The kid knew too much or maybe he shot the cop himself—I don't know—but he's some kind of pawn in this game, and Mick Abruzzo's behind it all."

Suddenly I couldn't catch my breath.

"Little Carmine's mother watched the kid go off to the mall yesterday. But airport security found his car in the long-term lot this afternoon with the trunk wide open and the kid's suitcase unzipped. With his cell phone on the top."

"The police checked all flights?"

"Of course they did. If Carmine left the city, it wasn't by plane."

"So you think Michael kidnapped him from the airport parking lot? Maybe the boy left with a friend.

Maybe he's gone to Atlantic City or the beach or . . ."

"Or somebody killed him."

"No," I said.

"Maybe they're holding Carmine hostage." Richard sat back to muse. "But why bother? Why keep a noisy kid around when it's easier just to pop him in the head and dump his carcass in the Atlantic? The Abruzzos aren't known for their humanitarian deeds. I'll bet his body's disintegrating in the ocean right now."

A swarm of bees began buzzing in my head. A cloud of them rose up around me, darkening the room.

Richard got out of his chair. His napkin fell through the swarm and disappeared into the blackness that had been the carpet. Next thing I knew, he had pushed my head between my knees and was telling me to breathe.

The waiter came back, looking anxious, as I sat up.

"Sorry," Richard said. "I guess I surprised her."

The waiter smiled uncertainly and backed away. The diners near us returned to their own drinks, studiously pretending I hadn't just made a fool of myself. I drank another swallow of champagne, but my hand shook too much to hold the glass for more.

Richard sat down again and leaned forward on his elbows. "Nora, this is serious business now. If you know something about Carmine Pescara, you have to tell me."

"I don't know anything."

"Think. There's got to be something you overheard. Even something you suspected?"

"Michael's not involved in this."

261

"He's involved," Richard said. "Up to his neck. In fact, he'd better be walking around in a bulletproof vest these days, because if he hurts Carmine, some other wiseguy is going to kill him. But you can help Mick, Nora. And if Little Carmine is still alive, you could save his life, too."

"But I don't know anything. I've never met the boy! I don't know anyone else in the family."

"Nora, I'm here to protect you now. I'll make sure you're safe. There's no reason to lie for him anymore."

My mind cleared very quickly. "Is this story so important that you would accuse me of lying to you?"

"I love you," Richard said, husky and intense. "Together we can put him behind bars and out of your life."

I put both hands over my eyes. "No."

"Nora—"

I felt a dull ache reach upward from inside me, and I wondered fleetingly if it was the pain of a breaking heart. I dropped my hands into my lap. "I don't know what to believe," I said. "Do you love me and want to marry me? Or do you want this story?"

"Yes to both questions. Look, you know Abruzzo isn't the right man for you. But marrying me can help us both. With you by my side, I could be the managing editor of the paper in a couple of years. And you'd be rid of him and free to do everything you want. You could be a real community leader. You want to make a difference, don't you? It's your destiny, but you can't do it chained to a mobster."

"But first you want me to help with this story," I said as everything became clear. "You're using me to get it, aren't you?"

Richard sat very still. "Of course not."

Unsteadily, I put my napkin on the tablecloth. "I need to be alone."

"Nora?"

"I'm going to the ladies' room," I said. "I'll be back."

But in the bathroom, I discovered the pain I'd felt wasn't my heart at all. There was a spot of blood in my underwear.

Chapter Fifteen

I phoned the doctor immediately from the telephone in the bar, but ended up speaking with her on-call associate. He asked me questions and listened politely to my answers. In the end, he tried to assure me that light spotting wasn't unexpected, but if it got worse I should get to the emergency room.

"Go home and relax," he said kindly. "Avoid sexual activity for a few days."

No problem, I thought. I planned to swear off sexual activity for the rest of my life.

I hung up, not feeling any less terrified than before,

and turned around to find Richard standing at the bar, leaning on his cane. He stared at me, white-faced with anger.

"You called him, didn't you? Abruzzo?"

Coldly, I said, "I'm finished fighting, Richard."

"You did," he said, sounding amazed as well as furious. "I can't believe it."

"I did not call Michael," I said. "I'm not feeling well. I want to go home."

For an instant, I could see he didn't believe me. Then he looked away, defeated, and said wearily, "I'll drive you."

"No. I'll take the train. Libby will pick me up at the station."

"That's ridiculous. I'll drive—"

"If we stay together any longer tonight, Richard, one of us is going to say something we can't take back. Will you get my coat? I'm going to call my sister."

In silence, he walked me to Suburban Station and bought my ticket. We barely spoke until the R5 arrived.

"Nora," he said, "I'm sorry—"

"So am I."

"This isn't the way I thought the evening would go."

He kissed my cheek as I stepped on the train.

Libby picked me up at the Doylestown stop to drive me to the farm over back roads. I thanked her profusely. Fortunately, she was too wrapped up in herself to ask about me.

"I couldn't help it," she said in her minivan. "I'm

264

weak! I've always given in to my most basic needs. It's part of my character—the insatiable hunger for satisfaction."

"You went off your diet," I guessed.

"Those damn cupcakes!" she cried.

The box from Verbena's bakery was on the floor between the front seats of her minivan. I noticed the string had been broken and the lid savagely torn open.

"I only ate half while I waited for your train," she confessed. "I couldn't stand it any longer! They were just too scrumptious looking!"

She showed me the demolished half of a cupcake, now unappetizingly squished into a Kleenex.

"It's all right," I said. "You can get back on your diet tomorrow. A little slip once in a while is natural."

She shoved the cupcake remains into her coat pocket. "I could kick myself! I was going to try the Chocolate-Cake Diet tomorrow, and now I can't." She burped and belatedly clapped her hand over her mouth. "Where did that come from?"

"Are you okay?" I noticed she was sweating. "You look kind of feverish."

Libby put the back of her hand against her damp face and frowned. "I don't know. Maybe I don't feel so good."

"No wonder. After a week of watching your diet, even half a cupcake could wreak havoc."

"You think?" she asked, sounding doubtful. "I don't know. . . ."

Suddenly, she braked and pulled over. The instant

the minivan stopped moving, she threw herself out the door. I heard retching.

She climbed back into her seat a moment later, shaking.

"Are you okay?" I passed her a handful of fresh tissues.

"N-no," she whimpered. "I feel really sick."

"Let's call Rawlins. He can pick us up. You shouldn't be driving."

"I think I can make it," she said uncertainly.

We stopped twice more before arriving at Blackbird Farm. Libby left the van running as she bolted for my downstairs powder room. I shut off the engine, gathered up our handbags and the box of cupcakes and followed her into the house. From the sounds Libby made behind the closed powder room door, it was clear we'd barely arrived in time.

I knocked. "Lib? Can I do anything?"

She groaned and didn't answer.

Behind me, Emma said, "What's going on?"

I turned to discover my little sister in full Dungeon regalia. She wore a black leather bodysuit and tall patent leather boots that reached her midthigh. The heels looked sharp enough to impale anyone who dared get within range.

"Good grief," I said. "You could scare the Hell's Angels in that getup."

"They visited last week. If you ask me, they're a bunch of sissies."

Libby interrupted us with another volley of vomiting.

Emma said, "Wow, that's pretty impressive puking. And in rehab, I heard some pros."

I wasn't in a joking mood. "She's really sick, Em."

Emma joined me listening at the door. "Does she have the flu?"

"She ate half a cupcake, that's all."

Emma frowned. "This sounds a little extreme."

I took a closer look at her outfit. It actually covered up Em pretty well, and the leather was very good quality. But I said, "Are you going to be late for work?"

"I was just leaving." She noted my disapproval. "You want to come along? You might see something interesting."

"No, thanks."

"For instance," said Em, "you might see Boykin Fitch."

"What?"

Emma grinned. She leaned against the bathroom door. "Surprised you, huh? I remembered where I'd seen him before. He's a regular at the Dungeon. He's one of the guys who wears a mask, but—"

I forgot about Boy Fitch. "People wear masks? Oh, Emma!"

"Only the ones who want to keep their identities a secret from the voting public. Your pal Boykin has a kink that might startle his constituents. Most people don't want a senator who likes to be spanked on a regular basis."

"It certainly puts his campaign in a different light, doesn't it?"

Emma nodded. "Yeah, but does it make him guilty of murdering Zell Orcutt?"

"Good detective work, Em."

"Just call me Watson."

Libby retched again, and we both winced.

I said, "Maybe Libby fibbed. Maybe she ate more than just half a cupcake."

"Sounds like she ate a dozen."

"She was feeling fine one minute, then this." A light-bulb went off in my head. "You don't suppose . . . ?"

"What?"

"The cupcakes came from Verbena." I told Emma the short version of what I'd seen at Cupcakes. "Do you think those cupcakes were tainted?"

"You mean deliberately poisoned?" Emma asked.

"Oh, my God." My knees wobbled, and I sat down on the bench in the hallway. "The police were going to question ChaCha this afternoon. Verbena must have hoped to prevent her from telling them something about Zell's murder."

"Did you eat any cake?"

"No."

A new siege of sickness reverberated in the bath-room.

Emma said, "That's it. We're going to the hospital." She pounded on the bathroom door. "Libby! Come on, we're going to the emergency room."

"I can't move," Libby croaked. "Just leave me here to die!"

Emma barged into the bathroom, mopped Libby's

face with a towel and then bullied our sister to her feet. Libby looked even worse than before—white-faced and perspiring so heavily that her hair hung in damp strands. She was almost too weak to stand. Emma grabbed her around the waist, and the two of them staggered out the back door. I grabbed coats for everyone and brought up the rear, armed with plastic bags and paper towels.

Emma stuffed Libby into the backseat of her own minivan and made sure I fastened my seat belt before she set off at high speed. In the backseat, Libby kept her head in a plastic bag.

We arrived at the Doylestown hospital in record time and found the emergency room blessedly empty but for an elderly gentleman who appeared to be sleeping in front of CNN. The emergency room staff remained calm except for a few suspicious glances at Emma's choice of wardrobe. Beneath our father's Burberry raincoat, her stiletto boots and dog collar were plain to see.

Then Libby upchucked in the middle of the waiting room, and everyone forgot about Emma. Libby got priority status as they whisked her away.

"Now," Emma said to me, "let's get you taken care of."

As luck would have it, my own doctor was in the hospital delivering a baby. Between contractions, she came down to the emergency room to see me, looking younger in blue scrubs than when she wore the more formal white coat in her office. Somehow, it was more reassuring to see her ready for action.

Dr. Stengler studied the notes already prepared by the resident who had thoroughly interviewed me, then gave me a quick exam before helping me sit up again. "No cramps, right?"

"Just an ache, really," I said.

"You haven't been eating much since I saw you last week."

"Not much," I admitted.

"Not good." She closed the file and slid closer to me on the wheeled stool.

I liked Rachel Stengler very much. She had a no-nonsense bedside manner, but a sense of humor I appreciated. Tonight, however, the humor was subdued.

She put her hand over mine. "We've talked about this, Nora. Sometimes we can't stop nature."

I felt my heart lurch.

"This pregnancy has been delicate from the start. I wasn't happy with your hormone levels at last week's appointment. And now this. With your history, we knew there was a chance things weren't going to turn out well."

"Am I losing this baby?" I whispered.

"Let's not talk like that yet." She squeezed my hand. "We need to take care of you, though. I want to admit you to the hospital, get some fluids into your body, make you relax for a couple of days. We'll watch your hormone levels."

"Okay," I said.

"Why don't you go home tonight, pack a few things, get your life organized? Come back tomorrow after-noon, and we'll find you a bed upstairs."

"Okay."

"Get a decent night's sleep tonight." She summoned a smile. "My patients tell me they don't get much rest in the hospital."

"Thanks, Rachel," I said.

Her beeper began to squeak, but she held my hand a little longer. "Try not to worry, Nora. We'll do what we can, I promise."

Rachel went upstairs to her other, luckier patient, and I got myself dressed. It took another half hour to go through the discharge procedure, after which I felt as if I'd run a marathon in high heels. I longed for my bed. I found Emma pacing in the hall.

"Bad news?" she asked upon seeing my face.

I told her what my doctor had said and that I was to return the following day.

"That's good, right? I mean, that you haven't lost the kid yet."

"That's as good as it gets."

But Emma wasn't really listening. She nodded, but said, "Tell me about the cupcakes Libby ate."

"Why? Is she okay?"

"She's going to be fine." Emma pulled me to some seats in the waiting room. "The doctors are pumping her stomach. They think she was poisoned, all right."

"Oh, God. By the cupcakes?"

"Either that or the four cans of Diet Coke she drank

or the nine rice cakes she ate this afternoon, but somehow I don't think those did it. What about you? You're sure you didn't eat any of the cake?"

"Heavens, no."

"Are there any left somewhere?"

"Yes, they're in a box on my kitchen table."

Emma jerked her head in the direction of the exam rooms. "The docs want to test them. I'll go back to the farm and—"

My brain began to function again. "Wait, I think there's part of a cupcake in Libby's coat pocket. It's in the back of the minivan."

While Emma went out to the parking lot to retrieve Libby's coat, I sat in the waiting room and thought about Verbena. Had she deliberately taken poisoned cupcakes to ChaCha to stop her from revealing something to the police? And if so, how did she imagine she could get away with such a crime?

Emma came back with a wadded-up tissue wrapped around an oozing chunk of uneaten cupcake. We looked at the lumpy mess, and Emma said, "Sit tight. I'll take this to the docs."

When she returned ten minutes later, she had a young resident in tow—the same young man who'd asked me questions about my pregnancy. He wore a long white coat with a latex glove dangling from the breast pocket and a stethoscope draped around his neck. He had introduced himself as "Tad," but his name tag read DR. SINGH. He carefully avoided looking at Emma's patent leather boots.

"Your sister has certainly suffered a mild poisoning," he told us as if he dealt with tainted cupcakes on a daily basis. "She has experienced a digestive disturbance that's annoying and a little scary, but not life threatening."

"What's the cause?"

"If I had to guess by the quick onset and amount of vomiting along with her current state of lethargy, I'd say it was probably something as simple as a small amount of ipecac syrup. To tell the truth, I recognize the signs because we see it a lot in bulimic teenagers."

"Libby's not bulimic."

"I didn't think so." Tad accidentally allowed his gaze to stray to Emma's collar, but he said, "People used to keep that stuff in their medicine cabinets in case of household poisoning. Nowadays, we don't recommend its use in the home, but families haven't disposed of the stuff. There's a lot of it around. It's harmless, but unpleasant."

"How soon will Libby be okay?"

"She'll be back to normal by morning. She would have recovered on her own, but we've made her more comfortable. In other words, she's going to sleep it off."

"Thank you," I said.

"We'll send the cake to a lab for assessment. In the meantime, we're required to contact the police about this matter. I know you're not feeling well yourself," he said to me, "but can you answer a few more questions for us?"

I didn't hold back. If Verbena was going around poisoning my sister, I wanted her stopped right away. I told Dr. Singh about seeing Verbena deliver the cupcakes to ChaCha Reynolds at Cupcakes earlier that day.

The doctor took notes. "Okay," he said at last, rereading his scribbled writing. "We'll keep your sister overnight. I expect she'll be just fine in the morning. Meanwhile, you should definitely go home."

"I'll take her," Emma said.

"Okay," Tad said slowly. "But it looks like you were headed someplace a lot more exciting."

"I dunno." She leaned closer and gave his latex glove a snap with her forefinger. "Looks like you have it worse."

In one of the exam rooms, Libby was snoring and barely woke when we said good-bye. Emma whisked me out of the hospital and tucked me into bed an hour later.

"You're late for work," I mumbled.

"Maybe they'll fire me," she joked from the doorway. "And maybe I'll have to start working for Pointy Fitch instead. Either way, I'll get to use the whip, right?"

In the morning, I awoke in a fog and fumbled the bedside clock off the table to discover I had slept for nearly twelve hours. I sat up and found a thermos of tea on the table along with a bowl of popcorn and a note from Emma saying she had gone to pick up Libby at the hospital and would return before noon.

Her last line read, *Stay in bed!*

I went into the bathroom, surprised not to be feeling as nauseated as I'd been on previous mornings. But I wondered if that was a good sign. A few minutes later, with my face washed and my teeth brushed, I climbed back into bed and opened the thermos of tea Emma had made for me. I was sipping my first cup of tea when the phone rang again.

It was Emma.

"Is Rawlins with you?" she asked without preamble.

"G'morning, Em. No. Should he be?"

"He's not here, either." She sounded distracted.

"Where, exactly, are you?"

"At Libby's place. I just brought her home from the hospital."

"How's she feeling?"

"Ecstatic. She lost four pounds yesterday. Amazing how a little poison can cheer up a person. Thing is, Rawlins isn't here. The twins were in charge of the asylum last night until Delilah showed up."

I sat up straight. "Are all the kids okay?"

"Yeah, Delilah spent the night. They ordered a bunch of pizzas and had a pig-out. Apparently, a week on Libby's diet put those kids over the edge. But Rawlins is AWOL and doesn't answer his cell phone."

"Where was he supposed to be?"

"Here. Looking after the monsters. But he walked out early last night and hasn't been heard from since. Maybe it's just as well he's gone. Libby's ready to kill him right now." I could hear Libby shouting in the background. Emma said, "Any suggestions?"

I squeezed my eyes closed to remember the name of the girl Rawlins had told me he was dating. They were scheduled to attend the Spring Fling tonight. "Shawna Greenawalt," I said. "Try calling her. I think she lives in New Hope."

"Okay." Emma hesitated. Then, "Did you see the news this morning?"

"I just woke up."

"Then this is going to rev your engine. Verbena Barnstable confessed."

I fell back against my pillow. "To poisoning Libby?"

"No. The police went to talk to her about the poison, and she started yammering how she was so angry about Clover being fired that she killed Zell Orcutt in a fit of rage."

"Verbena killed Zell?" I echoed. I fumbled through the bedclothes for the TV remote. "Why?"

"She came right out and said she murdered her step-father."

Which meant Delilah was in the clear, I thought at once. But common sense quickly replaced that thought. "Verbena killed him because he fired Clover? But he didn't do that—ChaCha did. Em, it doesn't make sense!"

"The police took her word for it. She's in custody."

"But—why did she try to poison ChaCha?"

"To stop ChaCha from talking to the cops, she says. She told the detective she needed time to think, so she gave ChaCha cupcakes laced with ipecac."

What secret had Verbena wanted to keep from the police investigators? Had Verbena believed ChaCha knew who Clover's father was? And why did that matter?

I said, "Okay, where is Delilah?"

"She took Keesa and went home. I think the twins creeped her out. Look," Emma said, "we're a little more concerned about Rawlins at the moment. Once we figure out where he is, I'm coming over to take you to the hospital."

"Thanks, Em," I said, full of gratitude that she was coping with all of our troubles today.

"One more thing. I left the rest of those cupcakes in your kitchen. Don't throw them away yet. The police want the rest of them."

"Gotcha."

I watched the television, waiting for some information about Verbena, but the news channels were covering the disappearance of Little Carmine Pescara. When Michael's mug shot appeared on the screen, I clicked off the set, got out of bed and puttered wanly around the bedroom, packing an overnight bag for my hospital stay and trying to make myself believe Verbena had murdered her stepfather. The mental picture of Verbena with his dead body in the herb garden was something I couldn't get out of my mind. She hadn't acted like a woman who'd just shot a man with a bow and arrow. She had been . . . afraid?

I opened my laptop computer and went online to learn more about Verbena's confession, but the news hadn't changed since Emma heard the first sketchy details. I still couldn't imagine Verbena's motive. Did Zell's death make any difference to the secret of Clover's parentage?

Mumbling to myself, I went into the bathroom and packed some toiletries into a makeup bag.

"Fine," I said to my reflection in the mirror. "If the police have arrested Verbena, she must have done it."

I had my own problems to think about.

I climbed back into bed and opened my computer again. I e-mailed my editor with the news that I was going to be out of action for a few days.

I thought I had enough material to keep the society page of the *Intelligencer* going until my return, and I sent it all to Stan. Some tidbits I picked up at the Kingsley's preview, a few lines about the reality show party and a few items sent to me by readers who wanted promotional mention of their upcoming events. I assured Stan someone would be able to attend the museum party on Saturday night, the high point of the week's social calendar.

After a few minutes Stan shot back his response. *Thanks*, he wrote. *There's plenty of junk to use. Don't worry about the museum thing. Get well soon.*

Junk. I stared at the word. Clearly, the newspaper believed my work had no value whatsoever.

I groaned and fell back against the pillows.

I closed my eyes and tried to imagine life without my job at the newspaper. Would a temp agency even consider hiring me? With my comprehensive knowledge of social etiquette, ballroom dancing, the art of the seating chart, exactly what employer would beat a hasty path to my door to hire me?

And what about health benefits? Could an unskilled woman with a baby on the way afford to pay for doctors and still eat or pay the electric bill every month?

I began to see the compelling logic of marrying a man with a steady job.

I found myself reviewing Richard's proposal. I gave him credit for offering to raise Michael's baby. But I couldn't imagine Richard truly accepting such a child.

Lying in bed—the site of the fiasco that had been making love with Richard—I wondered if I could stand a lifetime with a man who might choose his job over his family. I had no doubt now that he always would. Richard's ambition had been very clear to me last night. He didn't want a wife. He wanted someone who could help him reach the pinnacle of his profession.

The phone rang again.

"Sorry." Emma sounded more agitated than before. Her voice brought me back to reality with a snap. "We still can't find Rawlins. The Greenawalt girl says she was supposed to see him last night, but he didn't show up. Libby's having a cow."

In the background, I could hear that Libby's rant had turned into a wail.

Emma said, "Do you know the license number of the car Rawlins is driving?"

"N-no, I don't." I cursed myself for being stupid

enough to put the keys to a powerful vehicle into the hands of a boy who wasn't even out of high school yet. Images of a car crushed into oblivion crowded into my mind.

And I thought of Carmine Pescara. Missing. Presumed dead.

I said, "Michael would know the license number."

"Call him."

"Em, I—"

"I gotta go. Libby's crying again. Call me back," she said curtly, "as soon as you get the plate number." She hung up.

I didn't want to talk to Michael. But frightened for Rawlins, I dialed a few of Michael's many phone numbers. A surly voice I didn't recognize answered one of them, and I identified myself. "I'm looking for Michael," I said.

"Who?"

"Will you have him call me, please?" I decided not to say my name over the line. I added, "It's important."

The voice on the phone didn't respond. He hung up without another word.

Five minutes later, Michael telephoned. Whatever system of communication he had organized to protect himself from surveillance, it worked beautifully. Except when semihysterical ex-girlfriends called.

In a rush, I said, "I'm sorry. I know you don't want to talk on the phone. And this line is probably bugged, so—"

280

"It's okay." He sounded calm, even happy. As if he'd enjoyed his first cup of coffee and was considering splurging on a big breakfast. "What's up?"

"Rawlins is missing. It's not like him to disappear like this, but—"

Amused, Michael said, "He's a sixteen-year-old boy, Nora. Let the kid have one moment of teenage rebellion."

"He was supposed to be looking after his siblings while Libby went to the—it doesn't matter. He wouldn't just walk out without—anyway, now he doesn't answer his cell phone. Do you have the license number of the car he's driving?"

"Give me a minute," Michael said. "I'll call you back."

Less than sixty seconds later, he phoned again and read me the plate number. Then, still sounding calm, he said, "Have you called the cops?"

"Do you think we should?"

"They're the fastest way to track down a vehicle. You want me to organize a search party, too?"

"Michael . . ."

I was thankful for the reassurance in his voice and wondered for an instant what kind of catastrophe might terrify him the way my missing nephew did me.

He interpreted my silence as panic and said, "Take it easy. He's probably got a flat tire somewhere. Or he's with a girl and lost track of time. Some of my guys will poke around the neighborhood. Don't worry."

"Thank you." I could barely get the words out of my tight throat.

He said, "I'll come get you now. We'll look together."

"No, there's no need for that. Don't come. Emma's got things under control, and if we call the police— Michael? Michael?"

He'd hung up.

I threw myself out of bed and headed for my closet. With the receiver in hand, I punched in Libby's number and Emma answered. I gave her the license number, and she grunted her thanks before disconnecting.

I found a pair of jeans and a pullover sweater that would cover me up sufficiently, but it was too warm to wear as long as my heart was pounding so hard, so I slipped on a camisole and carried the sweater downstairs with me.

I had to clean all the evidence of my pregnancy out of the kitchen.

On the table alongside the box of cupcakes stood Libby's collection of maternity clothes, books and videos. Emma must have looked through the dubious collection because two books lay on the table. *Please Your Pregnant Partner* and *Yo-gasm*. Both covers left no doubt about the contents of the books. I stuffed them back into their boxes and shoved them onto the cellar landing.

I had time to eat a few handfuls of leftover popcorn before I heard Michael's car in the driveway. Then I threw on the sweater and glanced around the kitchen to make sure I had hidden any clues about my pregnancy. All clear.

I met him on the back porch, prepared to make a stand.

Chapter Sixteen

He came up the flagstone walk in jeans, boots and a leather jacket too snug to conceal a bulletproof vest. The wind blew his hair. Judging by the dark smudges beneath his eyes, I guessed he hadn't gotten much sleep lately. No rest for the wicked.

He carried a bag from a local doughnut shop.

"You shouldn't have come," I said when he reached the bottom of the porch steps.

"Rawlins showed up?"

"Not yet."

He came up the steps, giving me a look. "If I had a bunch of crazy women looking for me, I'd probably hide, too. Let's go inside where it's warm. You're shivering."

"No, I don't think that's wise."

He held up the doughnuts. "What, you're on a diet?"

"It's just better if we stay out here."

He smiled wryly. "Afraid somebody will listen to all our secrets?"

Shaken, I said, "What?"

"Is Clark Kent here?"

"No, he's not."

He reached past me and opened the door. "Inside."

I couldn't stop myself from obeying.

"I'll make coffee." He followed me into the warmth of the kitchen. "And you can tell me what you know. Any clue where the kid might have gone last night?"

"His girlfriend said he was supposed to meet her, but he never arrived."

"A girlfriend," Michael said, closing the door. "That's progress."

"Rawlins isn't as innocent as you think."

"Oh yeah? He's jaywalking now?"

"He had a brief encounter with one of the Cupcake girls."

"How brief?"

"Brief."

With a grin, Michael said, "Welcome to the modern world of dating."

But I wasn't listening. An idea had hit me, and I suddenly realized where Rawlins could have gone. "Good heavens," I said. "Clover!"

"Huh?"

I didn't know why I hadn't thought of it before. But I had seen Rawlins with Clover outside Verbena's tea shop. Perhaps, despite his protests, my nephew hadn't been completely unaffected by the pretty girl's come-on. "Clover Barnstable. The Cupcake Rawlins knows.

They bumped into each other when I—good grief, I wonder if . . . ?"

Michael unzipped his jacket. "You going to start making sense soon?"

"Sorry. I just thought of a place to look for Rawlins."

"So let's get going. After I have some coffee."

On a different sort of morning, I would have made him some breakfast, given him a chance to relax. But just having him in the house made me fear he could divine my condition by breathing the same air.

And then I saw my mistake. The bottle of prenatal vitamins sat on the windowsill beside my Christmas cactus.

Michael followed the direction of my terrified glance. "What?" he said. Then, "Oh."

He went to the window and reached.

I held my breath.

He picked the diamond ring off the cactus and looked at it in the light from the window. "I thought you were going to sell this thing."

"No," I said, shaking as if a high wind had just torn through the house.

He appeared to study the facets. "You could probably fix the roof for what it's worth."

"Take it," I said. "I don't want it here anymore."

Without a glance at me, he dropped it into his shirt pocket.

"Michael," I said, more calmly, "let's not turn this into a social occasion."

He had ambled over to the freezer and pulled it open. "You're worrying too much. Rawlins may be innocent as cherry pie at home, but he's got a few street smarts."

"We can find Rawlins on our own," I said. "Emma and I are managing just fine. Besides, you've got another missing boy to worry about."

He had located the pound of coffee he'd left behind when he'd moved out at Christmastime. Closing the freezer, he looked at me across the kitchen, no longer amused. "So you believe everything you read in the papers now?"

"Tell me it isn't true." Holding my ground, I asked flat out, "Did you kidnap Little Carmine Pescara?"

He looked down at the coffee label as if he might find a response printed there. "You never asked that kind of question before."

"I never thought I had to. Richard says—"

"Richard," Michael echoed. "Now I get it."

"We're not going to talk about Richard right now. Are you holding Little Carmine hostage, Michael?"

He glanced around the kitchen. "Okay, you really want to talk about this? First, let's make sure it's just you and me. Where's the transmitter?" He dropped the coffee on the counter and began to prowl the room.

"I can't believe you're behaving this way, Michael. I thought I knew you. I didn't think I was stupid, but—"

"You're anything but stupid."

"Naive, then." I dashed a tear from my cheek. "God

knows what you did before. I didn't care because I thought you'd put it all behind you. You were sorry, and you were helping people like Rawlins to—to atone or something. But now it's kidnapping? Or is there something worse going on?"

He checked the telephone receiver first, then the light switches, and finally he pulled out a kitchen chair and climbed on it to examine the chandelier. His search was businesslike and thorough, but I could see he was angry.

At last he got down from the chair and said, "Little Carm can take care of himself. When you grow up the way he has, you grow up fast."

"He's growing up the way you did," I said. "I get that. If he's so much like you, why aren't you more sympathetic?"

"I'm plenty sympathetic." Still looking for the bug, Michael hunkered down in front of my kitchen sink. "I'm a hell of a lot more sympathetic than you think."

"Is he alive?"

At that moment, Michael opened the cabinet door beneath the sink. As he did, three Jiffy Pop pans fell out onto the floor with a rattle and a bang. A dozen more were clearly visible inside the cupboard, tucked beside my recycling can like a stash of empty bottles hidden away by a secretive alcoholic. Michael reached to retrieve the fallen pans.

I took an involuntary step forward. "Wait—"

On a short laugh, he said, "What's this? You had a big popcorn craving last night?"

I couldn't come up with a quip. No clever, diversionary explanation came to mind, and for a split second, I let my guard down too far. He piled the pans on the kitchen counter. He hesitated, puzzled for only a heartbeat by my silence, and then he noticed the pharmacy bottle on the windowsill. He reached for it, and when it was in his hand, I saw the revelation hit him like a lightning bolt.

He said, "Nora?"

From across the room, his gaze met mine and sharpened.

"I—I like popcorn," I said.

Michael stared at me, bottle in hand, but transfixed by the fact that clarified in his mind.

I hugged myself and had the fleeting thought that I had never been so stupid in my life. But my brain couldn't downshift, couldn't gather the words to save me.

He dropped the bottle and came across the kitchen with the speed of a springing panther. I backed up instinctively to escape, but collided with the pantry door.

He stopped before me and said, "You're pregnant."

"I—"

"You are," he said, stunned.

I expected something different from him. Maybe joy. Maybe rage. Maybe some kind of loud Abruzzo fertility ritual that involved rolling out pasta dough and drinking a bottle of wine before noon.

I didn't expect him to grab both of my arms, his grip

biting deep as he pushed me hard against the door. His eyes burned bluer than butane. "Jesus Christ, who knows about this?"

"What?"

"Who have you told?"

"Are you kidding?"

He shook me. "Nora, it's important. Who knows? Your sisters?"

"Yes."

"Who else?"

"Michael—"

"A doctor? Nurses?"

"Why are you—"

"What about D'eath?"

"Richard? Yes, he knows—"

"Yes?" Michael demanded. "Dammit, Nora, you've told half the world but not me?"

"Stop it!" I glared up at him. "Michael, this child has nothing to do with you. I—I slept with Richard."

He released his hold on me and stepped back.

"Don't," he said, shaking his head.

"I'm sorry if that hurts you. You and I were finished, and I was trying to move on, so Richard and I—"

Michael put out one hand to stop me from speaking. "Don't bother. Don't bother even trying, Nora. You're carrying our child, not his."

"This child is none of your business, Michael."

His face was suddenly, truly ugly. "The hell it isn't."

I retreated, putting the kitchen table between us. "You made it crystal clear that we're not sailing into the sunset together, so I—I started something new with Richard. We've come a long way in a couple of months. We're very happy together."

Michael put his head back and laughed.

Which made my blood boil. "We're not just happy," I snapped. "Richard proposed last night. We're getting married."

He sobered fast. "No."

"Yes," I said, just as firmly. "We're starting a family right away."

He threw the kitchen chair out of his way and came after me again. "You are not going to marry Clark Kent. Not now."

"What's my other option?" I cried. "You? What kind of family life can you offer?"

"You don't love D'eath. He's just convenient."

"Convenient, maybe, but also safe and kind and—and he loves me. And best of all, he doesn't get himself arrested on a regular basis!"

"I haven't been arrested in months! And even then the charges were bogus."

"Do you hear yourself?" I cried. "Richard is a law-abiding, upstanding citizen with—with many good qualities. He's going to be around to tie shoes and play baseball and help with homework, not spend years locked up in jail for—"

"Fuck Richard," Michael exploded. "That smug asshole is not going to teach my kids how to tie their shoes!"

We'd both been shouting. With an effort, I controlled my voice. "Richard wants to marry me, Michael. And he's not running a crime syndicate. He's not kidnapping children or—or whatever the hell you're doing with all that cash in the trunk of your car. He doesn't have to check for hidden microphones or cameras wherever he goes."

Michael's expression hardened.

"You know he's a good man," I said. "The kind of man you'd want to raise your child, Michael. Admit it. If it were your decision, you'd choose Richard to be this baby's father."

A full minute ticked by during which neither one of us could breathe.

"Get your coat," Michael said at last, voice low again.

"What?"

"We're leaving."

"No. Look, I appreciate your willingness to help. But I have to—Rawlins is probably—"

"I don't give a damn about Rawlins right now." He slipped one hand under my elbow and pulled. "We have to get out of here."

"What do you think you're doing? Let me go!"

He hauled me across the kitchen to the peg where I kept my gardening jacket. He threw it at me. "Put this on. Is there—what else do you need?" He hesitated at last. "Any kind of—I don't know—baby stuff?"

"This is ridiculous. I'm not leaving!"

"Never mind, we can buy whatever you need. Come on."

"No!"

"Yes."

We slammed out of the kitchen and into a ferocious March wind. I fought him the whole way out of the house and down the porch steps. The wind whipped at us and roared in the branches of the oak trees overhead. I managed to break out of his grasp on the sidewalk and spun around to face him. "Stop this! I'm not leaving with you!"

He strode forward, chasing me up the walk to his car. "I'm not giving you any more choices."

"You can't bully me!"

"I'll throw you over my shoulder and carry you if that's what it takes. One way or another, we're out of here."

"I'm not going anywhere!"

"Dammit, don't you understand? It's not safe for you to be alone."

"What are you—"

Over the wind, he shouted, "Your whole house is broadcast central! Everybody from here to the Atlantic Ocean probably knows you're pregnant with my child. Everybody but me, that is."

"This isn't—"

"Don't you see how vulnerable it makes you?"

I caught my shoe and stumbled. "Vulnerable?"

"The Pescaras already think I snatched Little Carm. They're looking for a way to retaliate!"

"What does that have to do with me?"

"You still don't get it? Look around! Don't you see

292

how easy it would be to grab you? You're alone, sitting out here in the middle of nowhere, getting fat with the one thing I'd protect at any cost!"

"I am not fat!" I cried. "I'm pregnant."

He caught me in his arms, more gently this time, almost hugging me. "I know, I know. You're beautiful. You're smart and strong and you always try so hard to do the right thing. You're perfect. But you're so damn stubborn sometimes I can't stand it. I'm begging you now, Nora. Please, please, let me take you out of here. We can figure everything else out later. Let me take you someplace safe right now. Before something terrible happens."

I looked into his face, not handsome or refined, but battered and a little broken and nuanced in ways I understood deep in my heart.

"Trust me," he said. "Please. Just this one more time."

I said, "I have to find Rawlins."

"I'll help, I promise. Just let me take care of you first. Let me find you a safe place to be."

He let me go back in the house to get my overnight bag.

On the way out of the kitchen, I grabbed the cupcake box. I didn't want to leave it where someone might accidentally be poisoned, and I fully intended to see the cupcakes reached the police very soon. Michael locked the house behind us, and we got into his car.

"I have to make a stop first," he said. "Then we'll find Rawlins."

We didn't speak for ten minutes. I don't know what he thought about, but twice Michael looked at me as if trying to puzzle out a conundrum. Frightened, and not sure whether I might burst into a fit of laughter or tears, I couldn't speak, either.

He took the bridge across the Delaware into New Jersey, then wound down along the river to the unmarked road. We turned in. Two black SUVs blocked our path. One man who'd been lounging against a tree, talking lazily on a cell phone, got into one of the trucks and moved it to allow Michael to pass. We bumped along the narrow, winding road through the trees to the little house that was concealed by brush, rocks and trees from anyone who didn't know where to look. Michael's house, when he allowed himself the luxury of a home.

Today the yard was crowded with vehicles, and a handful of tough-looking men stood in the wet grass. They were the members of his ever-changing posse— mostly surly bikers, a couple of hulking thugs and one middle-aged, heavyset wiseguy named Aldo, who appeared to be supervising as he smoked a stubby cigar. Two of the younger ones leaned on shovels. A trench, six feet long, had been dug in the ground. They had heaped the earth messily on the grass nearby.

"Oh, my God," Michael said.

He got out and came around the car. His crew turned around to watch me climb unsteadily out of the passenger seat.

Aldo stuck his cigar in the side of his mouth and limped forward. "Hey, boss."

Michael slammed the car door behind me and glared at the hole.

"Hello, Aldo," I said. "How's the knee?"

After nearly a year of acquaintance, Aldo and I had reached the point where we could exchange a few sentences and understand each other. He shrugged. "Healing, I guess. Thanks for asking."

Michael said, "What the hell is going on here?"

Aldo shrugged again. "The kid, you know."

"What, he's giving orders now?"

"What are we supposed to do? After moving him around so much, you said make sure he got what he wanted today." Aldo's voice rose into a whine. "We couldn't say no to him. Maybe you thought keeping him happy meant some ribs and a few Pepsis, but things got out of hand."

"I can see that. You just dug up my basketball court."

Aldo swung around and stared at the grass. "Basketball court?"

With his jaw set, Michael said, "I was going to get the concrete poured in a couple of months. You had to dig a pit in the middle of it?"

Aldo looked a little surprised at Michael's tone. "Sorry, boss. We'll fix everything, you'll see. Good as new by tomorrow. You get the charcoal?"

Michael threw his car keys at Aldo. "In the trunk. Anybody else come visiting?"

"Nope. Like you said, they have other leads to keep them busy. And we've got two cars ready to take the kid out of here if we get word the cops are on their way. Nobody's gonna find him, boss. We're doing everything like you planned."

"Good."

"What about the other thing?"

"I'll take care of it later."

"Later?" Aldo glanced at me.

"Don't worry," Michael snapped. "I'll take care of it. Come on, Nora."

We climbed the wooden steps of the deck that ran around three sides of Michael's house. It was a chalet-style vacation home built by some New Yorkers as a weekend place along the river, and Michael had bought it for himself a few years ago. He could fish from his deck when he felt like it, and the constantly rushing river gave him some peace. In the autumn months, we had sipped wine, sitting in Adirondack chairs above the Delaware.

Inside, it was just one room on the first floor, a comfortable living area with a fireplace, a TV set big enough for a drive-in movie, and a full kitchen with a fancy stove and a counter with tall stools on one side.

Behind the bar, a young man with the sleeves of an Eagles football jersey shoved up over his elbows was pounding an enormous side of pork with his bare hands.

"What the hell are you doing?" Michael said when the door was closed behind us.

It was the teenager I'd seen with Michael at Cupcakes.

"Oh, you're finally back," said the boy. "Where's
the charcoal?"

"Outside." Michael made a short, frowning inspec-
tion of the slab of raw meat that lay on a sheet of
plastic on his kitchen counter. "I thought once you got
here you were going to smoke some ribs for everybody."

"I sent Vinnie for the meat, and this is what the
moron came back with. So I figured we'd have a pig
roast. Well, half a pig roast. Hi," he said to me with an
infectious grin.

He wasn't very tall, but had big shoulders along
with dark eyes and a wide forehead with curly black
hair that spilled down over it. The grin seemed a per-
manent part of his cherubic face. On the counter, he
had an enormous bottle of Mountain Dew, just as
Rawlins might have done.

Michael said, "Nora, this is—uh, Joey. Nora Blackbird."

Little Carmine smiled with dimples and started to
put out his hand to shake mine. But his palm and fingers were encrusted with an orange goo, so he pulled
back. "Sorry," he said. "It's a rub."

"A rub?"

"Like a marinade, only dry. A dry rub I've been
wanting to try. Garlic and mustard and some herbs,
you know, and a hell of a lot of brown sugar." Again,
the sunny smile. "I'm massaging it into the meat.

297

Then we're going to put it in the ground with some charcoal and mesquite wood chips. In eight hours"—he kissed his fingers—"perfection! All we need is some beer and cole slaw. Can I send Vinnie for some cabbage and stuff?"

"Sure, whatever," Michael said. "Just don't plan on rescuing the food if Aldo decides you have to make a break for it. If the cops or your dad even glance in this direction, the boys have orders to move you in thirty seconds, got it? We don't want anyone thinking you might be alive."

"Yeah, okay. You guys going to stay?"

"No," said Michael.

"May I have a glass of water?" I asked.

After one glance at my face, Michael got a pitcher out of the fridge. Equally fast, Little Carmine found a glass in the cupboard and filled it with ice. A moment later, I was sitting on a stool sipping water to settle my stomach while the two of them looked at me uncertainly.

Little Carmine said, "You okay? You don't look so hot."

"I'm thinking of becoming a vegetarian."

The boy nodded. "I know what you mean. I used to get squeamish seeing my meat so close to its natural, you know, state."

"You seem to be quite the accomplished chef, uh, Joey."

"I love to cook. You?"

"I prefer to eat," I said. "Usually."

298

"Cool. Well, if you come back later, there will be lots of eating going on."

He had a lovable gleam in his eyes, and I could see how tempting it might be to rescue such a kid from a life he hadn't chosen for himself.

"All right," Michael said. "I'll be back eventually. Don't do anything stupid."

"Okay, Mick. We'll save you some leftovers if there are any."

"Make sure there are."

As we left, Little Carmine Pescara was beating herbs into his dinner while Michael's crew put the finishing touches on their barbecue pit.

Chapter Seventeen

On the way into Philadelphia Michael made a series of phone calls. He said very little and listened quite a lot.

When he disconnected at last, I said, "You've organized quite an operation to make that boy disappear. Did he kill a police officer?"

"No."

"Does he know who did?"

"Probably. I didn't ask him."

"So you're protecting him from the police? Or from the cop killer?"

"Both," Michael said.

I'd suggested we start looking for Clover at Verbena's shop, but it was closed when we arrived. The door was locked and the lights were out. An all-woman television camera crew were packing their equipment into a van brightly painted with the logo of a local network affiliate. No doubt, the proprietress's arrest for Zell Orcutt's murder was going to put a dent in her business.

"Let's go around back," Michael suggested as we cruised by. "In these places, there's always somebody inside trying to pilfer a little something to pad the paycheck."

He was right. In the rear alley, we pounded on the door until it was opened by a heavyset woman in a dirty apron and a hairnet. Her arms were very red, perhaps from dish washing. She had a guilty belligerence about her.

I used all my social graces to find out where Clover might be.

Eventually, the woman decided we weren't there to cause her trouble and gave me the name of an apartment complex not far from UPenn. She said Clover had lived there for months.

We found it easily—a new complex of three-story buildings grouped around a center court with a "clubhouse" in the middle that appeared to do double duty as the rental office. I guessed the apartments appealed to graduate students or undergrads who could afford an upscale rent. Behind an aluminum fence, we could see the winter cover of a swimming pool flapping in the wind. Michael parked the car in front of a sign that read FUTURE TENANTS. Then he fished a baseball cap out of the backseat and put it on, and we got out of the car.

The apartments appeared to be laid out like a seaside motel, each unit with its own door that opened onto the balconies. On a weekday morning, no tenants wandered around the sidewalks. The place seemed deserted. From the roof of the clubhouse, the black eye of a camera watched us. Michael kept his head down and one shoulder turned to the camera. I hesitated, not sure I should go strolling into the rental office without a plausible story.

"Let's check the mailboxes," Michael said, reading my mind.

Each building had a freestanding kiosk of mailboxes at the base of the staircase that wound upward. Together, we scanned the names on the boxes at the first two buildings. I pointed at Clover Barnstable's name.

"Let's go," Michael said.

We headed for the open-air staircase. As we started up, two young men rounded the landing and came down toward us—beautifully groomed and leading a pair of equally perfect King Charles spaniels on matching rhinestone leashes. The dogs strained toward the tiny patch of grass beside the mailboxes. Their owners gave Michael his space.

One of them looked at my feet and said prayerfully, "Nice shoes."

We got to the second floor, and Michael said, "Nice shoes?"

"You should be happy," I said. "It's the only detail they'll remember about us."

We found Clover's apartment in the middle of a long line of evenly spaced doors—some sporting decorative wreaths. On Clover's door, however, someone had thumbtacked a cardboard silver star. The points of the star were beginning to curl.

I knocked. No answer.

Suddenly Michael said, "There's blood."

"What?"

He pointed. "On the door. Unless it's pizza sauce. But I think it's blood."

"Oh, God." I pounded on the door, louder this time. "Clover! Rawlins!"

Another door popped open several yards away, and a young woman put her head out into the hall. "You looking for Clover?"

It was Jane.

"Yes," I said, "do you know if she's home?"

Jane came out onto the balcony, barefoot and holding a baby on her hip.

She wore a shapeless pair of sweatpants and a sexless big shirt that camouflaged her body. We could hear the *Barney* theme song coming from her apartment. The baby sucked on one grubby fist and hiccoughed tearily, as if just finishing an exhausting tantrum.

Jane said, "Clover went out last night. She's not back yet."

"Do you know where she is?"

"She said she'd call this afternoon." Jane looked at me more carefully. "Don't I know you from some-place?"

"We're concerned Clover might be in trouble. Can you guess where she might have gone?"

"Nope." Jane began to gnaw on a hangnail.

Michael said, "Did she leave an extra key with you?"

"Yeah, sure. You want me to get it?"

"If it's not too much trouble," Michael said pleasantly.

"Gimme a minute."

She went back into her apartment and reappeared, still barefoot despite the cold, and padded up to us. The baby's eyes widened as she carried him closer. Someone had dressed him in a diaper and a T-shirt that was sopping with pink juice. He wore nothing else, and his nose needed to be wiped. When he saw she was getting too close to us, he burst into a howl.

"Shut up, Jackson," she said, not unkindly, adding to us, "He's teething. What a production."

Jane leaned over the doorknob with a key in her right hand. Michael's cell phone rang at that moment. He walked away and answered the call. The baby bawled and kicked. Jane couldn't manage him and the door lock at the same time, so I took the baby from her, tucking him inside my open jacket. I gathered his little bare feet in my hand and discovered they were freezing cold.

I suddenly wondered if I was holding Zell Orcutt's child.

His mother opened the door. "Clover? You home?"

The apartment was a wreck. Clothes had been flung to the floor where Clover stripped them off, shoes had been kicked off without concern for where they might land, and every piece of furniture was covered with handbags, accessories, fashion magazines and garbage. The smell of an unchanged cat box was over-whelming.

The television was on, blaring *The View*.

"Oh, God," I said.

"Don't worry, this is normal. Clover isn't exactly a neat freak." Jane called, "Kitty, kitty? That cat never comes out. He hides under her bed all the time."

We left the door open to let some fresh air inside. Because the carpet was completely covered with clothes, I walked gingerly. A lampshade hung drunk-enly askew. A bottle of nail polish lay on its side on a table, its glittery pink contents dried into a solid lump. On the television, Star Jones was laughing uproari-ously while her cohosts looked nonplussed.

I stepped on a pile of pastel cashmere and my foot struck an open cell phone, half hidden in the rumpled sweaters. Automatically, I bent to pick up the phone. The baby in my arms went quiet and reached out one chubby hand for it.

Michael came to the door and stopped, halted by the mess.

To Jane, I said, "Did you see Clover leave last night?

Did you hear her? Was she with anyone?"

"I heard her door slam about ten o'clock. She had a date."

"Do you know where? Or with whom?"

"Nope."

I handed the cell phone to Michael. The baby stretched to grab it again and began to cry when Michael took possession. Huge tears rolled from the child's eyes, and his face turned brick red.

"Oh, Jackson," his mother said.

I gave him back to her, which only made him cry harder.

I looked around the apartment while Michael clicked through some of the options on the cell phone. Clover had one bedroom and a bath cluttered with hot rollers, hairbrushes and a thousand makeup items, half on the floor. Brand-new appliances in the kitchen had never been used. In the kitchen sink, I found a dozen drinking glasses with lipstick on their rims, a serrated steak knife and spatters of blood.

On the glass window over the sink, someone had scrawled a message in red lipstick.

Do'nt call the pollice or Clover will dye.
We will contack you with a ransome not.

"Michael," I said.

He came into the kitchen, read the note and saw the blood in the sink. He said, "Don't touch anything else. It's time to call the cops."

Then he showed me the screen of the cell phone. It glowed with the telephone numbers of people whose names I recognized. Michael nodded. "This phone belongs to Rawlins."

"You shouldn't be here," I said. "If this is another kidnapping . . ."

He said, "Give me five minutes."

The first law enforcement officers to show up were not Philadelphia's finest, but two people in plain clothes. The woman wore a knit pants suit with a raincoat that caused some unfortunate static cling. The burly man wore a suit and tie. He was talking on his cell phone, but raised his eyebrows to Michael in greeting. We stood on the sidewalk beside the covered swimming pool. My overnight bag lay at my feet, and I held the cupcake box in my hands.

Despite the distracting static cling of her suit, I recognized Darla immediately.

She ignored me and stared meaningfully at Michael. "This isn't where you're supposed to be today."

"It'll happen," he replied. "But this situation needs my attention, too. What are you going to do about it?"

She sighed and looked at me at last. She shook her head. "I thought you were out of the picture."

"I am."

Michael said, "We need you to handhold the cops when they get here to investigate the Barnstable girl's disappearance."

Darla shook her head. "I don't think so, Mick. You, we can cut loose to do the thing. But her"—she nodded at me—"she's got to stay and talk to the cops. We'll take care of her when she's done, if that's what you want."

"This is nonnegotiable," Michael said. "I'm not letting her out of my sight."

A second sedan pulled up behind Darla, and two more men got out, leaving the engine running. They were also in suits, one with an earpiece that he pressed into his ear with one finger. It was Rudy, the man who had planted the bug in my kitchen.

"Mick, you can't stay here," Darla argued. "The cops find out you're connected to this kidnapping, they're going to bust you for Little Carmine for sure."

"So take care of it," he said. "Let us walk out of here, or the other thing you want done is screwed. Or maybe you don't have the clout you say you have?"

I said, "Let me get this straight. You're working with federal investigators? You're trying to solve the cop killing?"

Darla began to smile coldly. "You were right. She's pretty smart. Does she know where Little Carmine is?"

"Who?" I asked.

"You haven't found him yet?" Michael asked.

"We'll find him," Darla said testily. "Don't worry about that."

"I'm not holding my breath, Darla."

Her eyes narrowed. "You want us to believe that you don't have anything to do with Little Carmine, you're gonna have to trust us a little, too."

He shook his head. "Are you going to take care of the cops? If not, we've got to fly."

"Let us babysit your girlfriend if that's what you're worried about. We can put her in a safe place for a few days."

"I've seen your work," Michael said. "Why do you think I decided to help out?"

"Thanks bunches, Mick, but we were doing fine before you volunteered your services."

"We're wasting time. Nora stays with me. If that means the cops find me here, that's the way it goes."

"The cops will put you in jail. Then where will your girlfriend be? All alone in the big, bad city with nobody to carry her purse?"

"Hey," I said. "I don't need any of you. I'm calling a cab."

"Nora—"

It happened very fast. Darla's partner was talking on his cell phone one minute, and the next he snapped a handcuff on Michael's wrist. Michael twisted to escape before the lock clicked, but Darla was there with a stun gun. She hit him in the throat. The two other men swarmed around him, and Michael went down on the pavement.

"Put him in my car," Darla said. "She goes in the other vehicle."

Above us on the balcony, Jane yelled, "Hey!"

Rudy grabbed my arm and slapped his other hand over my mouth. He propelled me to the street, shoving my head down hard to throw me into the backseat of the second car. I fought him, trying to catch a glimpse of Michael, but the federal agent was very strong. Finally I bit his hand and he let go with a yelp. Panting, he got in beside me and closed the door. We were both breathing hard.

"Ow, that hurt!" He examined his hand.

I lunged for the opposite door handle and found it didn't function.

"Sorry about this," he said. "I'm Rudy."

I jammed myself against the door, to maximize the distance between us. "Let's forgo the introductions, Rudy. Let me out!"

"Sorry, I can't do that. Just sit here a minute, and then we'll get going. You really bit me."

"Going where?"

"Don't worry. You'll be fine." He tried to forget about his hand and straightened his tie. Then he looked at the container in my lap. "What's in the box?"

Another officer got into the driver's seat, and they took me to a nondescript office building that blended well into the financial district. The whole building was unmarked—not even a number over the door. There was no directory in the bland lobby, no Muzak in the elevator. Eventually we arrived in an office suite where the furniture hadn't been updated since Ed Sullivan's heyday.

For an hour, Rudy and I sat in an office decorated with football trophies, a nameplate that read G. P. BARLOW and a wall of framed photographs, all fea-

309

turing the same well-fed smiling man with a blond crew cut. On the desk, his face appeared in two separate pictures of both Bush presidents. It looked as if George Bush the younger was giving the man a noogie.

When the man in all the pictures came into the room at last, I noticed he'd put on a few pounds since his days of horsing around with presidents.

"Hello, Miss Blackbird," he said. "I'm—ah, sorry you've been detained so long. I'm George Barlow."

Three Georges, I thought. Behind him came Darla, looking very pleased with herself.

To her, I said, "Keep in mind it took four of you and a stun gun to make him cooperate."

She stopped smiling.

"Your—ah, friend is fine, by the way," said George as he sat in the nonergonomic chair behind the desk. Darla took the other plastic seat in the room, the one with the missing foot. The chair wobbled as she sat down, so she crossed her legs to steady it. Her pants were still clinging to her legs.

"Is Michael in this building? Or did you take him to a hospital?"

"His injuries were very temporary. At most, he'll have a headache. He has other business to attend for us later today, so he's—ah, elsewhere. But he's perfectly fine. A little ticked off, but fine."

"Am I under arrest?" I asked. "Either way, I'd like to call a lawyer."

"You're not under arrest." George feigned astonishment. "Who gave you that idea?" He sent an actorly glare at Rudy. "No, no, we're very—ah, grateful you could join us this afternoon."

"So why am I here?"

"Darla was under the impression you needed to be protected. We're—ah, wondering if that means you have some information about the disappearance of Little Carmine Pescara."

"Who?"

"You tried that before," said Darla. "And I didn't believe it then. Let's hear what you've got to say, sweetheart."

"You're the bad cop, I gather?"

George leaned forward on his desk. "Little Carmine has important information we'd like to hear, but that also means he could be in—ah, grave danger, Miss Blackbird. Frankly, we're afraid he's going to be—ah, killed if we don't reach him in time. In fact, he may already be—"

"I don't know anybody by that name. You are holding me against my will for no earthly purpose."

"She's got to know where the kid is," Darla said. "Mick's got him, or he knows who does. Mick's been stringing us along for two months now, but with Carmine suddenly missing he's either double-crossed us or something's about to happen. I'm damned if it's going to happen without us."

I thought I saw Rudy hide a smile.

"And now another young person, Clover Barnstable, has disappeared," George said. "What connection does Mr. Abruzzo have with this Barnstable girl?"

"None," I said. "Do the police know she's missing? Is anyone looking for her?"

"The police are sorting out that situation now. You don't need to concern yourself." George folded his hands on his desk. "Miss Blackbird, we must find out whether or not Mr. Abruzzo has kidnapped an innocent boy."

"Listen," I said. "I'm tired and I'm hungry and I don't know anything about a kidnapping. I want to go home, and if you don't let me do so this minute, I'd better be allowed to call a lawyer."

"You're hungry?" George looked surprised again. "Rudy, you didn't get this nice young lady any lunch?"

"None of us had any lunch," Rudy said.

"Darla? You didn't get lunch?"

Darla sighed. "Can we get back to business?"

George reached for his telephone. "Why don't we get some sandwiches sent up here? Would that make you happy, Miss Blackbird?"

I opened the box in my lap. "Why don't we just have a little snack instead?"

The three of them leaned forward to look at the cupcakes.

"Ah," said George. "They look delicious."

Chapter Eighteen

T he three federal agents fled George's office as fast as if they were being shot at by Al Capone. When all three disappeared into their respective bathrooms with minor digestive disturbances, I strolled out of the building and across the street to a coffee shop, my overnight bag in hand. I found a pay phone.

"Em," I said when she answered. "I need your help."

My sister arrived in less than an hour, squealing to a rocking stop at the curb in Libby's red minivan. I ditched the dry scone I'd been nibbling and went outside just as rain began to spit in the breeze. When I opened the passenger door, I discovered Libby had come, too.

"Oh, thank God!" With tears of joy practically spurting from her eyes, Libby seized me against her bosom. "I'm sorry I ever said you were fat! You found Rawlins!"

"No, but I have a good idea where he is." I wrestled myself free and climbed into the backseat of the minivan, pushing some of Libby's exercise equipment out of my way in the process. An Ab Buster recoiled at my shove, then bounced back and nearly hit me in the face.

Emma turned from the steering wheel to give me a

raised eyebrow. "Is it a felony to poison a federal employee?"

"I can't list the number of laws I think I've broken today." I gave up trying to tuck the Ab Buster out of my way and ended up holding the thing on my lap. "And it wasn't poison exactly."

Emma said, "Are we taking you to the hospital?"

I had spent the time in the coffee shop assessing my physical condition and decided I didn't feel any worse than I'd felt for the last two months. "I'll be all right. We need to get to Rawlins as quickly as possible."

Libby moaned, but Emma asked, "Where are we going?"

"I've been thinking. Judging by the bad spelling, I think Clover wrote her own ransom note. I think she's faking her own kidnapping, and she's got Rawlins with her. And they're probably at Fitch's Fancy. It's big, and she probably knows all its nooks and crannies. I bet it's the only place she'd think she would be unrecognized by her adoring fans."

"Are you sure?"

"No, but it's a place to start."

Emma threw the minivan into drive. "Hang on."

While she dodged traffic, I told both my sisters what I'd learned about Clover and Jane.

"That hussy!" Libby cried when I got to the part about Clover trying to entice her son on the sidewalk outside the tea shop. "What kind of girl throws herself at every man she meets?"

Emma took a breath to speak, but Libby rushed on,

"My Rawlins would never fall for such trashy behavior!"

Emma muttered, "I bet Rawlins wasn't crying for help."

"Not exactly," I agreed.

"That little sneak!" Libby's motherly concern turned on a dime. "What is it with men? I'm going to ground that boy the minute I see him."

"Relax," said Em. "You've given him a zillion condoms over the years. He's safe enough."

"Have you ever known a man to have one when he really needs it?"

By the time we reached Fitch's Fancy, the afternoon had begun to slip away and rain pelted the road in front of us. The lawn of the estate had grown in the few days since Zell had died, making the whole place look even more unkempt and neglected than before.

Emma touched the brake and peered through the rain-spattered windshield. "What are we going to do? Break into the house to look around for Rawlins and Clover?"

In the gloom of the descending storm, the mansion appeared to be empty—all the windows bare and no lights shining from inside. Even the ghosts of past Fitch generations had packed up and moved to more hospitable headquarters. The house had been abandoned. Suddenly I doubted myself.

"Do you think Rawlins is in there?" Libby asked, echoing my disappointment.

"Maybe the basement," Emma guessed. "You two stay here. I'm going to check."

"What's your plan?" I asked. "Are you going to knock politely on the door and hope Clover answers? Maybe we should call the police."

"And tell them what? That a dastardly teenage girl might be having wild party sex with our nephew?" Emma popped her door open. "We just need to find them, not get them arrested for lewd conduct. I'll break a window if I have to. Stay here, you two."

"Lewd conduct! I'm coming, too!" Libby cried. She flipped the hood of her tracksuit over her head.

The two of them bailed out of the minivan and slammed their doors, leaving me alone. I watched them scamper through the rain, up the garden path toward the house.

"Good luck," I said.

They were soon out of my sight, but I rubbed the condensation off the window anyway, in dread of catching a glimpse of bricks being thrown through the French doors. As the minutes passed, the rain began to ease, but the darkness continued to gather beneath scudding storm clouds.

Headlights flashed behind the minivan. I smothered a yelp as I pictured police intervention. Aloud, I said, "Please let this be a security company."

The car pulled up beside Libby's van and parked. It was not a police car or marked with a security logo, however, just a plain gray sedan. The driver got out. He wore a long, tailored raincoat over a dark suit and a red-white-and-blue-striped tie. He popped open a black umbrella.

Protected against the rain, the man came over to the minivan and cupped one hand around his face to peer inside.

Boykin Fitch in another patriotic tie.

I unlocked the passenger door and slid it open. "Hi, Boy."

"Nora, what are you doing here? Whose vehicle is this?" He came over to the door and stood there, blocking my exit. Rain pattered on his umbrella, and he looked at the Ab Buster in my lap, clearly trying to determine what the contraption was. "Is there anything wrong?"

"We're looking for my nephew."

"We?"

"Emma and Libby are searching for him right now."

Boy glanced up at the house. "I see. Has he run away?"

"No—at least I don't think so. He—well, this is a little embarrassing, but we think he might be with your niece, Clover."

"They couldn't be here," Boy said politely. "Clover doesn't live at Fitch's Fancy."

"I know, but—"

"Why don't you come into my car?" Boy asked. He reached for my arm. "You'd be much more comfortable there. The heater's running."

"I'm fine here. Em and Libby will be back any second and—"

His grip bit into my arm and he pulled. "I insist. Come with me, Nora."

"Ouch! Boy, you're hurting me."

"Stop that," he said when I resisted. His expression turned hard, but still a gentleman, he tipped the umbrella to shield me from the rain. "We're going to find your sisters, and then you're going to tell me what you're really doing here."

"I'm telling the truth. We're looking for—"

"Shut up," said Boy. "You're looking for evidence to incriminate me, aren't you? You're trying to prove I had something to do with Zell's death."

What can I say? After I'd poisoned three federal investigators, it was nothing to grab the Ab Buster and clonk a wannabe Senate candidate upside the head.

In one blow, I knocked him to the ground, where he landed on his knees in a puddle. His umbrella went flying. Despite his sprawl, Boy managed to reach one-handed across the floor of the minivan to make a grab for my ankle. With my other foot, I kicked his wrist until he released me. In the instant he drew back, I slammed the door. I slipped the lock, and—breathing hard—I figured I was safe.

Until Boy stood up and began to smash at the window with the Ab Buster.

I threw myself across to the opposite door. Fumbling with the handle for only an instant, I yanked it open.

"Stop," Boy yelled over the rain. He started around the hood of the minivan toward me, gripping the Ab Buster like Fred Flintstone with a club.

In jeans and flat shoes, I thought I could outrun him. I set off up through the garden, yelling for my sisters. Boy came after me, but his wing tips slipped on the wet stones underfoot.

Emma must have heard our commotion. She came skidding full tilt down through the garden. Her short hair was plastered to her head from the rain. "What the hell?"

"It's Boy," I panted. "He's gone crazy."

Emma's eyes widened as she looked past me at the sight of Boy charging toward us, waving the bent remnants of the Ab Buster over his head. She said, "Get out of here! I'll handle him. Go call the police!"

"Libby's got a cell phone. Where is she?"

"Stuck in the doggy door! I couldn't stop her and now she can't budge!"

There was no time for more information. Boy arrived and swung the broken Ab Buster at Emma. As graceful as a Musketeer, she ducked the blow, then came up and head-butted Boy in the solar plexus. He let out a strangled, "Oof!"

Emma grabbed the weapon from his grasp. I turned and ran.

The rain drenched me as I raced up the sidewalk to the kitchen side of the house. I could make out a figure kneeling in front of the kitchen door where the Fitch sheepdogs had once come and gone. Libby. Her backside was unmistakable in the lavender stretch pants. Her legs flailed as she tried to wriggle through a small pet door meant only for border collies.

I reached the door and crouched beside her struggling figure. "Libby! Libby, what are you doing?"

"What does it look like I'm doing?" she snarled from inside the house. "I'm stuck, dammit! Push me!"

I put both hands on her bottom and gave a tentative shove. No doubt about it, she was plugged tighter than a cork in a bottle. I tried locking my hands around one of her knees to pull her out, but she fought against me, yelling, "No, no! I'm almost through!"

"Libby, there's no way you're going to make it!"

"I'm almost in," she insisted.

I was looking at the largest part of her, which definitely wasn't going to squeeze through the tiny opening. No use arguing with her, though. There was nothing more determined than my sister when she was trying to delude herself. "Libby, where's your cell phone?"

"Here!" Her muffled yell came through the door. "It's in here with me."

"Call the police," I cried.

"What?"

"The police!" I shouted. "Call nine-one-one!"

"What for? I can wiggle out of here on my own!"

"Not for you," I bellowed. "Boy Fitch is here! He's fighting with Emma!"

"Why is she fighting him? I thought she was supposed to date him!"

I wanted to scream. "Libby, just call nine-one-one, will you? Say there's an emergency here!"

"I don't understand," she shouted. "Wait until I get

out of here, and you can explain—hey! I'm stuck!"

She tried backing out of the hole, but her bottom only bounced more frantically as she struggled. "Help!" she cried. "I'm really stuck!"

"I'll go get Emma," I said. "I'll be right back."

"Don't leave me!"

"You need help," I called. "I can't do this by myself. Just—sit tight and I'll come back. But call nine-one-one, Libby. Do you hear me? Call nine-one-one!"

I left her yelling and dashed back through the garden. In the brambles near the fountain, I spotted Emma wrestling Boy into submission. She had one knee on his back as she pinned him to the mud. If Boykin truly loved the humiliation of submitting to a powerful woman, he was probably in ecstasy. Emma, on the other hand, looked furious. Her face was smeared with dirt, and her clothing was soaked. I heard Boy whimpering as he struggled under her.

"Em, you're hurting a member of the legislature!"

"Get me some rope," Emma snapped, out of breath as she rode Boy's bucking body. "One of Libby's jump ropes from the minivan."

I ran back to the van. Just as I started into the back-seat to rummage through the junk, I heard a distant yell. A frightened human voice. I backed out of the van and listened intently. Besides Libby's muffled cries from the direction of the house and Boy's distinct baritone bellowing in the weeds with Emma, I heard another voice calling for help.

"Rawlins?"

I grabbed the jump rope from the minivan, threw it at Emma and headed toward the sound. It had come from the old sheep barn.

I ran down the lawn to the barn and came upon a set of tire tracks that had mashed down the grass. I followed them, climbed the low gate and slipped the last several yards to the barn. It hadn't changed much since I'd visited it as a child. But instead of a whole flock of sheep, just three woolly ewes stood huddled out of the rain beneath the overhanging roof near the door. I shoved through them and grabbed the slippery handle of the door. The tire tracks disappeared into the barn. Throwing my weight against the sliding door, I hauled it open. I saw the blue Mustang parked inside. As soon as the door opened just a foot, the sheep crowded through the opening, baaing in relief to be inside.

A feeble light glowed inside the barn. I peered ahead and saw a dusty lantern on a bale of straw. It was an antique, one of the lamps we'd used to hunt for champagne in the snowdrifts. Its small kerosene flame burned steadily.

"Rawlins?" I grabbed the lantern by its hot handle and plucked it off the straw, which was already smoldering. With my foot, I stamped on the straw, my pulse roaring in my ears. In another few minutes, the barn might have been in flames. And with the car parked inside, an explosion would have been certain.

Then I swung it to cast light around the interior of the barn. A series of wooden partitions about three feet tall divided the space into a series of stalls with a large open space in the center for shearing.

From the darkest corner came a croak. "I'm here, Aunt Nora. Watch out! She'll come out any minute!"

I headed toward his voice and came upon Rawlins in one of the stalls. He was shirtless and handcuffed to the low wooden fence. He had rubbed the wood to jagged edges by scraping the handcuff against it. A video camera had been abandoned, balanced on the top of the stall fence, pointed in the direction of my nephew.

"Rawlins! Are you okay?"

"Y-yes, I think so." His voice was hoarse from shouting.

He looked younger than his sixteen years and shivered in the cold. Bits of straw clung to his hair and jeans. I stripped off my jacket. "Oh, honey, you're freezing!"

His teeth chattered. "She's still here, Aunt Nora. She's still here."

"Who? Clover?" I set the lantern on the railing beside the camera and wrapped my coat around his quaking shoulders. "It's okay. We'll get you free in a minute. Your mom's here, and Emma, too."

"M-Mom? She's going to see me like this?" He looked more terrified than before.

"It's a toss-up whether you might see her first, considering where she's stuck right now. Where is the key to these handcuffs?"

Suddenly the barn was bathed in green light.

Rawlins shuddered beside me and gulped.

From behind the green light, Jane said, "I have the key in my pocket."

And Clover's voice said, "And we're not letting him loose until after we film the tribute."

"Oh, no," Rawlins moaned.

"Tribute?" I said.

The two girls climbed out of the Mustang, where they had been scribbling on a yellow legal pad. Jane carried the notepad in one hand, a heavy-duty flashlight in the other. Clover wore a bikini with a see-through baby-doll nightie over it, plus very high heels that made walking in the straw difficult.

One of the sheep panicked and butted past her, causing Clover to stumble. She cursed. "Who let the goats in here already? It's too soon."

Jane's flashlight had a plastic filter taped to it so that the eerie green light created an aliens-have-landed glow in the barn. She pointed the flashlight at me, extending the notepad to Clover. "Learn your lines, and we'll get started."

"I have to learn lines?" Clover assumed the classic pose of teenage irritation—one hand on hip, head cocked belligerently.

"What's going on?" I asked.

"They want to make a reality show," Rawlins said. "She thinks it's going to make her famous."

"A reality show?"

"Everybody's doing it." Clover snatched the notepad from Jane. "But mine will be very cool. You know, sexy girl meets handsome farmhand."

"Are you crazy?"

The words were out of my mouth before I could stop them. Both girls turned to stare at me while I hastily tried to think my way out of the situation. Clover bristled, not the least chilled by the nip in the air.

I looked at Rawlins, who hardly projected the aura of a handsome farmhand at that moment. The goose bumps on his chest were plainly visible.

I knew I couldn't overpower both of them and manage to get Rawlins out of the barn. So I said, "You don't plan on filming in here, do you? It's freezing."

"Where else could we film a farm?"

"We were going to do it at my apartment and make it like *The Real World*." Clover rolled her eyes. "But Raw kept yelling."

"We were afraid somebody was going to call the cops."

"They cut me!" Rawlins held up his free wrist to show me a wad of Band-Aids clumsily taped there. "They jumped me and put this handcuff on me, but it was too tight and then she tried to use a knife to get it off me, and—"

"You didn't have to act like such a scaredy-cat," Clover said.

"I was bleeding!"

"You could have waited for the key."

"Jackson had the key," Jane explained to me. "He kept trying to chew it, so it took me a few minutes to get it away from him."

"Meanwhile, I was bleeding."

"Not to mention making way too much noise," Clover said. "This is better anyway. There's a definite vibe."

"Ambiance," Jane agreed. She cast a filmmaker's glance around the drafty barn. "Very *Blair Witch Project*. It'll be like an indie film, you know? An art house flick."

"So we're starting with a tribute," Clover said.

Nodding, Jane said, "A tribute to tsunami victims to give, like, the whole movie some gravitas."

"Will you stop with the big words?" Clover complained.

"Where's Jackson?" I asked as casually as I could manage.

"With his sitter."

Clover said, "I told you, all you had to do was offer more money and you'd get a thousand babysitters camping out at your apartment like it's a *Star Wars* opening or something."

"I stood in line for *Star Wars*," Rawlins said.

"Of course you did," Clover snapped.

I asked, "What about the ransom note in the kitchen at your apartment?"

"That? Oh, a publicist lady told me about a Mafia kid who got kidnapped and all the media attention he was getting. I mean, why should some kid from Jersey get famous and not me? So I thought I'd try it myself. You know, for the publicity." Clover frowned at the notepad. "Can't we make these lines shorter?

There's way too much stuff to say."

"We already shortened it," Jane said.

"And what the hell is this word?" Clover jammed one finger down on the notepad and shoved it under Jane's nose.

"*Tsunami.*"

"Why can't you spell it right? Jeez! It's got a *t* in front of it!"

I said, "Did Zell know Jackson was his baby?"

Both girls looked at me again. I saw a flicker cross Jane's face.

"Of course he did," said Clover.

"And he paid child support? And for your apartments?"

"Well, yeah," Clover said testily. "He wanted us to share a place, but come on. Who wants to listen to a baby crying all the time?"

Jane reached for the video camera and began adjusting it. She avoided my gaze and spoke softly. "We really should start filming. The flashlight battery is going to die if we don't hurry up."

All the things I knew about Zell suddenly came together in my head.

I said to Jane, "When you slept with Zell, you did it for her, didn't you?"

Jane didn't answer.

Clover gave an allover shiver of exaggerated revulsion. "I certainly wasn't going to do it. I mean, yuck!"

"So you sent Jane instead. And in exchange, Zell

gave you everything you wanted. Money. Clothes. A car. Even a job at Cupcakes."

"My mother told him not to give me stuff. But I knew how to get around her." Clover smirked. "I knew what he wanted."

"Did he ever? When you were a child, did he touch you?"

"Hell, no. My mom kept me far away from that dirty old man."

"And after you had Jackson," I said to Jane, "he didn't want you anymore, did he?"

Jane took a step back, her eyes fixed like a spooked cat.

"He didn't," Clover said.

"And he stopped giving you money. Then ChaCha fired you, so you realized you were broke."

I could see how Clover tried to maintain her income. She had pushed Jane at Zell, hoping the cash stream would continue.

"But you figured a way to get all of Zell's money, didn't you, Clover? If he were dead, you thought you'd inherit."

"No," said Clover, but she was a very bad actress. "Look, my mom has an old will he wrote a lot of years ago that gives everything to her and me. All she has to do is make sure it's the only will anybody else sees, and I'll get all the money I need to get famous. So that's what I'm doing. Are we ready to do this?" Clover appealed to Jane. "Can't somebody else say the words while you just show me on camera?"

328

The only question that remained was which one of them had killed Zell.

But there was Rawlins to think about first.

"Kids," I said. "I respect your artistic choices, I really do. But the rustic look is passé."

"What does that mean?" Clover frowned.

I mustered an air of authority. "The latest style in television is definitely retro. A modern look would be much more effective on camera. More MTV. You want to be completely cutting-edge, right?"

Clover snorted. "What do you know about it? You always dress like you're going to church. Except what's with those jeans?" She glanced down my lower body as if mold had sprouted on the denim.

I said, "I have a friend with a beautiful apartment, very retro. She'd let you use it, I'm sure. For—uh—screen credit."

Clover's brow furrowed more deeply. "I don't know. I want this to be totally me. That's the point. Making me look good."

"Of course. So the background of your movie should enhance you. Make you look your best. Why don't we go take a look at some other locations?"

"But I'm all dressed! I had my makeup done!" Clover began to pout.

"All the more reason to find a suitably attractive place to do the filming."

Jane, who hadn't said a word, suddenly handed me a small key. I took it and unlocked the handcuff as quickly as I could manage. Swiftly, Rawlins slipped his wrist out of the cuff and sidestepped Clover.

"Hey!" She smacked him across the shoulder with her notepad. "Where do you think you're going? I need you!"

Quietly, Jane said, "I think he should go."

"You do, huh? And what makes your opinion count?"

"Rawlins," I said. "Go outside."

He hesitated.

"It's okay." Jane sounded resigned. "You won't tell, right?"

"Go," I said to Rawlins, and gave him a shove.

He stumbled through the straw, rousing the sheep again.

Clover said, "What's happening? Will somebody explain why we're not doing what I want to do?"

"Let's go outside," I said. "Do you have some clothes, Clover? Something a little warmer? It's raining. Let's get out of here and find somewhere to talk about this."

Cold-blooded as a reptile, Clover said, "Bite me."

I reached for her arm. Jane dropped the green flashlight. Rawlins slid the barn door open and let in a huge gust of cold air. Clover drew back to avoid my grasp.

Her elbow struck the lantern.

It skittered off the railing and dropped into the straw. We heard the glass break, and suddenly the small corner of the barn brightened. The confused sheep bolted around the Mustang.

"Now look what you've done," Clover said. "Jeez,

let me out of this place!"

Jane blocked her path. "We did a bad thing, Clove. We're going to get into big trouble now."

"Shut up!"

"What are we going to do? Everybody's going to find out."

"No, they're not."

"She knows." Jane pointed at me. "Your mom knows, too."

"She doesn't!"

I said, "Yes, she does, Clover. Your mother knows you killed your grandfather. She went to the police and confessed to the murder to save you."

"Then I'm in the clear, right? So get out of my way."

The straw on the other side of the partition ignited with an audible *whoosh,* casting our huge shadows on the barn walls. The panicked sheep couldn't find the door.

"I don't want anybody to know what I did," Jane said. "You have to help me, Clover."

"Let's all get out of here," I said to Jane. "We need to talk calmly about this—"

Clover hauled off and punched Jane so hard that the smaller girl fell backward into the straw. The flame from the lantern flickered more brightly, greedily consuming the fresh air and tinder. The sheep came dashing around the car and ran directly over Jane. She screamed, and the sheep wheeled away from her in tight formation. They saw the open door at last and leaped for it.

Clover stumbled away, shouting curses. I bent over Jane, reaching for her hands.

The flame reached the straw around her legs and she cried out, flinging her arms up over her face to avoid the heat. I grabbed her wrist and began to drag her away from the fire.

I saw Clover disappear into the darkness outside. I pulled Jane across the barn floor, heading for the door. Behind us, a wall of flame roared up as more loose straw caught fire.

Suddenly I couldn't see. I coughed on a breath of smoke and lost my footing. Jane felt like deadweight.

Then Rawlins was with me, calling my name and grabbing my arm. I shook him off, and he seized Jane's other wrist. Together, we pulled her outside. The rain felt like ice on my face, and the air was so sharp my lungs hurt.

I fell to my knees beside Jane. She coughed and began to cry. Rawlins had his arm around me, and he spoke, but I didn't understand him. He pulled us both up the hill away from the burning barn. Emma arrived, and suddenly everything was very bright. A fire truck's red light spun around us. Then a tremendous explosion rocked the world, and Rawlins knocked me down. I landed in the soft, cold grass.

"We're all safe," said Rawlins close by. "Everybody's going to be all right. Are you okay? Aunt Nora?"

Chapter Nineteen

When I swam up from the depths of a dreamless sleep at last, a nurse was bending over me. "Hi, there," she said. "Let me go catch Dr. Stengler."

I closed my eyes again and felt my body go dark. I surrendered to the murk, but knew I was in a bed, tightly wrapped in warmth and strangely floating. I heard no voices, felt no human presence with me. I felt alone. And empty.

It might have been a minute or an hour later when Rachel Stengler touched my shoulder. "I'm sorry, Nora," I heard her say. "It wasn't meant to be."

Later, in a private room with a television hanging from the ceiling, Libby said, "You'll have more chances. You'll have lots of babies, Nora. We all do, eventually. It's a Blackbird thing. But this one wasn't meant to be."

When another nurse came in to take my blood pressure in the dark, I heard her soothing voice murmur, but I did not hear her words until she sighed and said, "It just wasn't meant to be."

Much later, I woke up sharply when I felt someone's gentle hand in my hair.

"Michael," I said.

"Shh." He leaned closer so I could see his face in the

sliver of light that knifed across the bed from the hallway. "There's a very scary nurse who tried to kick me out once already."

Someone had hit him. A purple bruise had begun to swell around his cheekbone, but he didn't seem to care. His hair was wet and smelled like thunderstorms. I found his other hand and held on fast. "Don't let me fall asleep again."

"I won't." He squeezed my hand in return and then bent his head to kiss my fingers.

I whispered, "I'm sorry."

"Shh," he said again.

"It's my fault. I should have done something different—"

"It is not your fault."

"Don't say it wasn't meant to be, okay?"

"No," he said. "Because it was."

I touched his face and we bumped foreheads, and then we both wept a while, alone together in the dark. The soft sounds of the hospital—the quiet beeps and sighs and murmurs of life and death—pulsed around us. We held each other and wished for things that would not be.

At last I propped myself up on one elbow. "Are you okay?"

"Yes and no." His voice sounded thick.

"Did Darla get what she wanted? The cop killer?"

Michael ran his hand down his face—wincing only when he touched the bruise—as he tried to make sense of everything that had happened in the last twenty-four hours. He said, "My uncle. Lou Pescara. He's dead."

"Dead!"

"Maybe it's right—I don't know. One of Darla's guys shot him tonight. The thing went bad. It turned into a stupid confrontation, and I couldn't stop it. Now it's over, and maybe that's okay, but it feels—I don't know. I should have done something, but I don't know what."

"Your uncle Lou killed the police officer?"

"Yeah."

The whole mess finally made sense to me. Michael had pretended to go back to his family to help discover who among them had killed the cop last winter. He'd taken matters into his own hands again. He hadn't trusted the police to arrest the right man. I said, "You tried to do the right thing."

"I don't know. You can't go around killing people, no matter who you are. And a cop—that's more wrong than wrong. But now there's family stuff, too. The Pescaras thought they could get away with it. They were mad at me for not helping cover it up back when it happened, but now that Lou's dead . . ."

"I'm sorry, Michael."

"I know. Me, too. It's—I didn't expect anybody else to die. I don't like people dying, Nora."

"I don't like Darla."

He allowed a grudging smile. "Me, neither. She was assigned to make sure I played by their rules. You know that now, right?"

I kissed him again. "I think I always knew it. What about Little Carmine?"

"He had nothing to do with anything. He deserves something different."

"Is he safe now?"

"He will be." Michael hesitated, unwilling to give me more bad news just yet. "What about Rawlins? I hear he survived his brush with the Cupcake?"

"Clover tricked him, tried to use him to make a videotape. And she heard about the attention Little Carmine was getting, so she faked her own kidnapping."

"And she killed her grandfather?"

"Yes. She used her friend to get money from him. And when that ended, she thought she'd inherit his estate if he were dead. She wanted to use it to become famous."

"If there's a worse thing than being famous," said Michael, whose life had become the stuff of headlines, "I don't know what it is."

He found my right hand in the bedclothes and touched it gently. The IV was taped to the back of my hand. Above me, the machinery ticked. Michael glanced up at the IV.

"Please," I said, already aware that he had somewhere else to go. "Tell me what you still have to do tonight. Is it dangerous?"

"Not much. But after, I have to go away, Nora."

"No—"

"Things have to cool down," he went on. "Darla and

her cowboys are pissed, which is bad enough, but my father and my Pescara cousins—they need time to get used to what happened. If I stick around, it'll get explosive. Tomorrow's newspapers are going to be bad. I need to go away for a while."

"No," I said again, my voice strangled.

"If I stay, it will be harder for you, too."

"For me?"

"Nora." He took my hand in both of his, elbows on the bed beside me. "In my whole life I've never been as scared as I was today."

"Losing this baby had nothing to do with you, I promise. It was—"

"I don't mean that, although it's part of what you need to understand. I'm never going to be Richard D'eath, Nora. He can keep you safe. Just being with me is too dangerous for you."

"I don't want to talk about Richard."

"I can't put you in jeopardy again. And if we're together, it's going to keep on happening."

"But you're out of that life now. I know you went back to your family to expose the killer, but now that's over. You can—"

"I can't change who I am, Nora. I'm always going to be Big Frankie Abruzzo's son. And that makes me dangerous to be around."

"I need you now."

"I need you, too," he said. "But I can't be with you."

"Don't say that," I whispered.

"Richard's the right guy for you."

"He's terrible in bed."

Michael smiled, but didn't make a wisecrack. He said, "You'll help him."

"Don't go."

"I'll stay until you fall asleep."

"I won't," I vowed.

He kissed me good-bye and murmured, "Have a nice life, Nora Blackbird."

I don't remember when I slept. The anesthetic put me under again, and once I was in that dark place I didn't want to leave it. I tried to catch him, to slide myself into his slipstream and follow, but I couldn't do it.

In the morning, Lexie Paine arrived lugging a huge spray of pink lupine and roses in a Steuben vase probably worth more than my monthly paycheck. I was sitting in the chair by the window, looking at the toast and eggs on my breakfast tray and wondering if I was ever going to choke down food again.

"Sweetie," she said, hugging me with concern. "I'm so sorry. What can I do?"

"Keep my spirits up?" I mustered a smile.

"I'll bring gallons of chocolate ice cream this afternoon, I promise."

"Actually," I said with complete truth, "that sounds really good. But they're sending me home at noon. Nobody gets to stay in a hospital for long anymore."

"Are you sure it's wise to leave so fast? Sweetie, you're so pale." My friend cupped my cheek. "Maybe

I should speak to someone—"

I caught her hand before she stormed off to do a Shirley MacLaine at the nurses' station. I was grateful to have someone so willing to jump to my defense. "No, I'm ready. I'm tired of feeling sick. I want to go home and dig in my garden and eat ice cream around the clock."

"Sound medical advice, if you ask me." Lexie shoved the other flower arrangements aside to make space for her more spectacular offering. She plucked a card from a vase of particularly funereal lilies and read the message. "Who in the world is Darla DeAngelo?"

"Someone I'd like to forget, as a matter of fact. And you know how I hate lilies. Will you find those another home?"

"Of course." Lexie perched on the edge of my bed, her ankles crossed, her legs swinging cheerfully, which did not conceal her compassion. "You're going to miss the museum party tonight, you know."

"I'm sorry."

"No, you're not. I'll tell you all about it, though, so you'll have something to put into print when you feel up to it. Delilah's already on-site, working like a demon. She has little Keesa with her. What an adorable kid. And I've already heard from scads of people who are coming tonight. It's going to be a smash, just you wait."

I tried to smile. "I hope so."

Lexie stopped swinging her legs. "You want to talk

now, sweetie? Cry? Throw some dishes or something?"

"All of the above."

"I'm truly sorry, Nora."

"Thanks, Lex."

"You've had a hell of a couple of months."

"I'm sorry I didn't tell you sooner. About the baby, I
mean. I wasn't sure—I was afraid I might lose it, and
I couldn't face . . ."

"I understand completely."

"Tell me about Boy," I said. "Did Emma hurt him?"

"If she did, he's not pressing charges. But even
Kirby can't save his political career now. Boy helped
Verbena cover up a murder. They knew Clover did it,
and they tried to throw blame on Delilah. Boy planted
the earring and Verbena made the anonymous phone
call. They're both in custody now, charges pending."

"And Verbena confessed to the murder to save
Clover?"

"Looks that way. She tried to shut up ChaCha temporarily by making her sick while Verbena tried to get
rid of Zell's new will that gave much of his property
to ChaCha. Her plan fell apart when Libby took the
cupcakes instead."

"So ChaCha inherits Fitch's Fancy as well as Cupcakes?"

"I think so. The police want to talk to you about it
all, but Emma is keeping them at bay until you're
stronger."

"Where's Libby?"

Lexie shook her head in wonder. "She's fine. Emma says she managed to find herself a handsome fireman. Trust Libby to find a date during a disaster."

"And Rawlins?"

"Rawlins is looking a little shell-shocked, but he's fine, too."

"Did he make it to the Spring Fling?"

"A little late, I hear, but yes. He's got photos for you to see."

I smiled, but it didn't last. "And Clover? Jane? Where are they?"

"Clover has been arrested for Zell's murder. And Jane? Is that the shy girl? I don't know where she is."

Jane would need help, I thought. "You should meet her, Lex. She's going to need someone to talk to."

"Whatever you say, sweetie."

I touched the IV bandage on the back of my hand. "I don't want to turn into one of those women who just stares into space, but I feel as if I've been hit by a bus."

"You're allowed to stare for a day or two, but for after that, I have a better idea. Take my mother's yacht."

I laughed. "Just like that? And go where?"

Lexie grinned—relieved, I think, to see me smile. "You think I'm kidding, but I'm not. Mother wants to take a Mediterranean cruise in May, so she's having the dinghy moved from Venezuela to Turks and Caicos for its annual checkup. You could jump aboard at any island you choose in between and go along for the ride. What do you think?"

"Are you going?"

"Unfortunately, I have my job to keep me warm, and things are very hot right now. I might be able to join you next weekend, but that's about it. You could take anyone you like to keep you company, sweetie. Emma or Libby. Take Delilah. Take Richard, if you like."

"To tell the truth," I said slowly, "I'd rather be alone right now."

Although she kept smiling, there was concern in her face, too. "Well, then, what could be more perfect than your own private yacht? It would just be you and the crew and the deep blue sea. Even the chef will be aboard, so you won't have to think about a thing but your tan lines. Pack a few books and a bathing suit. I'm a firm believer in the restorative power of the sun. Let me take care of your banker while you're away. I've been known to have some influence with those guys. Relax on the boat for a week and see how you feel."

I felt the prickle of grateful tears in my throat. "You're very kind."

"So you'll go? You said yourself there's a lull in the social scene right now. The timing's right."

"I don't know. . . ."

I had to talk to Richard. And there was Libby's insanity to settle. And I wondered if Emma was still working at the Dungeon of Darkness or if she had started coaching Pointy Fitch instead. There was so much to do. I put my chin into my hand, feeling tired just thinking about all the difficult conversations I needed to have.

Lexie came over and touched my shoulder.

I said, "I'm going to break up with Richard."

Lexie waited.

"He was using me, Lex."

Lexie didn't show surprise. "His story about the Abruzzo family came out this morning. It certainly lacked . . . facts. It barely made sense. One of the uncles murdered a cop? The boy is missing, presumed dead? And lots of innuendo about Michael."

I didn't want to read what Richard had written. I understood the truth now, and I no longer cared what the rest of the world knew. Least of all Richard.

At last, Lexie said, "Do what you think is best, sweetie."

"It's best if I don't see him again."

"And Michael?"

When I didn't answer, Lexie smiled a little. "You've danced on the end of the diving board long enough, Nora. Is it time to take the plunge?"

I shook my head. "He's too much for me, Lex. I'd like nothing more than to come home every night to sew buttons on his shirts and raise his children, but he's not that kind of man. He'll never be the kind of man I should be with."

"So? Sweetie, Cary Grant is dead. And it's not about *should* anyway. For most of us it's about *want*. And you want him."

"No, I need a quiet life."

"If you say so." She checked her watch and got up. "I've got to run or the entire Chinese economy will collapse. But keep the yacht in mind, will you? I'd love to do you a good turn, and your very own Caribbean cruise might be exactly what you need right now."

I got up to give her a hug and reminded her to take the lilies. Lexie breezed out, but she left a surprisingly palpable charge of energy in her wake. Good friends might be hard to find, but the likes of Lexie Paine stuck around for good.

I went home that afternoon, and Mr. Twinkles greeted me warmly on the back porch. Emma promised to put him in the paddock after she tucked me into bed. I found I could see him from my bedroom window. As soon as her back was turned, I watched her wild horse jump the fence as easily as a swallow flitting through the sky. He headed straight for my porch, and as I lay in bed I heard him knocking at my kitchen door.

Libby telephoned. "I'll come over later," she sang. "I'll bring you all my potato soup and chocolate cake to build up your strength. I've given up on diets, and so should you."

"Thanks, Lib. What's this I hear about a fireman?"

She laughed gloriously. "His name is Sam! Isn't that delicious? And he's very strong. I'll bet he can carry me up a flight of stairs and still have energy to burn!"

On Monday, Lexie came to the farm. She and Emma packed a bag for me, and she drove me to the private airstrip of a family friend. I don't know why I let them bully me into going. Chaz Cooper claimed he had to fly to the Caribbean on business, but when we were in the air in his small jet, I wondered if he was making the trip just for me. The steward brought me lunch, which I devoured over the blue Atlantic, and then I sat back in the leather armchair and napped.

On the ground again, I kissed Chaz good-bye in the blazing Caribbean sun, and then I took a noisy cab alone from the airport to the docks where Lexie had told me her mother's yacht would wait for me.

The driver let me off at a block of storefronts—some souvenir and T-shirt shops, two bars, a bait-and-tackle establishment. There was a small grocery store, too, the kind that catered to people who lived on boats. The shops faced a small harbor crowded with perhaps two dozen vessels. The water was such a clear azure blue that I could see the sandy bottom from shore.

Anchored in the deeper water was a long, sleek, astoundingly expensive yacht with a gleaming white hull and cheerful yellow awnings over the salon deck. I'd spent some wonderful vacations on it with Lexie. She was an old-fashioned yacht—a little outdated now, but built in a day when boat builders knew what elegance and luxury were all about. Lexie's mother had bought the yacht from a Moroccan prince who had lavishly entertained movie stars aboard as he sailed from Monte Carlo to the Greek islands and back. A week aboard her meant seven idyllic days of comfortable cushions, sumptuous meals and plenty of solitude.

I could signal her crew from the harbormaster's booth, but I wasn't ready to do that. Not yet.

In front of the tackle shop, I sat down on a shaded wooden bench where I could watch the boats and decide. I put my suitcase on the ground and let the warmth of the bench radiate into the muscles of my back. Smaller boats bobbed along the quay, and the sun sparkled silver on the water around the yacht and beyond. I could hear tinny music from the radio of a wiry man in faded shorts who was painting a railing nearby. Two seagulls swooped around him, hoping for a handout.

A stocky boy on a Jet Ski revved his engine and zoomed out from the beach toward the open water.

I watched him go and looked out at the ocean, wondering if I'd been foolish to run away. That's what it felt like—as if I were trying to abandon my responsibilities, my family, my losses, and pretend they didn't exist.

But they did, and the dull pain in my heart didn't feel as if it was going to melt in the Caribbean sun. I should have stayed at home and fought, I realized. I should have figured out what I wanted, made a plan. Found a way to make myself happy.

In the tackle shop behind me, I could hear voices and the ringing of a cash register. An elderly couple in bathing suits and flip-flops climbed up a ladder from their small boat and strolled past me, holding hands and heading for a bar a few doors down. The woman laughed at something the man said and bumped her head fondly against his shoulder. Watching them, I was glad I could hide behind my dark sunglasses.

A man came out of the tackle shop and stopped still in the shade. He wore jeans and carried a duffel over one shoulder and in his other hand a bag of something that smelled like bait. I turned my face away to compose my expression and hoped he would walk away.

But he didn't, and I glanced up at last.

It was Michael, gazing at me with the same dumbfounded stare that must have been on my face, too.

"Lexie," we said together.

He hesitated, then put his duffel on the ground next to mine and sat down on the bench beside me. He said, "She sent you down here to sail around on her mother's boat?"

I took off my sunglasses. "Yes. You, too?"

"Yeah."

We sat, unable to speak or look at each other. I wondered if he could hear my heart beating in the silence that stretched between us. I wasn't ready. I hadn't decided how I should feel. And he couldn't say anything, either. So we sat.

"I'll go home," I said at last. "You take the yacht by yourself."

"No, no, you could use a vacation."

"You'll enjoy the fishing," I said.

"No, it's yours."

"Really, I was just sitting here thinking I'd rather be at home."

Another silence. Longer than before.

As if we were strangers making polite conversation, he said, "Isn't it snowing up there again?"

"Yes," I said, and took an unsteady breath.

We were talking about the weather.

The bruise on his cheek was almost gone now, but there was something new carved into his face. Something that made my chest ache.

He continued to look out at the blue, blue water, yet slipped one hand around the back of my neck. His touch felt warm, but sent a shiver of anticipation along my nerve endings. He traced his thumb along my hairline, and I felt every atom of my skin come alive.

I closed my eyes and said without thinking, "I've missed you."

Another minute ticked by before he said, "Watch this."

I opened my eyes. The boy on the Jet Ski was back. He cut a rooster tail in the water and skidded up onto the sand before killing the engine. It took him a clumsy minute to dismount and untie a box from the back of the Jet Ski, but then he headed up the sand, barefoot and wearing shorts and an oversized T-shirt with a necklace made of shells. The box, I thought, looked like a lobster trap.

It was Carmine Pescara with a sunburn. He carried the box into the bar and disappeared.

Michael said, "He's going to run his own restaurant.

With a Jet Ski rental on the side."

"Here?"

Michael shrugged. "Why not? It could be a good life for him."

"The restaurant didn't cost him eight hundred thousand dollars, did it?"

With a truly happy grin, Michael said, "If it did, he got ripped off."

I slid closer to him on the bench. He had managed to spirit Little Carmine out of a bad life and into a good one. Maybe a perfect one. At the sacrifice of his own happiness, perhaps, but Carmine Pescara was definitely going to live happily ever after.

"Sometimes I get things right." Michael put his arm around my shoulders and stretched his legs into the sunshine. "I watched that cruise ship come in and thought maybe a trip would be nice. But now I just feel like going home."

I knew how he felt. Relieved. Almost content. I said, "That's not a cruise ship, Michael."

"What?"

"That's Lexie's mother's yacht."

He stared across the water. "That big boat?"

"It's got three decks, see?" I aligned my thigh with his and pointed out the details of the luxury yacht. "The middle deck is completely private from the crew. There are chairs for deep-sea fishing and wonderful spots for sleeping in the sun. A very nice library and gold fixtures in the bathrooms. There's even a little theater with its own popcorn maker, although I don't think I'll ever eat popcorn again."

He took my hand.

I said, "The chef is from France, and he keeps an enormous wine cabinet on board. The owner's cabin was designed by a prince. It has mirrors on the ceiling over the bed."

"Oh yeah?"

I said, "Richard is moving back to New York."

Michael turned to me. "I do love you."

"I know." I touched his face and kissed him in the sunshine. "I love you back. And even though we're all wrong for each other, maybe we could take some time to work things out."

He began to smile against my mouth. "Like a week, you mean?"

"We could try to get to understand each other better."

Michael smiled. "For starters," he said, "what's your view on topless sunbathing?"

Center Point Publishing
600 Brooks Road • PO Box 1
Thorndike ME 04986-0001 USA

(207) 568-3717

US & Canada:
1 800 929-9108